It's IN THE Stars

JOANNE TRACEY

First published in Australia in 2023

by Joanne Tracey

https://joannetracey.com

Copyright © Joanne Tracey 2023

Print ISBN 978-0-6450587-1-3

Ebook ISBN 978-0-6459587-0-6

Cover design by Louisa West

A catalogue record for this book is available from the National Library of Australia

For Grant and Sarah...
Always

CHAPTER ONE

The whirr of a camera shutter marred the poolside serenity as a man wearing a Hawaiian shirt so loud it screamed took photo after photo of a woman climbing gracefully down the ladder into the water. She was wearing one of those bottom-baring bikinis that only the most perfect bums can wear, and her long, straight dark hair fell like a waterfall down her back, stopping mere millimetres above the water. I'd never considered myself one of those women intimidated by the looks of another – you do you, and I'll do me – but this woman had such a haughty beauty that although I was desperately in need of a swim, I wasn't getting into the water while she was there. Others sunning themselves on the surrounding lounges obviously had the same idea; the pool was effectively off limits to us.

Pretending to be scrolling through my phone I discreetly snapped a photo of her on my phone and contemplated sending it to my friends Callie and Tiff for a laugh, although it was probably one of those stories that wasn't amusing from a distance. I deleted the photo and sent them one of my feet with the pool and palm trees in the background instead.

You haven't been on holidays until you've taken a #footselfie

As the woman swished her hair from side to side and turned her shoulder towards the camera, I was vaguely aware of someone throwing a towel and sunglasses on the lounge a few down from me. He muttered, 'For fuck's sake,' and launched himself off the pool's edge in the best 'bomb' I'd seen in years. The resultant splash drenched the swimsuit model, who emerged dripping from the pool, glaring at the perpetrator and sputtering (what I assumed to be) expletives in a language I didn't recognise.

Muffled laughter came from the other sun lounges and the man who'd caused the ruckus calmly swam to the other side of the pool and, tanned biceps flexing, hoisted himself out of the water in one swift movement to sit on the ledge. When the giggle I hadn't been able to suppress turned into something else, the world stopped turning. As our eyes met across the pool, everything else disappeared. My heart was beating so loudly that I was sure he could hear it too. Inside I was reeling, breathless, my stomach was churning, and I swallowed a beery burp.

It was as if it was all playing out in slow motion: the water dripping down his broad chest and following the line of his flat stomach to the vee that disappeared into his flamingo-covered board shorts; more drips clinging to his biceps. He shook his head, and droplets sprayed around him like a halo, glinting as the sun caught them. A grin broke slowly across his face, and he slid back into the water, disappearing under it to reappear right at my feet. Not wanting to contemplate his view, I straightened, closed the book I'd been pretending to read and moved my legs slightly to the side.

'Alice Delaney,' he drawled. 'You're the last person I expected to see here.'

It was Luke Macarelli – the man who'd broken my heart so thoroughly it had, for a long time, resembled one of those thousand-piece jigsaw puzzles with way too many patches of sky.

In the months since I'd last seen him, I often wondered how it would be if I saw Luke again and had developed what I thought to be the perfect reunion fantasy.

We'd bump into each other in one of those hidden laneway bars Melbourne does so well; the ones where you walk past the entrance four or five times without realising there was a bar behind that unmarked door or that garbage skip. I'd be with somebody tall, dark and gorgeous – not my boyfriend Tommy, who, with his nice and ordinary looks and mousey-brown hair that had an endearing way of flopping over his spaniel eyes, didn't fit that description. I had established this fantasy way before I'd begun dating Tommy nine months ago.

Luke would stroll into the bar, and our eyes would meet. I'd be flaunting what I've got in a red dress that dipped low enough to show the curve of fabulous creamy breast before falling around my hips and flaring down to my calves. The sort of dress you could imagine a dominatrix striding through a room and slapping a whip against her jersey-clad thigh would wear. Not that I'm into that sort of thing. My high black boots would make my legs even longer, and my red curls would have none of the frizz I usually battle.

Luke, on the other hand, wouldn't be doing nearly as well. There'd be some silver peeking through in his black hair, or maybe, if Karma had anything to do with it, even some hair loss. Where previously his stomach was washboard flat, now there'd be some belly fat, and he'd have lines on his face from the stress of keeping up with his sales targets at work.

He'd approach a little hesitantly, not sure of his welcome and intimidated by the aura of success and strength that was oozing from my date. At first, he'd be lost for words – due, of course, to my utter gorgeousness and the depth of his feeling – but I'd take pity on him and smile and tell him it was nice to see him. I'd even lie and say how good he was looking. We'd talk a little, and he'd tell me how he'd heard I'd landed on my feet since leaving Sydney and corporate life behind and say he'd seen me featured in the in-flight magazine in a story on Australia's sexiest astrologers. (I hadn't gone as far as deciding where I'd rank – simply making the list would be achievement enough.) Then he'd tell me he'd caught my radio program that morning in the taxi from the airport. (As befits a proper fantasy, my five-minute weekly slot on *The Toast Team* would now have expanded into my own weekly talk show or perhaps even a podcast.) Finally, he'd say how much he missed me and how he regretted taking my job and getting married without telling me.

As for me? I'd say we must catch up some time, but not mean it. I might even make the 'call you' signal with my hand in the phone position at my ear like he used to do when he had no intention of phoning me.

Then I'd toss back my hair – worthy of any shampoo advertisement – turn on my heels with a swish of my dress and rejoin my adoring lover all without a backward glance. If I had turned back, I'd have seen Luke gawping after me with a wistful 'what could have been' expression on his face.

Even before the credits rolled on my perfect reunion scene, I had to acknowledge that the real-life scenario unfolding now was wrong on so many counts.

Instead of a sophisticated bar in Melbourne, I was wallowing on a pool lounge in a resort in Ubud, wearing an enormous straw hat with my hair – which was full of frizz and knots – tied back and shoved roughly under it. My faded black one-piece bathers appeared to have lost whatever suspension they once had; my normally pale skin (the curse of the redhead) was – despite the enormous hat and gallons of sunscreen – tending towards lobster-esque, and the bottle of the local beer on the table beside me was suddenly too gassy. As for Tommy, who hadn't, until now, figured at all in my fantasy, he was back in our room having an intimate conversation with the toilet bowl after what he feared was a dodgy satay from a hole-in-the-wall warung in one of the back streets earlier this morning.

Yet, despite all the deviations from my fantasy reunion, everything about the moment seemed inevitable. Like unfinished business often is. Inevitable. And Luke Macarelli and I had always been unfinished business. As I looked into Luke's eyes, so dark brown they were almost black, it felt as if someone had walked past and tipped a whole chunk of the jigsaw onto the floor.

'Nice splash,' I said when Luke flopped onto the lounge next to me, towel and sunglasses retrieved.

'It was, wasn't it?' His grin was wide and cheeky. 'I just did what everyone else lying here was wishing they'd done. It's been like this every day we've been here. They'—he tilted his head towards the glaring cheeky bum and her photographer/lover— 'treat it as if it's their own private pool and forget that, unlike them, the rest of us have paid for the privilege of being here. She's one of those social media influencers,' he added. 'You know the ones? Get all sorts of shit for free in return for a few photos.'

I chuckled at his accurate assessment. 'I know. We saw her holding up foot traffic on the bridge the other day.' Tommy and I had watched as she ran laughing across the little bridge that connected one part of the resort to the other. Lithe and tanned and dressed in a high-cut jungle-print bikini with a sheer kimono thrown over the top, she'd looked back at the camera and laughed as if she'd only just noticed it was there.

Tommy had alerted me to her online status. 'I think she's one of those social media influencers,' he said. 'Hundreds of thousands of Instagram followers.' He fiddled with his phone for a few seconds. 'Here she is, and here are the photos from yesterday on the bridge.'

'How did you find that?'

'I looked at the most recently tagged pictures for this resort. Too easy.' He shrugged the shrug of a man who found it difficult to believe I hadn't thought of doing the same.

There cheeky bum was: one perfect leg extended out of a petal-strewn bath, her hair piled into an artfully messy topknot, her smile almost embarrassed as if the camera had intruded upon a private moment.

Luke took in the waterlogged beauty, a smirk playing around his mouth. 'At first, it was a bit of a laugh, and the view was good, but I was over it today.' The smirk became a grin. 'Plus, we copped them at breakfast this morning. They were filming, and no one else could get served because the staff were so busy running around after her. You should've seen it. She was in the pool surrounded by platters of fruit and pastries, and she put her hand to her ear and said, "Listen to that." Then she looked at the camera and smiled and said, "That's the sound of Bali."' He mimicked her accented English and plastered a funny look on his face as he recounted the moment. I belly laughed as if it were the funniest thing I'd heard in ages.

We. He'd said it a few times. It shouldn't have surprised me. Of course it would be we. Back then, Luke had gone on holiday for two weeks and come back married. In those same two weeks, my life had completely unravelled. Remembering that allowed me to push aside the thought of how the drips of water were still running down his body and how much I wanted to reach out and touch them, my finger following their progress. Instead, I took a swallow of beer and asked the question I already knew the answer to: 'Is Sasha here with you?'

He raised the little cloth flag on the table between us to summon a drinks waiter, ordering another beer for me and one for himself, waving away my protests as he billed it to his room. Correction: their room.

'Yes. She's out shopping. I hope there's a new suitcase on her list because, man, she's bought some shit so far.' He laughed at his own joke and I forced a smile in response.

Our beers arrived quickly, and he leant over to clink his bottle against mine. 'Here's to catching up with old friends in unexpected locations.' He took a long drink from his bottle, his face suddenly serious. 'What happened to you? You disappeared off the face of the earth,' he said. 'You didn't go back to whatshisname?'

'Hayden? No. That was finished.' I'd ended my engagement with Hayden as soon as I realised my feelings for Luke went beyond officer banter.

He nodded as if he understood. 'Your family's in Brisbane, aren't they? I thought you might've gone there.'

'They're a little further north – on the Sunshine Coast – but no.' I shook my head. 'I live in Melbourne now – Prahran. I like it.'

He raised his head and met my eyes. 'Why didn't you ever phone me?' He was looking at me in the way he'd used to look at me and it had the same effect on my hormones it used to have.

'After everything that happened, I needed a clean break.' I lifted my bottle to take a sip, but my hands shook and I missed my mouth, the beer dripping down my chin and into the valley between my breasts. His eyes followed the drips until they disappeared. I wiped the beer from my chin, ignored what his eyes were doing and put my hands firmly in my lap where they couldn't give me away. 'Anyway,' I countered, 'you could've called me if you wanted.'

'You wouldn't have taken my call.' He picked at the edge of the label on the bottle.

'That isn't true,' I said. He wasn't to know that there were still days I picked up my phone hoping (or fearing?) to see a missed call or a text from him.

He shrugged. 'Maybe.' He was rolling each piece or torn label into a tiny ball.

'By the way, thanks for not giving me the heads up on the wedding.' I closed my eyes briefly, grateful for the dark lenses of my glasses.

'I was going to tell you—'

'But you didn't. Instead, Ainsley St James, took great delight in telling me about it –just after she gave me my marching orders.'

He laughed, an uncomfortable nervous-sounding laugh. 'We were never good at talking about the "us" sort of stuff, were we?'

'Luke, there was no "us". It was all a mistake.' I pushed some stray pieces of hair back under my hat.

There was an awkward pause. On the sun lounges at the other end of the pool, the bikini babe was towelling her hair dry, still spitting out curses. She must've sensed my gaze and glared at me.

'You knew I wouldn't be there when you got back,' I said. 'Ainsley said you'd already accepted my job.' She'd enjoyed telling me that too.

'Maybe.' He ripped some more of the label away. 'I knew what was going to happen, and I knew it was because of what happened between us. Ainsley told me.'

I nodded. 'I don't know how she knew about us, though.' Then the penny dropped. 'You told her.' How had I ever trusted this man?

Avoiding my scowl, he shuffled on the lounge. 'That was in confidence.'

'It was Ainsley – nothing was ever in confidence. Everyone knew that. *You* knew that.'

He waved my words away. 'It wasn't fair you lost your job, though.'

I slowly shook my head. 'And that you got it?'

He lifted a shoulder. 'I've thought a lot about you and what happened and what could've been,' he said. Even behind his glasses, his gaze felt as though it was boring into mine.

He was waiting for my response, but I couldn't find the words, nor could I look away from him. And the shivers were running up and down my spine in a way they hadn't done in ages. All the months of missing him, of waiting for calls that never came, of texts and emails that weren't sent were in that look. I'd never felt those shivers with Tommy, and that had suited me just fine.

The thought of Tommy brought me to my

senses and reminded me of the additions I'd made to my personal rulebook since the last time I saw Luke. Additions that had been necessary to stop something like Luke – and the fallout from Luke – ever happening again.

I took a deep breath and straightened my shoulders. 'You don't get to miss me. Besides, I've moved on too. I'm here with someone. His name is Tommy, and he's an IT guy at the radio station I work for. We're happy, and I don't need you interfering with that. Not that you could interfere with that because I'd have to still care for you, and obviously, I don't. In fact'—I managed a shrug that was supposed to be nonchalant but instead knocked my hat into my eyes— 'I've barely given you a thought since it all happened.' Lies, lies, lies.

By the time I'd finished talking, he was grinning at me as if I'd given him the response he'd wanted. A woman I assumed was his wife, Sasha, arrived and saved me from saying anything else.

'Hey babe, I thought I'd find you here.' She placed her hand on his shoulder and leant down to kiss him, but she focussed her eyes squarely on me.

In all the time we worked together, I'd never seen a photo of Sasha. Sure, I'd done a minor amount of Facebook trawling (doesn't everyone?), but until today, I'd only had an image in my head: a blurry picture of a blonde-ish woman doing *that* pose in front of the Leaning Tower of Pisa on one of their holidays. After that, I'd stopped in case anyone had invented an application that tells you who your Facebook stalkers are. According to Tommy, that application is being secretly developed right now, along with one that allows you to recall drunk texts.

Sasha was sleek, like a cat, and just as graceful. She wore a short, loose white linen dress that showed a more than a reasonable amount of perky and tanned cleavage. Her hair was perfect too. It wasn't blonde but light brown with caramel and blonde highlights and lowlights, the result of a good hairdresser and some clever colouring and layering. I wished that my hair, thankfully shoved up under my hat, wasn't in dreadlocks by now and that I'd made the time to buy new bathers.

'Sorry, babe,' Luke said, 'I was talking to Alice. I haven't seen her in ages.'

He turned back to me. 'Al, I don't think you ever met Sasha?' He knew damn well I hadn't. 'Anyway, Al-Sasha, Sasha-Alice …' He made the introductions with a wave. It all seemed strange, an almost formal introduction with him and me sitting here half-naked in bathers while she stood over us, dry and gorgeous.

Sasha smiled in response and pulled up another chair. 'It's lovely to meet you, Alice. I wish I could say I've heard a lot about you, but Luke hasn't mentioned you at all. How do you two know each other?'

'Al and I used to work together, but she left Chartered Pacific a couple of years ago. Has it been that long?' He gave a knowing chuckle as he asked the question.

I nodded in response. 'Almost.'

'That explains why I haven't heard about you. Luke has always liked to keep his personal and work lives separate, haven't you, babe?' He smiled tightly.

Then there was nothing left to say. The three of us sat there in awkward silence. Luke played with his pile of ripped-up beer label; Sasha fiddled with her phone, and I tried valiantly to swallow another beery burp.

Luke rushed to fill the gap. 'Why don't you and Tommy join us for dinner tonight? There's a place in town we're keen to try. They do both western and local food, and I've heard it's good.'

I hesitated. Did I really want to let him back into my life?

'Although if you'd prefer not to—'

'No, it's not that. It's just that it's our last night, and Tommy wasn't well this morning. A dodgy something or other.' I laughed, and they laughed with me. 'I'll need to check if he's up to it.'

'Sash and I are going to have a few drinks in the bar here first, so join us there if you like. Shall we say six? If you change your mind, text me. Do you still have my number?'

'I'm not sure,' I lied. I made a production of going

through the contacts on my phone. 'It's okay, here you are.' I forced surprise into my voice.

'Great. Well, unless I hear from you, we'll see you and Tommy for sundowners.' He turned to Sasha. 'Are you ready to head back to the room, babe?' He reached out and stroked a hand up her leg, the look in his eyes leaving me in no doubt what they needed to get back to the room for.

Once they left, I finished my beer. Luke was here in Bali, the absolute last place I'd expect to see him. I wanted to text Cal and Tiff to tell them but had no idea what I'd say. They knew I'd been in (what I'd thought was) love with him, and I'd told them how it had ended. I'd never told them what a fool I'd made of myself, though; how I'd believed everything he'd said to me and how I'd pictured a life together. So what if he still made my heart beat faster? He was off limits and, despite what he'd said, obviously hadn't given me a second thought. He'd come out of the whole sorry mess with a happy ending and a promotion, and I'd paid the price of our relationship by losing my job.

Neither of them had passed any judgement when I told them the bare bones of what had happened, even though Callie especially would've disapproved. While Tiff had never thought Hayden and I were suited, she'd also worked with Luke at CP and had nothing good to say about him, declaring him arrogant and trouble. 'Exactly the sort that I'd expect you to behave like this with,' she'd said, although she'd smiled when she'd said it, so she knew I'd beaten myself up enough without adding her two cents worth to it as well.

No, I couldn't tell the girls. Besides, tomorrow we were checking out and heading home. After tonight, I wouldn't need to see Luke again. If I were lucky, Tommy would say that he didn't feel like going out and I'd be able to avoid him altogether.

CHAPTER TWO

I wasn't that lucky. Tommy was tapping away on his laptop when I returned to our room. He turned when I clicked the door shut and smiled that slow sweet smile he has, his tawny hair flopping over his brown eyes in its usual way.

'Hey you,' he said. 'Good swim?'

I walked over to where he sat, pushed his hair out of his eyes and kissed his lips. 'Yes, although that Instagram babe was down there having photos taken, so I couldn't spend much time in the water. How are you feeling?'

'Lots better, thanks. I've drunk a heap of water, and my stomach is almost back to normal.'

'That's good.' Even to my ears, it sounded unenthusiastic. Of course I was happy Tommy was on the mend. I took my hat off and hung it on the hook behind the door.

His laptop lid snapped shut, and his chair scraped across the tiled floor as he stood and stretched, unfurling the kinks from his lanky limbs. He yawned and lifted the bottom of his loose grey T-shirt to scratch his flat stomach, his skin tanned from our week in the sun.

I mentally shook myself. 'I ran into an old friend I used to work with in Sydney.' I paused and took a breath. 'He's here with his wife, and they've asked if we want to have dinner with them, well, drinks first, but … yeah … he asked if we could catch up.' I reached out and stroked the side of his cheek, the bristles of his holiday beard rough against my palm. 'I'll understand if you're not feeling well or want to spend tonight together – seeing as though this is our last night.'

A smile curled at the end of his lips, and he pulled me close. 'I'd like to meet one of your friends. Besides your family, I've only met Callie in real life, although I have seen Tiff on a laptop screen. I was beginning to think you were hiding me away.'

'Oh no! It's nothing like that! Besides, it's difficult for you to meet Tiff when she's hardly ever in the country. And Luke isn't like that, not like Callie and Tiff. He's more like … he's just someone used to work with. He's no one, really. I thought it might be nice – or not – it's up to you.' I was rambling but couldn't seem to help it.

'Hey,' he said gently, 'it's okay. I'd like to have dinner with your friend and his wife.' He pulled the short dress I'd put on to cover my swimmers over my head. 'But there's something else that I'd like to do first.'

'Are you sure you're well enough?' I teased.

'Absolutely.' He took my hand and led me to the bed. I kissed him as if he was the only man I could possibly be thinking about, and when he made love to me, I pushed all thoughts of Luke and how he'd looked at me this afternoon out of my head and concentrated instead on the man I was with.

'Is this your first time here in Bali?' asked Luke.

We'd finished our meals – *Kari ayam* (chicken curry) for me, steak for Luke and Tommy and a burger for Sasha which she'd barely touched – and were sitting back in our chairs nursing beers. Although the sun was long gone, the warm evening wrapped around us, and the rhythmic sound of the gamelan hung in the air. At the back of the restaurant, a Beatles tribute band played 'Yesterday', and the table beside us sang along with gusto.

We'd got through dinner without many awkward moments. I was beginning to think I'd been worried about the evening for no reason and wished there wasn't something about Sasha's possessive hand on Luke's leg that made me feel both sorry for her and guilty, although, as far as I knew, she wasn't aware how close we'd come to ruining her life.

'No,' I replied. 'We were up here last year to escape the winter. There was an astrology workshop that I went to here in Ubud. I loved it so much – Ubud, that is, not so much the conference – that we came back.'

Luke raised his eyebrows while Sasha looked bored. 'You at a conference? I seem to recall you hating groups and complaining whenever we had an offsite to attend.'

He was looking at me the way he did this afternoon, and it immediately took me back to the evening during one of those off-sites when he'd kissed me for the first time. It wasn't long after he'd told me he and Sasha were finished, and he wanted to be with me instead. There was something in his look that said he was remembering the same event. I took a long mouthful of my beer.

'It's my fault,' said Tommy. 'We were in Queensland at her brother-in-law's birthday party, and I told her I wanted to come here to do some diving off one of the islands. When Alice mentioned there was an astrology conference on at the same time—'

'It was so weird; I'd literally received the email only the day before,' I added.

'I suggested she come too and we spend some time together before and after.'

'And I couldn't say no because of Project Yes.'

'What on earth is Project Yes?' drawled Sasha, the first time she'd shown any interest in the conversation.

'It was this idea that Tiff came up with during the winter to get Callie and me – Tiff and Callie are my two oldest and closest friends – out of our comfort zones and dating again. Her theory was that if we said yes to every opportunity that came our way, we'd find out what we *really* wanted. Callie had been through a nasty break-up, and I hadn't dated since I broke up with my fiancé—' Cursing the beers I'd drunk, I pulled myself up as I remembered who I was talking to. 'I'd been concentrating on getting my business off the ground and hadn't had time to go out much.' What had held me back was the fear of repeating the mistake I'd made with Luke. Even as far as my mistakes went, that one had been a doozy.

'But here you are with Tommy,' said Sasha. 'So it must've worked.' There was an edge to her voice that made me wonder if she knew why I'd broken up with Hayden.

'I'd had my eye on her for months but asked her out at exactly the right time,' said Tommy. 'When she couldn't say no.'

'Your timing certainly was perfect.' I reached out and placed my hand on his leg. He lifted my hand to his lips and pressed a kiss on my palm. Luke watched us, and Sasha watched him.

'What about your friend?' Sasha asked.

'Cal? Well, she got what she wanted – or rather who she wanted – then realised she didn't want him anymore. Isn't that always the case? Anyway, that all worked itself out, and she's dating my older brother now.' Thankfully, Callie had seen through her ex-boyfriend Jamie before it was too late. She and Matt were made for each other.

'And Tiff?' Luke asked. I peered at him in the darkness, but there was no expression on his face. Even though they'd worked in different parts of the business, there'd always been underlying competition between Tiff and Luke. 'Did she get what she wanted?'

'You know Tiff. Doesn't she always?' I said lightly.

'She seems to, yes. She certainly caused a ruckus when she walked away from her job last year.' He paused and drained his beer, signalling a passing waiter to bring another. 'Did you hear they gave Ainsley the boot because of that?'

'Because Tiff left?'

He nodded.

'There's no reason I would hear,' I said. As much as Ainsley had been the reason I'd lost my job and as much as she'd made Tiff's working life difficult once she'd moved to Melbourne, Ainsley's career had meant everything to her, and I couldn't help but feel sympathy.

'There were other rumours—' he began.

I shook my head. 'I don't want to hear them,' I said firmly. 'Have they replaced her?'

'You truly haven't heard?'

I shook my head. 'Why would I?'

'I'm now heading up that division,' he announced, his eyes watching mine for my reaction.

'Aren't the staff all based in Melbourne?'

His lips curved in a sardonic smile, his gaze burning into mine. 'Yes, they are.'

'It's fortunate they've allowed you to manage it from Sydney then.' In my lap, my fingernails were digging into my palms.

A brief pause, during which his smile grew wider. 'They haven't.'

I swallowed hard. 'So you've relocated?'

'We have.' My tummy, which had felt as though it was teetering, fell. I couldn't help the little gasp that escaped me. Luke in Melbourne? Sasha looked up from her phone at the sound; her eyes narrowed on me suspiciously.

After a short and uncomfortable silence, while I searched unsuccessfully for something to say, Luke beat me to it. 'You mentioned this afternoon that you and Tommy work for a radio station; are you doing the same sort of work as you did with CP?'

I kissed goodbye to another part of the fantasy – so much for keeping tabs on me and my brilliant, new and extremely successful-and-happy-without-him life.

Seemingly oblivious to the undercurrents at the table, Tommy answered him with a wide grin. 'I head up the IT team, and Alice does an on-air slot with the breakfast show.'

'Sami and Joe,' I added. 'They call themselves *The Toast Team*, and in the ads on the side of trams, Joe looks like he's done something unbelievably naughty, and Sami has her arms crossed and is shaking her head in much the same way that my sister Laura shakes her head when one of her umpteen boys does something unbelievably naughty.' Inwardly I grimaced, knowing that Luke and Sasha probably had no interest in the tram ads for *The Toast Team* or my sister and her children.

'Her segment rates well,' said Tommy.

'Her segment? What is it you do?' asked Luke, his brow furrowed in bemusement.

'These days, I'm an astrologer, but I also do freelance writing and radio work. It's all good.' I waited for the inevitable joke to follow.

'The planets finally aligned for you, hey?'

Was he laughing at me? It didn't matter. 'They sure did. I'm happy with the way things have turned out, and it's nice being out of office politics.'

He grinned at that. 'I never noticed it bothering you too much in the past. You never cared who was who in the zoo when it came to sharing your opinion.'

'I know,' I groaned. 'It's something Ainsley was quick to point out in that last discussion.'

Before Luke could respond, Sasha jumped in. 'Answer me this, Alice. Why is it you never see the headline: Psychic Wins Lottery?' She paused for the punchline. 'I bet you saw that coming, didn't you?'

I smiled tightly. I'd heard it all before. My night would be complete if she mentioned something about tarot cards and alignments with Uranus.

'Seriously though, are you a psychic? Or do you

read the cards?' There it was. The woman was an absolute riot.

'No,' I said, resisting the urge to clench my teeth.

'Can you let me know when Mercury is retrograding into Uranus?' Luke laughed as he said it, almost as if he was trying to break the sudden tension between his wife and me. Tommy, god love him, seemed to have no idea what was going on.

Sasha, however, wasn't taking the hint. 'If you don't read the tarot and can't tell me my lottery numbers, what is it you do?'

Her question didn't have a simple answer.

'Contrary to popular opinion, I don't sit around in a pointy black hat gazing into crystal balls and stirring up cauldrons of bubbles and trouble, and I don't turn up to appointments on the back of a broomstick. In fact most of the time, I talk to my clients via video conference and am still wearing my pyjama bottoms.' I laughed but Sasha's expression remained impassive. 'Seriously though, I assist my clients in identifying potentials and challenges, talents and roadblocks, and help them work with those,' I said. 'I help people make the most of their opportunities and have more good days, or at least better days,' I finished.

'Oh.' She stifled a yawn. 'That's not very exciting.'

'Perhaps not, but it's what I do.' The band was getting into the 'na na na nah' part of 'Hey Jude'.

I'd suddenly had enough of pretending to make

conversation with this woman who I'd decided I didn't like and who was welcome to Luke and said to Tommy, 'Are you right if we make a move?'

'I'm ready when you are.'

I stood to leave, and Luke did the same, coming around the chairs to kiss my cheek. 'It was good to see you, Al,' he murmured in my ear. Tommy was saying something to Sasha, so I didn't think either of them noticed, although as soon as she could, Sasha's eyes whipped around to check on us. She might not have known what had happened between us, but she certainly suspected something. The band was now crooning 'Let It Be'. How appropriate.

'I want to see you again,' Luke whispered. 'I'll text you.' I pretended not to hear him and moved across to where Sasha was now standing.

'It was nice to meet you,' I said. 'Enjoy the rest of your holiday.' It wasn't all a lie. I meant the part about the holiday.

'Likewise,' said Sasha. 'It's a pity that you're going home tomorrow.' She didn't mean a word of it.

'It is, isn't it?' Nor did I.

'Perhaps we can catch up some time in Melbourne,' Tommy suggested brightly.

Luke said, 'That sounds like a great idea.' Sasha smiled tightly and turned away.

'Over my dead body,' I muttered under my breath.

CHAPTER THREE

Back in our room, I began throwing shorts and tees into my suitcase. Tommy checked his emails, then sat on the end of the bed watching me. 'Luke and Sasha seem nice,' he said. 'How did you say you knew them?'

I concentrated on folding the sun dress I'd picked up off the floor. 'Luke and I used to work together in Sydney. I've never met Sasha before.'

'That's all?' he asked with raised eyebrows. 'I thought you must've dated,' he said. 'That would explain the undercurrent between you. Plus, Sasha was watching you like a hawk whenever he spoke to you.'

Not trusting myself to lie to his face, I instead rummaged through the wardrobe for clothes to wear on the plane. 'No. We didn't date.' As the words came out of my mouth, I screwed my eyes tightly shut. Tommy and I had only been together since last winter, so we were still in the first year of our relationship – my first proper one since Hayden. Was I going to start lying to him already? I mightn't be in love with him – yet – but Tommy was a nice guy and deserved more than that from me.

I turned around to face him. 'We didn't date, although there was a time when there might've been something between us, but I was with Hayden, and he was with Sasha, so it didn't go anywhere.' I shrugged as if it hadn't mattered.

'Is that why you broke up with Hayden?'

I slid a dress off its hanger and folded it. 'Yes. Even knowing I was tempted by Luke told me I was being unfair to Hayden.'

I'd been lucky that Hayden had already put two and two together and let me go easily and with less fuss than I'd deserved. I'd heard since that he'd met someone and was engaged again. That was the thing about nice guys like Hayden – they deserved a lovely woman who wanted to get married and settle down, not someone like me who has trouble spelling the word commitment and has a closer relationship with Temptation than I should, and it's not a positive relationship. Temptation had whispered in my ear, and I'd buckled. Hayden was well rid of me.

'I see.' He dropped his eyes to his phone, turning the screen on and off. 'And now? How do you feel about him now?'

'There's nothing between us. Seeing Luke today was good, but I don't care if I never see him again.' As I said it, the goosebumps ran across my chest at the memory of the words he'd whispered in my ear. *I want to see you again.*

I tossed the dress into the suitcase and moved over to the bed. I took Tommy's phone out of his hand, sat it on the bedside table and pushed him back onto the bed, straddling him. Leaning forward, I kissed him hard. 'Not only do I not care if I never see him again, but I don't know what I ever saw in him.'

Straightening, I pulled my strappy dress over my head and tossed it towards my suitcase. My bra followed soon after. Tommy's eyes followed my movements, and his hands held my hips in place so I could feel how interested he was in what I was doing. I leant forward again and sucked at his nipple through his T-shirt. 'I don't want to talk about Luke anymore,' I said. 'Do you?'

He swallowed hard, then rolled me over onto my back. 'I don't want to talk at all,' he groaned.

Sometime later, curled beside him, I remembered what had been lurking around the edges of my brain. 'Tommy?'

'Yeah?' he murmured.

'You told Sasha tonight that you'd had your eye on me for months before asking me out. Was that true?'

'It certainly was. I can still picture the exact moment the boss introduced us at work. From that day, I couldn't stop thinking about you and looked forward to those days you'd be in the office, just so I could get a glimpse of you.'

'Really?' I pulled back to examine his face. It was full of honesty and a touch of shyness. 'You never said.'

He ran his finger up and down my arm, leaving little trails of sensation. 'I didn't think I had a chance in hell with you. A geek like me and a woman like you – you were never going to pay me any attention. All I could do was look on in wonder.'

It flattered me, although something made me uncomfortable about him watching me in silence all those months. I wondered what had prompted him to speak up. 'But you found the courage to ask me out.'

'I did. I figured if I didn't ask, I'd never know. I got lucky when it coincided with your Project Yes thing.'

'You certainly couldn't have timed it any better.' I laughed.

'No, I couldn't.' He stroked my hair as I drifted to sleep. 'Alice?'

'Mmmm?'

'You're sure there's nothing between you and Luke?'

My eyes snapped open at the uncharacteristically possessive tone of his question. 'Completely.'

Soon after, he was asleep, but I was wide awake. Once his breathing slowed and became rhythmic, I pulled away and rolled onto my back.

I want to see you again.

The conversation in my head started. *Maybe Luke's changed*, whispered Temptation. *He wouldn't come back into your life unless it was Destiny's doing.*

Don't even think about it, argued Reason. *He's trouble and married, so regardless of whether he's happy with his choice, that makes him off limits.*

I want to see you again.

The image of Luke this afternoon with water dripping down his biceps and chest flashed into my head. I tried to push it away, but when I squeezed my eyes shut, the picture was clearer: muscles, tanned skin, dazzling smile, wet… I forced my eyes open to stop the movie from playing behind them.

Beside me, Tommy was snoring softly, his hair flopped over his eyes. I reached out and gently pushed it away. Tommy was so perfect for me, so why didn't he make my heart race? Luke was trouble, and I'd fallen for all of it before. Last time it had lost me my job.

Extramarital affairs – even though neither of us was married and (technically) we hadn't had an affair – were deemed to be potentially compromising for the Chartered Pacific brand, so once word had spread to management about us, one of us had to go. They could use a no fraternisation policy everyone ignored and that only got pulled out when management needed an excuse to get rid of someone. Given my argumentative reputation, it was always going to be me.

To ensure I didn't take the issue further, risk media exposure and bring out examples of those far more senior flouting the same no fraternisation policy (the stories I could've told!), CP paid me out and promoted Luke into my role. Within the space of a couple of weeks, my entire life had imploded. I'd gone from being engaged to Hayden with a house in the suburbs to having no job, no fiancé and nowhere to live. It was probably no less than I deserved.

On the bright side, it was, however, an opportunity for a new start, so I'd dusted myself off, packed up my rescue dog, Stella, and a car full of stuff and headed down the Hume Highway to Melbourne. As brave and carefree as I'd pretended to be, I'm not sure what I would've done if it wasn't for Tiff and Callie. They'd picked me up, let me cry and pretended to believe me when I said I was over him – Luke, not Hayden, that is. I'd barely given Hayden a thought since we parted, something else I wasn't proud of.

But that was last year, and today I was stronger. I wasn't the heartbroken girl who'd arrived on Tiff's doorstep eighteen months ago with Stella and all my worldly goods. Now, I had my own business, a little house with a herb garden and random vegetables, and a park over the back fence where I walked Stella. I also had a new set of rules in place to stop things like Luke from happening to me again. All I had to do was stick to those rules, and whenever Temptation whispered in my ear, remind myself how badly he'd hurt me last time.

It was close to two when I finally drifted off, yet when I woke, it was as though I hadn't slept at all. It was Tommy's tuneless whistling as he made a coffee for me that reluctantly forced my eyes to open.

'Hey sleepyhead,' he said, sitting on the side of the bed and smiling down at me. 'I was beginning to wonder if you'd ever wake up.'

I groaned and rubbed at my forehead, the beginnings of a dull headache behind my eyes. 'What time is it?'

'Just after eight,' he said sounding way too jaunty for this hour of the morning, although at least he wasn't showing any of last night's insecurity. The direction my thoughts had taken last night were not ideal; I didn't want the guilt for any part I might've played in the insecurity he'd felt and had kept to himself.

We'd managed to get a late checkout from our room and decided to spend the morning wandering the lanes in Ubud one last time and the afternoon by the pool soaking up the Bali sunshine. I was waiting in the lobby for Tommy – who'd returned to our room for a hat – when my phone buzzed with a text from Luke.

Hey Al. It was good to see you yesterday. I meant what I said; I'd like to see you again. If I can arrange to get away from Sasha, can you leave Tommy for an hour or so?

As Temptation rubbed her hands together, my finger hovered over the reply button for only a second before I deleted his text without responding. Then I deleted his number. Luke was now finished business. Done.

CHAPTER FOUR

'You're what?' I hadn't even taken the first sip of wine when Callie dropped their bombshell.

'We're getting married,' she said, turning to Matt and smiling at him, love surrounding her like an aura. As for Matt, he was wearing a goofy smile and holding on to Callie's hand as if she was in danger of slipping away from him. No one in the rooftop bar of the Fitzroy hotel where we sat could've been in any doubt of their happiness.

As I struggled to process the information and swallow my wine, a cloud descended over Cal's face. 'I thought you'd be happy for us,' she said quietly.

'Oh sweetie, I am,' I said, putting down my glass and reaching for the hand my brother wasn't holding. 'I'm so happy for you both; you're perfect for each other. It's just a shock, that's all. You haven't been dating for that long.'

After having a brief flirtation many years ago, Cal and Matt had found each other again last June when we all visited my parent's house on the Sunshine Coast in South-East Queensland. At the time, Cal had been seeing someone else and Matt was living in Hong Kong, but by September, they'd got their respective acts together and acknowledged their love for each other. They did the long-distance thing for the first few months until Matt moved back to Australia earlier this year. But engaged already? That was fast work, even for my brother, who'd always been a fast worker.

'When you've found the right person, there's no reason to wait,' said Matt, raising Cal's hand to his lips and feathering a kiss on her knuckles. That's when I noticed it.

'Oh. My. God. Check the size of that ring! Way to go, Matt!'

Callie's pale cheeks blushed a soft pink. 'It's lovely, isn't it?'

I wrestled her hand from Matt's, inspecting the ring more closely. In rose gold, Celtic knots embraced a round pale pink gemstone, with elegant scrollwork making its way around the band. To say it was wildly romantic would be to understate it.

'It's gorgeous.' I nodded in approval. 'But what's the stone? Is it a pink diamond?'

'No,' said Matt with all the knowledge of one who'd obviously spent hours choosing the perfect stone. 'It's morganite.'

'I've never heard of it before, but nice work. Did you choose it yourself?'

He nodded slowly in satisfaction at a job well done. 'I had some help from Tiff.'

'Really? When?' Tiff had left Melbourne to travel with Jake, her travel writer boyfriend, several months ago. She'd only been home sporadically since, but Cal and I still spoke to her regularly via video calls.

'I caught up with her and Jake in Hong Kong back in December. She saw the ring I'd originally picked out and made me take it back.'

I grinned across at Callie. 'That sounds exactly like something that Tiff would do.'

'I'm sure it would've been lovely too,' said Cal, catching Matt's eyes and making me feel as though I was intruding on a private moment.

To cover my discomfort, I said, 'So you've had it for months?'

'Yes,' he said. 'I told you after that first weekend in June last year that Callie was the one for me; I just needed to make sure she knew I was the one for her.'

'I think she's always known that,' I said, smiling across at Cal, whose radiant cheeks made her look even prettier than usual. 'Even if she took a little while longer than you to believe it. So, go on then, tell me about the proposal. When did it happen?' I risked another sip of wine.

Callie looked shyly across at Matt and blushed again. 'About two hours ago.'

This time the wine snorted out of my nose, and

I scrambled for a serviette. 'This morning?' Callie and Matt nodded, both beaming. 'And you came here straight afterwards?'

Matt seemed to grow a little taller in his chair as he waited for Callie to share how clever he'd been. I raised my eyebrows slightly and shook my head in mock exasperation.

'So,' started Cal, 'we were at Rose Street Markets. I wanted a shawl from the alpaca lady, you know, the one who can tell you which alpaca each ball of wool comes from?' I nodded. 'Anyway, there was this artist there doing caricatures. Matt said it would be fun to do a picture of the two of us. And I'm like, no, it wouldn't be fun at all, but he was *so* insistent.' I suppressed a giggle at the animation on Callie's face as she described the scene. 'We sat there, me feeling like an idiot. The artist wouldn't show us what he was drawing as he went along, so I'm thinking he's made my cheeks like apples or my boobs huge or something.' She paused and smiled again at Matt. All this smiling was making me hungry. 'And then he showed me the picture.' She bent over and pulled out a tube from her bag. Unrolling the paper carefully and beaming and crying and blushing all at the same time, she showed me.

As I looked at it, my throat closed and my nose prickled and before I could stop myself, I was crying too. I leant across and punched Matt's arm lightly; he, too, had tears in his eyes. 'You old romantic,' I said.

'That's bloody brilliant.'

The artist had drawn them, although not in the clothes they were wearing today, but in what they'd worn that night at the surf club when they found each other again. Callie was in a rose-pink vintage-style dress with a tight bodice and full skirt. He'd drawn her with stars around her, her blonde hair almost alive under the beams of light from a disco ball hanging overhead. Matt was rumpled after flying for hours from Hong Kong. The sleeves of his white shirt were rolled up, and his tie was loosened and hanging crookedly. He was on one knee holding out a ring box, a speech balloon above saying: Calliope Jones, will you marry me?

'And then,' she said through her happy tears, 'when I looked up from the drawing, he was on one knee holding the ring box out, right there in the middle of the market. I was so overcome I almost forgot to say yes.'

'I'd met with the artist during the week and told him what I wanted,' said Matt. 'I told him how she'd been dancing to some daggy pop song, whirling around in a dress that was a sort of pink colour that looked like it had been once owned by a Hollywood star. She'd looked so beautiful as if she'd burst out of a million stars and come to earth out of a mural to make me fall in love with her because that's what muses do, and Calliope was a muse like in that bad movie with the soundtrack you girls loved.'

'*Xanadu*,' said Callie, who was an eighties pop music tragic.

I shook my head at the goofy expression on Matt's face, the same one I'd often seen since they'd gotten together. 'The artist must've thought you were mad.'

He gave a one-shoulder shrug. 'It's probably why he charged me so much, but it was worth every cent.'

Callie rolled the picture back up. I stood and embraced her while she sat, my cheek against hers, our tears mingling, then kissed my brother on the cheek. My best friend and my big brother, it was all beyond perfect.

'Does Tiff know?' I asked.

'Not yet,' Cal said. 'We'll text her later this afternoon.'

A thought occurred to me. 'Is that why you were so keen to meet me today, even though you knew I'd still be jet-lagged?' I directed my question to Matt. He'd called yesterday after my flight had landed and insisted I come to lunch with them.

He nodded. 'I wanted us to celebrate with someone.'

Through my leftover tears, I smiled at him. 'I'm glad. But all this emotion has made me hungry. Do you think you can get us some snacks? And a bottle of something bubbly for Callie and me.'

'I have you to thank for dragging Calliope to Mooloolaba for Mick's birthday. If it wasn't for that, I might never have found her again, so you, my dear sister, can have whatever your heart desires and as many bar snacks as you like.' With that, he headed in the direction of the bar.

'And to think I only made you come with us because I wanted to get you away from Jamie for the weekend,' I said, referring to Callie's awful ex-boyfriend. 'But I'm happy to take all the credit regardless.'

Callie twisted the ring on her finger and said, 'You don't think we're rushing into it, do you?'

'Oh sweetie, you know what Matt's like – once he decided he was ready for the happy ever after thing, you didn't stand a chance. Besides, I think you're made for each other, so why wait?'

'I wish you'd found your perfect match, too, and don't tell me it's Tommy; we both know you're trying too hard to make that work.'

I contemplated telling her that Tommy was my perfect man but knew she'd see straight through it. 'You're right, of course. He's perfect on paper, but'—I shrugged— 'my heart has never known what's good for it, so I might as well—'

'Don't you dare say you might as well settle! You know you get bored easily, and that's when the trouble starts with you. There's someone out there who will excite you without being a dickhead like Luke. Just don't follow your rules too closely, though, or you might miss him. And,' she lowered her voice, 'take care not to hurt Tommy too badly.'

She gave me her version of a stern look, which wasn't very stern at all but was enough for me to take her seriously. I gave a quick nod, and the return of Matt saved me from saying more.

'As requested, I bring you bubbles. The food isn't too far away,' he said. 'I told them to keep it coming.'

'Good man.' I held up my glass. 'A toast, I think. To Matt and Callie, I love you both so much'—my throat tightened— 'and I couldn't be happier you found each other again; so, here's to years and years of joy; you both truly deserve it.' My words came out sounding squeaky. 'Just not too many kids, hey? Laura's five—' I turned to Matt. 'It is still five, isn't it?' He nodded, and I continued, 'Okay, you never do know whether our sister has managed to pop another one out without us noticing. Anyway, her five already send me broke with presents, so you're limited to, um, three.'

'That sounds like a nice number to me.' Matt touched his glass to Cal's and leant across to kiss her, and again, my insides twirled. It was a weird feeling, almost as if there were hollow parts that bar snacks would never fill. Inwardly, I shook the feeling away and said, 'Have you given any thought to the wedding?'

As Callie said, 'No, we haven't had a chance to,' Matt said, 'Yes, actually.'

When Cal and I turned our gazes on him, he said sheepishly, 'I might've rung the surf club at home to find out if they had any availability in July.' As he said it, his eyes maintained focus on the champagne flute.

'Next year?' Cal choked.

'No, this year,' he mumbled with half a smirk.

'That's two months away,' I said, darting a quick look to see whether Cal had registered that.

He shrugged one shoulder. 'They can't fit us in until the end of July, and we're only a few weeks into May, so that's technically almost three months.'

I did the maths in my head. 'It's technically ten weeks,' I said.

'That's almost twelve weeks,' he said with a straight face.

I shook my head in exasperation. 'You're incorrigible.'

I couldn't help but laugh at the look on Callie's face. It was so typical of Matt. Once he'd decided on a course of action, it didn't occur to him to wait for anyone else involved to catch up. It wasn't that he was selfish – Laura and I had made sure he'd grown out of that – it's just how he was. While being with Matt for too long could be exhausting, Callie was the opposite. Her calm, sweet nature was a foil for his energy, yet she had enough strength to put her foot down if needed. Besides, he'd walk across fire for her.

'You've got an entire lifetime of this, Cal,' I said. 'A wedding in under three months; how hard can it be?'

Cal was still speechless, and Matt's confidence slipped. 'If you need longer, darling, that's fine, and if you want to get married here in Melbourne, I'm okay with that too. I got carried away and—'

She smiled and touched his arm lightly, and he relaxed again. 'A wedding in July sounds lovely, and the surf club is exactly where we should get married.' She looked across the table at me. 'As long as you and Tiff can be beside me, that is. You will be my bridesmaid, won't you?'

'That goes without saying,' I said, happiness radiating across my chest. 'And I'm sure Tiff will make sure she's back too.'

'When we were choosing the ring, she told me we can't have the wedding without her,' said Matt. 'And I'm not brave enough to try!'

After a couple more hours of wedding talk, Callie and Matt were eager to return home and begin their more private celebrations, so I left them to it.

Although I was over the moon with happiness for them – their joy truly was my joy – that weirdness was back in my stomach. To shake the unwelcome feeling, I walked into the city to catch the tram back to my cottage in Prahran, stopping along the way in one of my favourite vintage stores.

As I meandered along the footpath, the feeling came back, and this time, I gave it a name: envy. Not a lot, but yes, there was a little bit of envy, and I didn't like myself very much because of it.

Matt had said he was grateful to me for taking Callie to our brother-in-law's fortieth birthday party and thereby helping them get together, but all the credit should've gone to Tiff. It was Tiff who'd told him Callie would be there, and it was Tiff who'd introduced Project Yes in the first place.

Tiff's rules for Project Yes had been simple: we had to say yes to every opportunity that came our way, providing it was law-abiding and consensual, of course. Cal had been reluctant but had accidentally ended up embracing the challenge. She'd thought it would help win her ex-boyfriend back, and she had, only to finally understand that she didn't want him in her life. She'd also taken up belly dancing and fell in love with Matt. Everything had worked out for Cal as it was meant to.

As for Tiff, she'd said she was perfectly happy with her life. Unlike Cal and I, she thought she knew what she wanted – most of it was based on career success. She'd said she didn't believe in love, and then she met Jake. A travel journalist, Jake didn't meet any of the criteria on Tiff's checklist, but despite that, or maybe because of it, she'd fallen completely for him and, within a few months, had left her corporate job behind and embarked on an adventure with him as a travel photographer. He wrote the words, and she took the photographs to accompany them. It was the career she'd dreamt of when we were all at school together; I couldn't be happier for her either.

Not trusting my heart to make the right decision, I'd utilised my training as a project manager and conducted the equivalent of a post-implementation review, analysing what had gone wrong with every relationship I'd ever had. When I finished, I had a list of attributes the right man for me would have – with stability and reliability at the top of the list – and Tommy satisfied every one of them. I'd designed myself the perfect boyfriend. So why wasn't I as deliriously happy as my friends?

The answer was simple. Despite Tommy's perfect boyfriend status, I wasn't in love with him. I cared about him and had tried so hard to fall in love, willing myself to feel the butterflies when he looked into my eyes. I'd thought that love might come with familiarity, but all that had come was, well, familiarity. It wasn't Tommy's fault; he hadn't put a foot wrong. The heart wanted what the heart wanted, and my heart had made its mind up some time ago. No attempts on my part to convince it otherwise would change its mind. Callie was right; it was cruel to keep him hanging, hoping I'd feel more for him when I was never going to. My stomach churned at the thought of it.

Nor was Luke the problem. My heart might've raced when we met the other day, but with the rationality of hindsight, what I'd felt for him hadn't been love; it had been only a transitory crush and would've burned itself out. But Luke hadn't only let me down, he'd humiliated me, and that's why it had hurt so much for so long. The goosebumps when we met in Bali were simply Temptation flexing her muscles.

CHAPTER FIVE

As I rode the tram to Prahran, I pondered the situation; then, I pondered it some more as I walked from the tram to home. Once home, I refused to think about it anymore and was instead pondering the lack of biscuits in my pantry when the doorbell rang.

With the front door wide open, smiling at me with that wide, crooked grin of his, was my neighbour, Mac, and Kevin, his (mostly) black (mostly cattle) dog. It was then I remembered why all the pondering and wondering was pointless. The reason I couldn't love Tommy was standing in my doorway and had been since the day we met.

Even though I'd tried as hard not to be in love with Mac as I'd tried to be in love with Tommy, I'd failed dismally. The problem was that allowing myself to love Mac would break every rule in the book, rules I'd put in place to guard my heart against such temptation.

As I stood there gawking at him and his ridiculously sexy grin with the little lines at the side of his blue eyes crinkling, he said, 'I thought you must've forgotten about Kevin and me.'

I groaned inwardly and looked at my watch as Kevin bounded in and nuzzled my legs in greeting. I'd lost track of time and missed the usual walk we took with the dogs most Saturday afternoons. 'Ha, you did forget! Where've you been?'

'To lunch with my brother and Cal,' I said, going to the back door to let Stella in. She jumped all over me before bounding to Mac and Kevin. 'I'm just back and haven't even had time to change.'

'Why don't you do that, and I'll put the coffee on?' he said.

'Thanks, I'll only be a second.'

'No hurry.'

As I walked down the hall to my bedroom, he went into the kitchen to switch on the coffee maker, both dogs following him. 'Good holiday?' he called.

'Fabulous. Did you miss me?' I teased.

'Absolutely.'

In the kitchen, cupboard doors squeaked opened and banged closed; their contents moved around as he rummaged.

'Are you right in there?' I asked, coming back up the hall, having swapped my maxiskirt and boots for gym tights and trainers.

'Your biscuits aren't in any of your usual hiding spots.'

I leant on the doorframe and watched him. 'Nope.

If they aren't there, I can't eat them.'

'That's why I thought you hid them,' he said. 'So you wouldn't have to rely on willpower.'

'Hmmm, that was the idea, but it didn't work so well; I knew where to find them.'

He laughed, throaty and deep. 'I can't imagine how.'

'You won't find anything in there either,' I said when he opened the fridge and peered inside. I poured hot water into two coffee mugs, and he tipped some milk into each.

'There's plenty of actual food in here,' he said, taking another look in the fridge, 'but nothing for nibbling on. Weren't you on deadline last night?'

'Yep, September horoscopes due by midnight.'

'Where's the deadline pizza? Any leftover?'

I sent him a pitiful look. 'As if. The copy was due at midnight Los Angeles time, so I set my alarm for stupid o'clock and finished that and the pizza this morning.'

He let out a short laugh. 'Of course you did. Does it ever occur to you to start writing when you get the commission rather than leaving it until the last minute? It's not like you don't know when these are due each month; you'll get caught one day.' He picked up his mug of coffee and blew it on the top. 'What happens if, say, your laptop crashes the night before the deadline?'

'If it does, I'm dating my IT specialist, so no

problem.'

'What if your flight had been delayed and you were stuck in Bali?'

'No problems, I had my laptop and my IT specialist with me.'

'Right you are.' He sipped his coffee, eyes wandering around the room and falling on the calico shopping bag I'd left on the table. 'What's this? Post-deadline purchases?' He reached inside. 'Cool scarf. It's like a *Doctor Who* scarf, circa Tom Baker.' He pulled it from the bag and wound the narrow-striped scarf around his neck. 'What else is in here?' He pulled out the khaki wool felt hat I hadn't been able to resist buying but would probably never wear. Putting it on, he said, 'I feel very *Man From Snowy River* now; all I need is a horse and a whip to crack.'

I snuck a look at him and giggled. With my scarf around his neck, his sexy stubble-lined jaw, and the country-style hat on his head, he looked quite rakish and way too shaggable. I shook my head to remove the image that was firmly planted there.

'Seriously, though, Ally, I've never known anyone who's as disorganised as you when it comes to deadlines yet have so many rules you follow at the same time.'

'I don't have that many,' I said, annoyed he'd been able to see right through me. 'And I never miss a deadline; I hit every single one.'

'True'—he nodded— 'but right at the last minute.

And the deadline pizza and post-deadline vintage shopping?'

'Not rules, but habits,' I said, trying to keep a straight face as he twirled the end of the scarf.

'Perhaps, but you never attack a deadline without them. What about your first-scorer after-half-time rule?'

'Have I ever been wrong? Besides, that's a theory and not a rule – there's a difference. The team to score first after half-time always wins.'

'What about Richmond last weekend? Scored straight after half-time and the Swans still beat them.'

'That's because they scored a single point instead of a goal. The same applies in rugby – it's about scoring tries. Penalty goals and field goals don't count.' I shook my head in exasperation; we'd been through this many times.

'Okay, that one might be a theory, but the rest are rules. Like the one about underwear and alcohol?'

'That's just common sense,' I scoffed. 'And trust you to remember that one.' One night we'd had pizzas and too much to drink, and I'd blurted this one and another few out.

The rule in question is related to those all-in-one bodysuits with a little row of hook and eye fastenings so you can use the bathroom without having to undress completely. As I told Mac, these should be avoided whenever you intend to consume more than two standard glasses of wine. Your ability to coordinate the undoing and doing up of those things while remaining upright is inversely proportional to the amount you've drunk and how badly you need to pee. I'd learnt that rule the hard way.

A wicked grin split his face. 'Hello, it involved underwear; of course I'd remember it. I don't get why someone like you, who likes a certain amount of chaos in their life'—he nodded towards my office, which he knew would be messy— 'has so many rules in place. Take your garden, for instance. You plant flowers amongst herbs and salad leaves wherever there's a spare spot. That's not the garden of someone who is naturally disciplined, and that outfit you were wearing before didn't conform to any of the usual fashion rules.'

'What's wrong with what I was wearing?' Admittedly, the tie-dyed long-sleeved T-shirt I'd pulled on with my patchwork maxi skirt had been chosen more because it was clean and didn't need ironing and less from any actual fashion decision. What can I say? I was still jet-lagged. And the riding boots were handy and able to be pulled on when laces or buckles seemed a step too far for my post-deadline, still-jet-lagged brain.

'Nothing,' he said. 'It was very you.' He tipped his head to one side to study my face. 'And that's my point. It seems to me, sweetheart, that you've put all these rules in place to try and keep the real you under control.'

I straightened. 'Since when did you become my therapist?'

'I don't want to be your therapist; I'm just interested. We've been friends for how long?'

'About eighteen months,' I said, swallowing the last of my coffee.

'And in all that time, I've wondered about the rules. Why so many?'

I sighed and put my coffee cup into the dishwasher. 'You know how you have this little voice in your head? The one that says 'don't go there' and warns you when you're about to do something reckless or stupid and suggests you think twice before doing it?'

'Yeah, of course I do.'

'Well, I don't. Mine gave up talking to me when it realised no one was listening. So after my last big mistake, I decided I needed more boundaries – that's why I have the rules. They make sense.' I'd said more than I intended and reached up and took my hat off his head. 'And there's nothing wrong with what I wear; I just don't like things to match. Now, give me back my scarf and let's take these dogs for a walk.'

It was the dogs who had first introduced us. I hadn't long moved down from Sydney and was still bruised by what had happened, yet determined to make a completely new start. I'd got into a habit of walking Stella in the park behind my semidetached cottage most afternoons, but that day we were later than usual. Spring was in the air, and some trees had that first tinge of green, almost like a watercolour smear across the bare branches. It's the sort of green that doesn't exist at any other time in the year. Like the blue of jacarandas and the purple of lavenders, that green was a hopeful colour, and I so wanted to feel hopeful again. I'd allowed Luke to take enough from me; I wasn't letting him get away with taking my hope as well.

Over those early weeks of visiting the park, Stella and I had got used to the usual suspects: the groups of outdoor training or 'boot camp' participants, social soccer teams, runners, and others like me who sauntered and let their dogs do most of the running. This time as I threw the ball and Stella streaked past me low to the ground in pursuit, a dog of even more questionable breeding took off after her. As they raced through the park, the man leaning against a tree straightened, put his phone in his jeans pocket and called after him.

'Kevin!' he yelled.

I'd laughed, a big belly laugh. And it was strange because I couldn't remember the last time I'd laughed and there was no reason for me to be laughing. But there, on that afternoon in Fawkner Park, I couldn't stop. The man approached me with a reluctant smile.

'Please tell me that isn't your dog's name,' I sputtered. Who names a dog Kevin?

'Yep, Kevin by name, Kevin by nature,' he said.

As I wondered how a dog could be a Kevin by nature, I took a quick, hopefully not obvious, look at the owner. Tall and lean, dressed in a pair of loose-fitting jeans that had seen better days and a faded blue T-shirt, sporting the logo of a popular surf-wear shop, that hung off his just-broad-enough shoulders in the way it was designed to. Rubber thongs on his feet and sunglasses pushed into his dark-brown wavy hair completed his look, but it was his eyes – deep blue against a lightly tanned face – that I'd had to drag mine from to concentrate on the rest of him.

Judging by the light peppering of grey through his hair, I took a stab at him being somewhere in his late thirties or early forties. Oh, but those eyes. I reckoned he had a good idea of the impact of that gaze on an unprepared female, and I was certainly one of those. The impact on me was like a blow to the solar plexus – my hormones were obviously out of practice.

Kevin came wagging up to his owner, panting hard and wearing a doggy grin, closely followed by a triumphant Stella who'd won the ball. She dropped it at the man's feet and rolled straight over on her back for a tummy rub. Dogs can do things like that and get away with it.

As the man squatted down to oblige her, Kevin jumping all over me in a pleased introduction, he looked up at me.

'Seeing how our dogs have got to know each other, I guess we should as well.' He stood up and held his hand out to me. 'I'm Mac, and my dog, Kevin, you've already met.'

I shook his hand, which felt weird with dogs jumping around us. 'I'm Alice … and that wanton hussy is Stella.'

'Pleased to meet you, Alice. Kevin and I live just over the way, so we walk through here most days. I'm surprised we haven't seen you before this'—he paused— 'or does that sound a little too much like "come here often?"' He leant against the tree and grinned leeringly at me to illustrate.

I'd laughed at the goofy look on his face, and we'd talked for a long while that afternoon, realised we lived a few houses apart, and swapped phone numbers. We met up again the next day in the park, went for coffee afterwards, and now Mac is one of my closest friends.

After the Luke debacle, I have rules about sleeping with friends, so despite Temptation still occasionally whispering a little too loudly in my ear, most of the time, I can remind myself of all the reasons I can't contemplate being anything more than his friend. Aside from making my heart race, Mac is also everything that's landed me in trouble in the past – charismatic, gorgeous, the sort of man a woman could be tempted to tear her rule book up for. There are, however, moments where I'm completely honest with myself and admit that being more than his friend is what I want more than anything, not that I'd ever told anyone else that.

Mac, of course, doesn't feel anything for me other than friendship. To him, I'm a friend and the sort of friend that doesn't come with sexy benefits. More's the pity.

We text and we talk; we meet for breakfast, for coffee, to walk our dogs. He leaves Kevin with me when he goes away, which he does a lot. If I go away – which I do much less often – I leave Stella with him. He tells me about his dates – he's a man, it would seem, in demand – and I tell him about Tommy, and most of the time, I do an excellent job of reminding myself not to be in love with him. More importantly, I'm almost sure he has no idea how I feel about him.

Being with Tommy had helped me push my feelings for Mac to one side. Every time I forgot to remind myself not to be in love with Mac, I forced an image of Tommy into my head, and all was well again. But seeing Mac at my front door this afternoon, I'd felt exactly as I had done on that spring afternoon when we first met. I wasn't sure whether it was having seen Luke again and finished that unfinished business or being immersed in the loved-up aura that was Matt and Callie, but I feared that the guard I'd placed around my heart to protect it from Mac had some cracks in it … and I had no idea how to mend them.

CHAPTER SIX

'How was lunch?' asked Mac.

I pulled lightly on Stella's lead to remind her she should be walking beside me and not trying to tear ahead. 'Good. We went to that rooftop bar on Brunswick Street.'

'Nice. You're lucky the weather held. How were the lovebirds? Still love birding?' While Mac had never met my friends, I'd told him plenty about them.

That weird empty feeling was back. 'They certainly are. Would you believe they're engaged?'

Mac gave a low whistle. 'Already? They've only been together for two minutes.'

I shrugged. 'It depends on when you're dating it from. They first got together last June but didn't cement the deal until September.'

'Even so, your brother's a fast worker.'

'He says that when you know, you know, and there's no point waiting any longer.' I snuck a look across at Mac. 'He reminds me a bit of you in some ways.'

Mac grinned. 'How's that? Is he as irresistible as me?'

I pretended to consider the question. 'Maybe not quite as irresistible as you.' I laughed so he wouldn't take me seriously, not that I thought he would. 'No, there's something else. I think it's in his certainty, the way he goes after what he wants. Although I've never seen him as uncertain as he was when he let it slip to Cal today that he's booked a July wedding for them.'

'Next year?'

I shook my head.

'Not this year? Not the July that's less than three months away.'

I nodded.

He let out a low whistle. 'How was she about that?'

I lifted a shoulder. 'She loves him, and she'll make it happen.' I smiled as I thought of my friend. 'You know, when she was mooning after that dickhead she used to go out with – Jamie Aldridge – it would've been easy to dismiss her as being weak, like a victim even, but she's so strong underneath. Somewhere along the line, Cal found her confidence. My brother will never be able to walk all over her – although I suspect he'll allow her to walk over him.' I chuckled at the thought.

'I know you've talked about Cal and Jamie before, but I didn't know you meant Jamie Aldridge.' The look on his face was one of concern.

'Do you know him?'

'Unfortunately. He came in for an interview once, but his reputation preceded him. Let's just say he wasn't the right fit for our company.'

Mac rarely spoke about his work, so I tried not to show my surprise. 'What is it you do again? IT, isn't it? Like Tommy?'

'I'm more on the sales and management side than the technical side,' he said. 'Anyway, if her ex was Jamie Aldridge, she's well rid of him. I assume you'll be a bridesmaid?'

Mac's change of subject was so neat that I almost imagined it. 'Yes, with Tiff. Hopefully, she'll be able to get back from wherever she and Jake will be. Not that Jake would be game enough to try and stop her from coming back.' I shuddered at the thought of Tiff's reaction if Callie and Matt even contemplated getting married without her presence.

'I suppose you'll take Tommy.' Mac stopped walking to allow Kevin to sniff at something that might once have been on the ground, which meant Stella also had to stop and sniff it too. It gave me time to consider my answer. Before I could speak, though, he'd turned to face me. 'You are taking Tommy, aren't you?'

I sighed. 'I'm not sure.'

'Trouble in paradise?'

'Hardly paradise,' I scoffed. 'I just think it's run its course.' I shrugged so he'd think it wasn't a big deal and pulled on the lead for Stella to start walking again.

'I see,' he said. 'I thought you were happy with him. You've just been on holiday together.'

I shrugged again. 'I'm not unhappy with him, and we had a lovely time away together, but there's more to it than being not unhappy, don't you think?'

His laugh was derisive. 'Are you telling me you believe in the fairy tale where you're both ecstatically happy all the time? Come on, Ally, I thought you were more practical than that.'

'I am,' I said. 'I know there are ups and downs, and it's what happens after bin night that's important; it's just that—'

His rumbling laughter interrupted me. 'Sorry, what's this bin night thing? Is this another of your rules?'

'No, of course not. I'm talking about when that first burst of lust wears off and everyday life sneaks in, like arguing about who takes the bins out. You can't expect that first flush to last – it'd be way too exhausting. But the thing is, I didn't even have that with Tommy.'

By the look on his face, he was trying not to smile. 'Are you telling me that the lust wasn't there? I seem to recall you being hungry, horny and itchy before you began seeing him.'

I pushed the memory of how close I'd come to giving my feelings for *him* away last winter.

'No, I'm not saying that; I'm just saying I'm hungry again. You should've seen how many bar snacks I demolished at lunch today. Tommy's lovely, but he's, I don't know, too nice.'

'Don't tell me you want someone who's going to treat you badly?' He stopped walking for a second and stared at me as if he was seeing me for the first time. It wasn't so much surprise as disappointment written on his face. 'I didn't think you were that woman,' he said with a little shake of his head.

'I'm not! And that's not what I meant.'

'What did you mean then? You're the one who told me that Tommy was perfect for you on paper, that he was everything you needed in a man and that he was the opposite of all your biggest mistakes. That's what you said.'

'He is … was. But since when does it matter to you who I do or don't date?'

'It doesn't, but—' He must've seen the hurt I couldn't hide. 'That came out completely wrong. Of course I care. The last thing I want is for you to be so wrapped up in someone that you don't have time for me.'

I recognised the statement for what it was, an attempt to lighten a conversation that was getting more heated than our conversations tended to get. 'And it's all about you, isn't it?'

'Shouldn't it be?' I smiled at his conceit. We walked

a little further in silence.

'Seriously though,' he said. 'What's the real problem?'

I opened my mouth, and the words slid out before I could stop them. 'I don't love Tommy, and I think he might love me.'

'Aaah. I'm guessing you don't think you can learn to love him?'

'I thought I might be able to, but I don't think I can. I like and care about him a lot, but I know I'll never love him.' An involuntary smile came to my face.

'What's funny?'

'Not that, obviously. It just sounds like the lyrics to an eighties pop song. Cal would know which one.' I shrugged. 'I don't want to hurt him, Mac, but I think it's too late for that. He said something when we were away that made me think …'

He was silent for a few steps. 'Then it's best you let him down quickly and kindly,' he said.

'I know. I feel bad about it, though.' The thought of what needed to happen made my stomach churn again.

He shrugged one shoulder, not to show that he didn't care but as an indication that he understood. 'I'm sorry about that,' he said, 'but stringing it out and letting him hope if there isn't reason to hope is cruel.' He stopped, Kevin immediately sitting beside him as he'd been trained to do. 'And you're not a cruel person,

Ally.' He smiled briefly and began walking again. 'How do you think he'll take it?'

'He'll be fine,' I said confidently. 'He's never given me any cause to think he's the type to go all weird on me. He's never shown any jealous tendencies—' Even as I said the words, I remembered the incident in Bali and dismissed it just as quickly. Even then, he hadn't been jealous or possessive, more insecure. 'No,' I said, 'He'll be sad, but he'll understand.'

'I hope you're right,' he said simply. 'Are you seeing him tonight?'

I nodded. 'What about you?'

'No,' he said seriously, 'I'm not seeing Tommy tonight.' I punched his arm lightly. 'I am, however, seeing Bree.'

'Who's Bree?' I ducked my head as I walked. That hollow feeling was back again, and I feared it would show on my face.

'Someone I met in the airport lounge the other week when I was heading to Brisbane. One thing led to another, and … well, you know how it is.'

I snuck a look at him. The self-satisfied smirk he wore made my chest hurt. Mac rarely saw anyone more than a handful of times, yet if memory served me correctly, he was last in Brisbane for an overnight stay a month ago. I should know – I looked after Kevin while he was gone.

'I see,' I said, nodding as if I knew how it was

when I had no idea. 'A repeat date,' I said, forcing lightness into my tone. 'Next thing you know, we'll be talking about *your* engagement.'

He chuckled. 'For your information, this will be our …' He stopped and counted on his fingers. 'Fifth date.' He grinned wickedly. 'I'm not counting the first few times as dates.'

An image of him in a hotel room with Bree flashed before my eyes. She'd be blonde, I decided, no, that was too cliched, brunette. With hair so dark it was almost black. She'd be slim, of course, and wear designer business clothes with sky-high red-soled heels. I shook my head to remove the image. She'd be everything I wasn't.

'Earth to Ally …' he was saying.

'Sorry,' I said. 'I have no idea where I was.'

'Knowing you, probably already rehearsing what you'll be saying to Tommy,' he was grinning, but there was something else in his expression. Concern perhaps?

I let out a short laugh. 'Something like that.'

'Are you sure everything else is fine?' The dogs pulled us to the side of the path to investigate a stray tennis ball. 'You are happy about the engagement, aren't you?'

I almost told him about seeing Luke again, yet Luke was something we'd never spoken of. I wasn't sure whether it was because the story wouldn't show me in a good light – I had, after all, broken off an engagement because I'd had feelings for a man who was already with someone else – or whether because talking about it would make it more important than it was. What Luke and I had had was a flirtation, nothing more. Yet I'd lost a fiancé and a job because of it. In all honesty, Hayden and I probably wouldn't have lasted anyway, and I'd outgrown the job, but had it all needed to have been so dramatic?

So I told him none of it. 'I couldn't be happier,' I said with a fake smile. 'And Tommy will be fine, I'm sure of it.' If I told myself that often enough, it would be true.

CHAPTER SEVEN

I kept telling myself that for the rest of the afternoon. Tommy would be fine; he'd understand. He was so laid-back he might not even notice. Then I remembered work. Oh god, we had to see each other at work. He'd be okay with that too, I decided. We'd simply move from dating back to friends, not that we'd truly been friends to start with, but it would be fine; we'd be fine. Everyone at the station knew we were seeing each other even though we'd never done the public displays of affection at work, so if we were civil with each other – and I had no doubt we'd be able to be – people would soon forget we ever dated. Besides, I was only in the office once a week and tended to be out before anyone in IT began their day.

I kept that thought as I prepared for our date that evening, and I kept that thought when Tommy rang the doorbell and when he kissed me hello and as we walked to the restaurant on nearby Greville Street.

'How was lunch with Matt and Callie?' he asked when we were seated and our drinks orders taken.

'Good. No, great, actually. They're engaged.' I managed to smile sweetly even though my head was on other matters.

His face lit up, and he pushed his hair up and out of his eyes. I'd miss his floppy hair and eyes and how they turned down a little at the edges, almost like spaniel eyes. There was a lot I'd miss about him. Maybe there was still hope; if I tried hard, maybe I could fall out of love with Mac and into it with Tommy.

'That's great news,' he said. 'I'm so happy for them, and to think we were there at the start.'

His smile was so open and hopeful that inwardly I groaned but forced a smile back. 'We certainly were.'

'When are they getting married?'

'July.' As he opened his mouth to probably ask the same question I'd asked and Mac had asked, I added, 'This year.'

He raised his eyebrows. 'That soon.'

'Uh huh.' I scanned the menu again. 'Have you decided what you're eating? I know there's a lot of garlic in it, but I'm leaning towards the *L'escargots* and the *Coq au Vin*.' I called the waiter over and placed our order.

Tommy couldn't hide the little wrinkle of his nose. He wasn't a garlic fan, and I'd only gone and chosen the dish with the most garlic in it as my starter. In fact, we only came to this French restaurant as often as we did because I loved it. Come to think on it, nearly everywhere we went was my choice. Tommy rarely offered an opinion on anything; he simply agreed with me, or if he didn't agree, he didn't say anything. It meant that we didn't argue, but now I wondered, perversely, what it would take to have him assert himself or stand up to me about something. Anything.

Last September, he'd put on denim dungarees and played Elton John to my Kiki Dee at Mum's sixtieth birthday party – without any argument. Callie thought it was sweet, but subconsciously, I think I was testing him. Even though he said nothing, I knew it annoyed him how often I met up with Mac to walk the dogs – especially on the weekends – and how frequently I had Kevin at my place. Tommy wasn't a dog person but tolerated Stella because I loved her. I even knew that he didn't understand what I did – and probably didn't believe in it – but kept his opinions to himself and went along with me. It's what he always did.

'Are they getting married down here?' he asked.

I shook my head and reached for a piece of baguette, slathering on the butter. Depending on what sort of bridesmaid's hell Callie wanted to subject Tiff and me to, I'd better go easy on the snacks … from Monday. 'No, it will be on the Sunshine Coast. Matt has already booked the reception at the surf club, and Callie mentioned she'd like to have the ceremony on the beach.'

'And you'll be a bridesmaid?'

'Yes, Tiff and I.'

'Where's Tiff now?'

What was with all the questions, and where was our food?

'I'm not sure – I can't keep up with them. I think they're still in Asia somewhere.'

'Will she be happy for Callie?'

I swallowed my impatience with another slice of baguette. Tommy's face was open, guileless; he was just interested in my friends. He smiled and swept his hair back again. 'I'm asking too many questions, aren't I?'

My annoyance turned to guilt. 'I'm sorry, Tommy, I don't know what's wrong with me tonight.'

He reached across the table for my hand. 'It's okay. I know sometimes it can be difficult.'

My brow furrowed, but I didn't get to ask what he meant as the waiter arrived with our food, snails for me and pâté with thin rounds of toast for him.

It wasn't until I was dipping what was left of the baguette into what was left of the parsley and butter sauce that I picked back up on our conversation.

'When you said you understood it could be difficult, what did you mean?'

At first, he looked perplexed, but then he caught up. That was another thing I'd miss about Tommy, how his face showed his every thought. 'I know it can be hard for women when their friends get married,' he said. 'It must make you wonder whether it's your turn.'

I didn't know whether it was because what he'd

said wasn't that far from what my thoughts had been earlier today, but I couldn't stop myself from snapping. 'That's ridiculous. The thought of getting married hasn't even occurred to me.'

I almost groaned aloud as his face fell, disappointment and hurt written all over it. 'I'm sorry, Tommy, I didn't mean for that to sound like it did.'

'It's okay.' His smile was tentative. 'You haven't thought about marriage?'

'No,' I said, running my finger around the edge of the dish to capture a final lick of garlicky butter.

'Is it that you haven't thought about marriage, or you haven't thought about marrying me?'

I sighed and leant back in the booth, allowing my head to tip back and my eyes to close as I scrambled for words that would hurt him – but words I needed to say. This wasn't going according to the script I'd practiced.

'It's me, isn't it? You haven't thought about marrying me.'

His voice sounded so empty; I brought my eyes back to his. 'I'm sorry, Tommy, but no.' I said the words quietly and gently, hoping to soothe him even though they hurt him. 'I like you, but—'

'But you don't love me,' he finished.

For the briefest of seconds, I contemplated lying to him, but that would've been cruel too. I shook my head, hating myself for hurting him. 'No, I don't love you – not like that.'

He nodded once, more of a half a nod as if he was having difficulty conveying the message to his head to nod. 'I understand,' he said. 'I do. And I know I can't make you love me back.' He paused before adding, 'This is it, isn't it?'

My throat closed over at the pain in his eyes, something he was trying to hide with the barest of resigned smiles. 'Yes, I suppose it is. I'm so sorry.'

When his hair flopped over his eyes, he let it stay there. 'I know you are, and I'm sorry too, but it's been fun, hasn't it?' His attempted smile was tremulous.

Guilt at the hurt I'd caused was replaced by relief (which I immediately felt guilty again for) he was letting me off so lightly. 'Yes, it has been fun.'

'We can still be friends?'

Even as I knew he hoped that being friends might lead to being something more than friends again, I smiled back at him through the tears I couldn't stop. 'Absolutely.'

He walked me home, both of us saying little along the way, and at the gate to my cottage, he stopped and kissed my cheek.

'Thank you, Alice,' he said.

'What for?'

'For the last ten months. It's been fun.' He paused and added, 'At least I've enjoyed it.'

I smiled at him in the darkness, dear sweet Tommy with his floppy hair. I'll miss him. 'Yes,' I said softly, 'I've enjoyed it too. It's been lovely – you've been lovely. I wish …' I couldn't finish my sentence. I was sure he knew what I wanted to say, that I wished I was in love with him.

'So do I,' he said sadly.

I kissed his lips briefly, finally, and stroked his cheek before stepping back. 'Take care.'

'You too.'

And then he turned and walked away, his hands in his pockets, his shoulders slumped. My heart ached for him, but at the same time, I'd done the right thing, and there'd be someone out there who was right for him – as there had been for Hayden. It made me wonder, though, if I was ever going to get this whole love thing right. So far, it seemed, the man I loved didn't love me back, and the men who loved me I couldn't love in the same way, and in between, I bounced from ridiculous crush to even more ridiculous crush. It seemed so easy the way it happened for other people, yet I couldn't get the hang of it. Even Tiff, who didn't believe in happy ever afters, had found hers, so why couldn't I?

The ringing of my phone jolted me out of my pity party for one.

'Good, you're still up. Can you believe that idiot brother of yours is expecting to organise a wedding by July?' Tiff's face filled the screen; she typically didn't bother with the pleasantries.

'Where are you?' I asked.

'You don't want to know,' she said, and the way she said it told me she *really* wanted me to know where she was.

'Go on,' I urged, 'let me travel vicariously through you. Where are you?'

'Guess,' she said, turning her phone to show me around her room.

'South-East Asia somewhere?' I guessed. 'Bali?'

'Close,' she said. 'Ubud, to be precise. We arrived this afternoon. It's a pity we couldn't have coordinated better and been here when you guys were. We're in this gorgeous little boutique resort a few kilometres out of town. What is it with throwing the name "boutique" in front of everything at the moment? Once upon a time, a boutique was where your bought clothes; now it's anything from resorts to breweries and pizza bars.' She shook her head slightly as she struggled to understand the concept. 'Sometimes I think you could pop a four-poster bed into a two-hundred room hotel and it would qualify as boutique. Check out the bed here.' She swivelled the phone around again so I could admire it. 'Would you believe they change the doona cover for the day, then put the white one on at night? And no, I have no idea why. It seems like a lot of extra linen changing and washing to me. And how much mosquito netting do you need? I'm convinced I'm going to get caught up in it when I get up for the loo in the middle of the night. Oh, and there's a deck that backs onto the rice paddies. It's too dark for me to show you, though.'

'You're right; I didn't want to know. It sounds like that place I stayed in the first time I was there – where the fireflies darted through the rice at nighttime. It was all terribly romantic.'

She panned the camera past where Jake was seated at a desk, tapping away at his laptop, a bottle of Bintang, the local beer, on the table beside him.

'Hi Jake,' I called.

'Hey Ally,' he said. 'All good?'

'Absolutely.'

'Yes, it's all very romantic with Jake working on a story and me on the phone to you.' She laughed, and I laughed with her. Tiff was a different woman since meeting Jake and taking off with him into the great unknown. She might no longer need the designer handbags and shoes, but she seemed lighter, happier and infinitely more fulfilled, although Tiff would be quick to tell me that was purely the result of their sex life.

'Speaking of all things romantic,' she said, 'is Matt serious? Does he honestly think Cal can organise a wedding in two months?'

'I think he does,' I said. 'He's already booked the surf club, organised a photographer he knows up there and pointed out that it's technically almost three months.'

'He must've been pretty sure she'd say yes,' said Tiff.

'You know Matt,' I said. 'It wouldn't occur to him that once he'd thought of it, everything and everyone else wouldn't fall into line.'

'True. He's certainly a force of nature, and Callie is the only woman in the world who can deal with him without being burnt out by him.' Despite their having been involved in an on-again, off-again casual hook-up type of arrangement in the past, Tiff said it with affection. 'They're perfect for each other, but so soon? And you and I are to be bridesmaids. Is she also having her sister?'

'Apparently not. She's spoken to Clio about it, and because Lennox will only be about six months old and she'll still be breastfeeding and whatever, she said she'd prefer that Cal leaves her out of the wedding party.'

Tiff chuckled. 'It's a pity I don't have the same excuse. Anyway, what sort of a name is Lennox?'

'Apparently, it's Scottish and has something to do with a tree. An elm, I think.'

'Right you are. It's probably fortunate he wasn't a girl and didn't get named after another of the muses.'

When Callie and Clio were born, Cal's mother was studying ancient history and had been fascinated by Zeus' muses. Calliope was the muse of poetry and Clio the muse of history, or was that the wrong way around? Luckily for him, by the time their brother

Angus came along, she'd moved onto family history, the Scottish side.

'Very fortunate – as are we to be Cal's bridesmaids,' I said. I tried to sound stern even though Tiff would've hated being left out of the wedding party.

'Do you know who the groomsmen will be?' Tiff asked.

'I don't think Matt's thought that far ahead yet,' I said. 'Are you going to be able to make it back?'

'We will. Jake's already been onto his editor. We were due to be in New Zealand in August, so we'll go via the Sunshine Coast and maybe spend a few weeks up there.'

'I can think of worse places to be during winter,' I said with a chuckle.

'Yeah, me too. It's been years since I was there, probably not since those summers we spent at your holiday house when we were kids. We'll also spend a few nights in Brisbane with Dad and Mary. It's probably about time I introduced Jake properly to them. He's met Dad via Zoom, but it's not the same.'

'No,' I said, 'it's not. He's met your mother, though, hasn't he?'

'Yes, when she was in Thailand earlier in the year. Anyway, why aren't you out somewhere with Tommy tonight?'

'I have been, but—' My bottom lip trembled, and (not for the first time) I cursed video calls.

'Oh Ally,' she said, immediately understanding. 'You did it?'

'You're not surprised?'

'No,' she said. 'You were trying too hard to convince yourself it was perfect.' She shrugged. 'It was just a matter of time.'

'Yeah, but how did you know I dumped him? He might've dumped me.'

'No, sweetie, it was always going to be you as dumper and him as dumpee. I might have only met him once via FaceTime, but anyone could see he was devoted to you.'

'He was the perfect boyfriend on paper,' I said. 'I don't know why I couldn't make myself love him. Maybe I'm destined to always fall for the men who don't deserve me and overlook those who do. Take Tommy, for instance, he was everything he was supposed to be, and I took him for granted. He didn't like garlic, yet I insisted on dragging him to that French place I love in Prahran tonight. Last week we lined up for ages to get into my favourite Asian place in Flinders Lane even though I know he doesn't like spice—'

'He doesn't like garlic or spice?' Jake piped up from his desk. 'Get rid of the man immediately.'

'If you'd been listening to the entire conversation rather than random bits of it, you'd know that she has gotten rid of him,' said Tiff. 'Ignore him,' she said to me. 'Now, how did you do it? Was it okay?'

'It was fine,' I said. 'Much better than it should've been.' I relayed the evening's events. 'I haven't told Cal yet. I didn't want my issues to dampen her celebrations.'

'She knows it's coming, though,' said Tiff. 'We've both known it was coming.'

'Yeah, well, now it's done.'

We were silent for a second before Tiff brightened again and said, 'What has Cal told you about the bridesmaid's outfits?'

'Apparently we can decide for ourselves. Semi-formal, she said.'

Tiff screwed up her nose in disbelief. 'It can't possibly be that easy. Callie's been dreaming of her wedding since we were in primary school.'

'And you said you'd never get married, and I said … I can't remember what I said.' How was I so clear about what my friends wanted from life and so murky with my memories?

'You used to say you didn't care whether you ever had a ring on your finger, but your forever man had to make you laugh and love dogs.'

'That sounds like something I'd say.' Then there was a brief silence while I thought about how much that description fitted Mac.

As if she could read my mind, Tiff said, 'Maybe you should fall in love with Mac. I know I haven't met him, but from what you've said, he ticks those boxes.'

I made myself laugh and said, 'Now, there's an

idea, except for my rule about not falling for friends—'

'On account of if you break-up, you lose both your lover and your friend?' Tiff finished.

'Exactly.'

'Some rules were meant to be broken,' said Tiff. 'After all, look what happened with my checklist?' She walked over to where Jake sat and kissed the top of his head. He reached up and grabbed her hand, planted a kiss on her palm and smiled at her in a way that hurt my bruised heart.

'I saw Luke the other day,' I blurted.

Tiff's head jerked up, her attention back on me. 'Where?'

'In Bali, the night before we came home.' I lifted one shoulder in a show of nonchalance. 'It was okay; Tommy and I had dinner with him and Sasha.'

Tiff's mouth was open, but no words were coming out.

'He told me that Ainsley is gone,' I said.

'I don't care about Ainsley, although, in hindsight, she did me a favour.' She drew a deep breath and said, 'Please tell me you didn't finish with Tommy because of Luke.'

'No! Absolutely not!'

Tiff raised her eyebrows, and if you could hold a stare through a phone screen, she was doing just that. 'Really?'

'Really!' I shook the image of Luke climbing from

the pool from my brain. 'I felt nothing for him.'

Tiff nodded slowly as if deciding whether she believed me.

'He's got Ainsley's job,' I said.

'What the fuck?' The words exploded from her. Jake turned, his eyes following Tiff as she stalked around their room. 'Does that man make a career of jumping into other people's jobs? What's the bet he was offered it before Ainsley even knew she was on the way out? God, they're ruthless!'

'Isn't it a good thing you're out of it then, babe?' said Jake soothingly.

'Exactly,' I added. 'After all, you have no regrets ...'

'None at all,' she dismissed. 'It's the principle of the matter.' Her brow furrowed. 'Hang on, does that mean he's in Melbourne now?'

I nodded. 'Apparently so.'

'Are you seeing him again?' Tiff's eyes had narrowed.

I shook my head. 'No. He texted me, but I didn't reply. I even deleted his number,' I declared proudly.

She nodded with relief. 'Good girl. But back to Callie, even if I can't be at the bridal shops with you guys, you must message me all the pics and, whatever you do, don't let her walk out with something that makes her look like a toilet roll doll.'

I laughed and promised her she'd be involved every step of the way. When she hung up, I gave into the tears that had been threatening ever since I said goodnight to Tommy. It might've been my decision, but that didn't mean I felt good about it … or myself.

CHAPTER EIGHT

I woke on Sunday morning feeling as dull and sorry for myself as I had on Saturday night. The day was as grey as my mood, so I marched up to the markets and stocked up on vegetables before returning home to make batches of soup. By the time I'd finished, I had stashed enough lunches in the freezer for the next few weeks. I was also exhausted and blamed it on emotions and jet lag. Stella must have felt the same as she scarcely moved from her position on the mat near the kitchen where she could keep a good eye on me.

When the rain pelted down in a way that said it was here to stay for the rest of the day, and Mac texted to say he and Kevin would give their walk a miss, I was relieved not to have to see him. I wasn't sure if I could force some sunshine into my mood and didn't want to inflict myself on him – or anyone – while I felt like this. One day, I promised myself, you get one day to get this, whatever it is, out of your system.

I replied:

It's miserable out. How was your night?

Mac: *Yeah, good. We went to a new rooftop in Little Lon – a mate of mine designed the garden for it. How did you go with Tommy?*

My finger hovered over the phone for a few seconds as I considered my reply.

It was fine. Sad, of course, but fine. I think he might've been expecting it.

Mac: *And you're okay?*

Me: *Just a bit sad – it's for the best, though.*

Mac: *Want to catch up for comfort pizza and red wine tonight?*

My heart quickened. For a second or two, it felt almost as if he was asking me out on a date. Then I remembered he'd spent the previous night with Bree – and would probably repeat that next weekend – and realised he was just being a friend.

Me: *Thanks, but I think I'll have an early one. I didn't sleep well last night and have a busy week ahead.*

Mac: *No probs. I'm heading into a busy one too. See you Saturday morning? Brekky?*

Me: *Sounds good.*

Even though I probably should've got a start on next week's deadlines, I pulled a throw rug out of the closet and retired to the couch to feel sorry for myself in the company of Inspector Barnaby and the rising body count in *Midsomer Murders*.

The first half of the week had me busy with client

bookings, leaving no time to think about Tommy, Mac or even Callie's wedding plans. I also worked on a commission from one of the mainstream lifestyle magazines for an article about finding your career mojo in your Sun sign that I was keen to submit before the end of the week deadline. While I'd pitched and had stories accepted by this editor before, this was the first time Catherine (or, indeed, any editor) had approached me, and I didn't want to let her down. Also, it was through her acceptance of previous articles that I'd been approached to do the radio gig.

The first article I wrote for her – a piece on how you can use your Sun sign to help with weight management, *Is Your Sun Sign Making You Fat?* – had led to me being approached by three radio stations to do a short interview on the subject. The same happened with my next contribution about using astrology to manage workplace stress and make the most of your day. This was quickly followed by a call from one of the producers of *The Toast Team*, and the rest, as they say, was history. None of it would've happened if Catherine hadn't accepted that first pitch from me, so I owed it all to her. When she emailed me on Wednesday afternoon to let me know she'd received the copy and was pleased with it, I breathed a little sigh of relief.

On Wednesday night Callie came round, and we opened a bottle of bubbly and dialled in Tiff, who was still in Bali, for a preliminary wedding discussion.

Once Callie had oohed and aahed over Tiff's villa and we'd toasted the bride-to-be, Tiff, in typical fashion, went straight to the point.

'How the fuck are you going to organise this wedding so quickly, sweetie?'

I choked on my mouthful of sparkling, but Callie serenely said, 'It's completely doable. Matt and I are taking the week after next off, and we'll head up to Mooloolaba and get as much organised as we can. We have a meeting booked with the celebrant, and she's already begun organising the licence and any permissions we need for the beach. We'll also see the events manager at the surf club and run through menu options. Your mother'—she nodded towards me—'has already spoken to a couple of potential suppliers for the cake, and the photographer is a friend of Matt's.' When Tiff made to interrupt, Callie calmly cut her off. 'I'd love for you to do the photos, Tiff, but as bridesmaids, you and Ally will have enough to do.'

Tiff nodded her agreement. 'Fair enough. What about your dress? Actually, what about our dresses?'

'If Ally's free, I thought we could go looking on Saturday?' Her look was a combination of hope that I'd come with her and recognition that wedding dress shops were probably my idea of hell.

'Sure,' I said. 'It should be fun.' I injected a tone of excitement into my voice.

'I know you don't think that,' Callie said, 'but I love

that you said it anyway. As for you guys, you've both got completely different tastes, and the whole thing will be quite casual anyway, so you can choose your own dress.'

'Do you at least have an idea about your colours?' I'd seen a fabulous burgundy vintage eighties-style pantsuit in Fitzroy a few weeks ago that could fit the bill. It had filmy long sleeves with a deep vee, a cinched waist and wide legs. Some platform shoes and …

'I don't think she means vintage,' said Tiff. How did she know what I was thinking?

'Alice can wear vintage if she wants,' said Callie, and I shot Tiff a 'so there' look. 'It will be on the beach so it will be barefoot. Even though it's winter—'

Tiff snorted. 'Whatever passes for winter in South-East Queensland, that is.'

Callie chuckled. 'Yes. With luck, the day will be mild, but you'll probably need a wrap or something for the evening. Matt, Alex and Todd—'

'Who's Alex and Todd?' I broke in.

'Matt's groomsmen. Alex, his best man, is an old friend. I think he went to uni and worked with him in Hong Kong at one stage, or was it Singapore? I've never met him. And Todd is another friend from uni. You know him, Tiff. Matt said he's dating a friend of yours – Andi, I think he said her name was.'

'Not Todd Reynolds?'

'Yes, I think so,' said Cal.

'Small world,' said Tiff, nodding slowly.

'We're keeping the guest list fairly small,' Callie continued. 'Matt wants to have a dinner in the next couple of weeks to introduce you to Todd and Alex,' she said to me. 'Andi will probably be there, but I don't know if Alex has a plus one,' she mused. 'You can bring Tommy along.'

I turned my head, but not before Tiff noticed. 'You haven't told her?' she accused.

'Told me what?' asked Callie, frowning. Then the penny dropped. 'Oh Ally, you did it.' She reached out to pat my hand. 'How are you? How was it?'

'It was … it was okay,' I said. 'As okay as can be expected. I have to see him tomorrow morning, so I hope he's still fine.'

'Did you tell Callie you'd seen Luke?' asked Tiff. I scowled at her through the screen. 'What?' she asked, her face a picture of innocence.

'I didn't want to worry her,' I said.

'I am still here and in the room with you,' said Cal. 'What's this about Luke?'

'She had dinner with him when they were in Ubud. He's got Ainsley's job and is living in Melbourne now.' Tiff finished with a little shrug of her shoulder.

'And you didn't think you needed to tell me that?' Cal rounded on me. 'That didn't have anything to do with—'

'With why I broke up with Tommy?' I glared at Tiff. 'No. And it wasn't like Tiff made it sound. *I* didn't have dinner with him; Tommy and I met him and Sasha for dinner. And I've deleted his number from my phone.' I added the last for effect.

'Did you still feel anything for him?' asked Callie, her face a picture of a concerned friend.

'No,' I said. 'Absolutely not.'

'Ally?' Cal raised her eyebrows as if she didn't believe me.

'Okay, when I saw him, it felt weird, and I thought it was all starting again, but I think that was just muscle memory. My heart thought that's how it was supposed to feel, so it did. Do you know what I mean?'

Callie nodded sagely. 'Yes, I know. That's how I was with Jamie.'

'Sasha is welcome to him,' I added for effect.

'Did you notice she didn't say she'd blocked his number?' said Tiff with another lift of the shoulder.

'Seriously?' I stared down at the screen. 'Only because I didn't think about that. Besides,' I added, 'I never pick up calls from numbers I don't recognise, and now I've deleted it, I can't go back and block it,' I added with a 'so there' tilt to my head.

Callie nodded slowly. 'I'm worried about you, sweetie. We both are.' She dipped her head towards Tiff. 'I remember too well how you were when you arrived here.'

I smiled at her, suddenly choked for words. Taking a deep breath, I said, 'I'm fine and won't be seeing him again, but I have to be awake at five, so I reckon we need to wind this up.'

Tiff rang off, but before Cal left, she said, 'You're sure you're okay?'

Impulsively, I hugged her. 'I am, sweetie.'

'I just want you to be happy, you know?'

'I know.' I attempted a determined smile. 'I'm fine,' I said again. 'And I'm so happy for you and Matt. My turn will come. I know it will.'

She squeezed my arm and kissed my cheek. 'I know it will too.'

I hoped rather than believed she was right.

Thursday didn't start well. A five am alarm call is never welcome and breakfast radio is unforgiving and challenging at the best of times.

Contrary to my client bookings, where we look at their personal chart as a whole, pinpointing opportunities and potential ways of working with challenges, on *The Toast Team*, it was a combination of popular astrology, what was happening in the sky that week (Mercury's about to turn retrograde, so it's a great idea to back up your hard drives and delay, if possible, signing any major contracts or purchasing technology) and an ancient form of question-and-answer astrology known as horary.

For hundreds of years, this was the bread and butter of astrologers. At its simplest form, the astrologer would draw up a chart for when the question was asked and look to it for answers. Of course it's more complex than that, but that's the general idea. Back in the Middle Ages, the questions might be around the grain harvest or the location of the cow that had gone missing, the identity of the scoundrel who'd ridden out of town with your daughter, or the result of a dispute. Kings and queens even consulted astrologers in those days, eager to know about the outcome (or preferred timing) of battles and other important events. Back then, doctors even used the position of the planets to help with diagnosis and treatment.

In some ways, things haven't changed. It's been said that certain members of royalty and even presidents and billionaires have consulted astrologers, and the questions they ask are the modern-day equivalent of what was asked back in those days. The type of calls I get on *The Toast Team*, though, could be considered by some to be a tad more trivial than queries relating to investments and elections.

The segment has, however, proven to be popular, and while it wasn't my favourite thing to do each week – and not just because of the five am alarm – the money helps, and my client bookings had grown in the twelve months I'd been doing it, so I couldn't complain.

I usually got the list of listener's questions thirty minutes before my airtime slot and had a short window to separate the one-line responses from the ones which could make good radio, selecting four or five questions to take to air and phoning the rest afterwards. This morning I had the usual group of suspects:

- Mark from Hawthorne wanted to know if he'd get the job he applied for (yes, they'll love him).
- Tash from Brunswick was concerned about her husband's infidelity (no, he *is* just busy).
- Donna from Richmond wanted to know if her house would sell (yes, but hold off putting it on the market for a couple of weeks until Mercury was direct again).
- Daniel from Balaclava wanted to know if he'd win the major prize in the TattsLotto this week (most probably not).
- Nina from Toorak wanted to know if she would ever get together with the man she says is the love of her life.

We breezed through the first few with no major surprises. Nina, though, was a different issue.

'I'm sorry, Nina, but the answer is no. All indications are that you two will be good friends.'

'Oh.' I was sure all of Melbourne heard the disappointment in that single syllable. 'Did you ask the chart if we'll ever get together, or just whether we will get together soon?' I gave her full marks for persistence.

'There's definitely something or someone else in the way.' If I was a betting person, I'd have put money on the love of her life already being married.

'But how long is the answer for? I feel like we have a connection. Maybe if you asked whether we would just kiss and not … you know?' Hope flooded the airwaves.

'Hook-up, you mean?' jumped in Joe, the male half of *The Toast Team*.

The producer was now waving madly at me to keep her on the line and Sami, the other half of brekky central, jumped into the fray. 'Nina, you sound disappointed. You must truly like this man?'

'I do, Sami. I feel that he's my soulmate. Perhaps we're meant to be together in another life,' Nina replied with a catch in her voice. I rolled my eyes. Thank goodness for radio.

Joe said, 'Maybe he doesn't fancy you, and you need to get over it?'

'Joe!' scolded Sami, immediately springing to Nina's defence. This was radio gold; I shook my head at the grins both were wearing.

'I can't get over it,' Nina's voice broke. 'I have to believe we're meant to be together.'

'Can you think what the commitment or obstacle is that's standing in the way of this relationship?' Sami asked the question gently.

'No,' said Nina miserably. 'If we were careful, my husband would never need to know – and his wife is always too busy with their kids to notice anything!'

Nina let out a little half sob, and in the studio,

Sami and Joe choked back laughs. Through the glass wall, the production team were almost rolling on the floor with laughter. The ensuing banter took them through to the end of the slot and the next song.

As much as everyone was laughing at poor Nina, I couldn't. It felt too unkind and too close to home. I remember only too well how I was when I had the crush on Luke and wondered now whether I'd been so infatuated with him because I was looking for a reason to break from Hayden. Back then, though, Luke was all I could think about.

It was at that time that I began taking my interest in astrology more seriously, telling myself that it was because I wanted to learn more about myself. It wasn't, though; it was because I wanted to know who I fitted with.

I'd buy books and go straight to the chapter on Sagittarius and read about who my perfect match would be, only to worry then because it was never Hayden. Just like I had with Tommy, I tried so hard to convince myself that Hayden and I were right together, even though in my heart, it didn't feel right. Luke and I were never going to be a match made in heaven – I didn't need to be an astrologer to know that. These days I knew that relationship astrology was so much more complex than a simple Sagittarius-goes-with scenario.

I remember casting 'what does he think of me?' and 'will we hook-up?' charts over and over, waiting for the Universe to slam her fist on the table and scream at me: 'Not you again! For the last time, this isn't going to happen!'

On the bright side, doing so many charts had been great practice for me. These days the results I get for clients are scarily accurate, yet when it comes to relationships, the answer is rarely accepted without further discussion – especially if it isn't what they want to hear. Like Nina, we look for loopholes and hope that maybe one day our dreams might come true.

It's why I couldn't laugh at Nina – I'd done the same.

So while Sami and Joe and the rest of the team giggled over poor Nina's predicament, I remained quiet and excused myself from the studio as soon as the segment was done and called the listeners who'd left their details and hadn't made it on air, booking in appointments for the following week with two of them.

I'd left the studio and was heading to the car park when I literally bumped into Tommy. He reached out automatically to steady me, his hand holding my arm for a second longer than needed. As if realising that, he snatched his hand away, his eyes dropping to his feet, his face colouring. 'Sorry,' he mumbled.

'It's okay,' I mumbled back, not sure where I should look or what I should be saying. 'I wasn't watching where I was going.'

'Neither was I,' he said. Then we stood there,

avoiding each other's glances, the awkward silence filling the space between us.

'How are you?' I asked.

'In the few days since we broke up, you mean?' He looked up, met my eyes and sighed heavily. 'I'm sorry, that wasn't called for. I know you wish things were different almost as much as I do.'

I nodded wordlessly.

'And I'm sure it was tough for you to say it,' he said, smiling tightly. 'Possibly almost as tough as it was for me to hear.'

I nodded again. 'I wish things had been—' I started.

'Different?' he finished. 'So do I, but it's not, and I meant what I said the other night – I hope we can be friends.' He held out his hand, and I shook it gratefully. Then, with a wave, he continued on his way. There. It was done, the first meeting. We had to do it eventually, and I was glad it was sooner rather than later.

CHAPTER NINE

When I finally got home, it was to find that my website was down and probably had been for most of the night. I relied on traffic from the US to bolster my statistics, so effectively, plenty of potential views had been missed. After being relatively stable for the last year or so, there had been a lot of downtime since the weekend. A quick call to my provider ended in a server reboot to get me back online.

As I was settling down to start on another article (due by the close of business Friday, London time), my phone rang. This time, it was my sister Laura. I adore Laura but also know that a call from her cuts straight through work time. Like all older sisters, she wants the best for me, and in her mind, wanting the best for me this time coincided with her suggesting I go home to the Sunshine Coast for a visit. Also, like all big sisters, she knew the best way to manipulate me into doing what she wanted was to use one of my nephews as leverage.

'I can't persuade you to come up for Newton's

birthday?' she asked. 'He'll be so disappointed …'

'Laura, it's not like he's even going to notice if I am there or not,' I reasoned. Newton was now nearly four.

'Come up next weekend while Matt and Callie are here,' she tried a different tack.

'Somehow, I don't think they need me there while they're wedding arranging,' I said.

'Maybe not, but it would take your mind off things.'

I almost snorted down the line. 'You've heard then.'

'About you and Tommy? Yes, Matt told me this morning. Why didn't you tell me?'

I exhaled. 'I knew you'd be disappointed. And Mum, too.'

'What's Mum got to do with it?'

Lauren hadn't denied it. I shrugged even though she couldn't see me. 'She wants more grandchildren.'

'Maybe,' Laura conceded, 'but she also wants you to be happy. Besides, I can't see Matt and Callie waiting too long to pop a couple out. I reckon the pressure will be off you for a while.'

'True.' I chuckled. 'Have you told her? Mum, that is … about Tommy?'

'No. Not yet. I wanted to talk to you first. What went wrong?'

'Nothing,' I said. 'It was just—'

'You had to try too hard to be in love with him?' she guessed.

'Yeah,' I conceded.

'Then you did the right thing,' said Laura. 'Tommy's nice, and we all like him, but even Mick said he thought you were attempting to convince yourself he was Mister Perfect. How was the sex?'

'Oh my god! Do we have to talk about that?'

'Why? Wasn't it any good? If that's the case, it's probably a good thing you decided now.'

'The sex was fine,' I reluctantly said.

'Only fine?'

'Okay, it was good. How would you like it if I asked you the same question?'

'Mick and I have always been great together. Why do you think we have so many kids?'

I shook my head and laughed. 'I figured that was because you hadn't yet worked out how it happened.'

'Oh, ha, ha. No, I don't like taking the pill, and there have been several times—'

'Five?' I scoffed.

'Where we haven't been able to stop for a condom,' she finished, unabashed.

'Is that how you knew he was the one?' I asked, suddenly serious. 'Because you couldn't keep your hands off each other?'

She paused before answering. 'It's important, but it's not everything,' she finally said. 'Do you remember when we split up for a while?'

Laura and Mick had begun dating when Laura was still at school. Mick had declared he'd wanted to marry her very early on, but even though she'd also fallen for him, she'd said she wasn't ready and wanted to live and work in Brisbane for a time. They'd split up for a few months, but it wasn't long before they were back together.

'Yes, I remember ... vaguely,' I said.

'Well,' she hesitated briefly, 'I went out with someone else for a while.'

'Really?' I'd always assumed that Mick had been her one and only.

'It was just a few months, and it was so exciting. But then I came home one weekend, and I ran into Mick. He was so familiar, but at the same time, I had this rush of, I don't even know how to explain it, but I knew in that moment that even when the lust died down, it would still be there, if that makes sense.'

When I didn't reply, she added, 'I knew he was the one I wanted to share everything with – all of it.'

'What about the other guy?' I asked. 'Do you ever think about him?'

'No.' Had she hesitated? 'Seriously, though,' she said. 'As exciting as the alternative might seem, don't underestimate the ordinary.'

'Are you saying I shouldn't have split from Tommy?'

'I'm not saying that. You still need that rush, even if the everyday gets in the way. All I'm saying is that the rush without the everyday just leads to trouble.'

'I see.' At least, I thought I did. While the sex with Tommy was good, I didn't want to share the ordinary with him. And as exciting as Luke had been, even back then, I knew that any relationship would be fleeting. There was nothing of substance underneath the attraction to sustain anything more. What I needed was a combination of the two – someone I could share both the excitement and the ordinary with. A picture of Mac's face floated before me, and I pushed it away.

'I know we don't talk often enough, Ally,' she said, 'but I'd like us to … if you want to, that is.' When I didn't answer, she added, 'I know you have Callie and Tiff, but I'm here too.'

'Thanks.' I squeezed the word past the lump in my throat. 'I'd like that too.'

'And you'll think about next weekend?'

'I will,' I promised, already knowing I'd be on that flight with Matt and Callie.

Between the traffic, the website and Laura, my morning was shot to pieces. By midday, I gave up on *Elements and the Change Management Cycle* (something had to be done to add some pizazz to that title) and wandered over to Commercial Road for the tram down to St Kilda Beach. Maybe lunch and some people watching would do the trick.

Aside from anything, the day (for now, after all, this was Melbourne) was too nice to spend inside. It was the bright blue that only exists outside of summer, with Port Phillip Bay having a weird green colour seen on the windiest, bluest days when the water is a mess of white, choppy waves. The palm trees were swaying in the wind, their leaves rustling together as seagulls hovered above, seemingly held in place by the wind.

The occasional jet-ski scooted across the top of the chop, and on the horizon, container ships made their way out of the bay into open waters while the kite surfers were doing their thing further up the beach. A loved-up gorgeous couple glided by on a tandem bike with a fluffy grey designer pooch nestled in the basket.

Callie had asked me the other week whether I ever missed Sydney. It was on one of our regular video calls with Tiff, who was in a hotel room somewhere and had scoffed at the question.

I'd laughed and said I had everything I needed here, but I missed Sydney Harbour, especially on a clear blue day in winter when the water shimmered with a million diamonds and the sails of the Opera House gleamed. I remembered being able to watch the Wednesday afternoon yacht races from the boardroom in the office and the walks through the botanical gardens on the harbour foreshore on those rare days when I managed to get out for more than half an hour at lunchtime. Yet, despite the beauty of Sydney Harbour, on a day like today, nothing beat St Kilda's particular brand of therapy.

When I first moved down and felt particularly low, I'd stand at the edge of this pier with Stella a few times a week. I hadn't visited as much lately – I hadn't needed to.

I sauntered up the pier past the anglers with their rods and abandoned bikes, stopping every so often to make the sort of conversation you make with pier fishers:

'Caught anything?'

'Nah, not today, love.'

'It's a good day for it, but …'

'That it is.'

Reaching the end of the breakwater, I stood at the edge, letting the wind rush through me and blow all the cobwebs away. Maybe now I'd freed all this space in my head, I might be able to work some magic on that title. I roughly bunched my ponytail back into its elastic and shoved it under the hood of my jacket before retracing my steps.

After choosing a café on the beach, I sat outside and caught the eye of a waitress and ordered a glass of white wine and a trio of dips and Turkish bread.

Letting St Kilda work its usual magic on my soul, I sipped, spread dip onto bread, and watched the passing parade on the esplanade. It felt like missing school for the day or phoning in sick at work. I should be at home working, but being out in the fresh air was doing my soul so much good.

This is why, when my phone rang, I answered it automatically without looking at the number.

'Hey, Alice.' My heart sank – it was Luke. At my continued silence, he said, 'It's me, Luke.' Then he laughed as if it was unthinkable I should ever not recognise his voice.

'Oh, hi,' I said, trying to sound more nonchalant than I felt. 'How was the rest of your holiday?'

'Yeah, it was great. Bali is always a good idea, although we had to buy another bag to get all the shit Sasha bought home.' He laughed again. 'What about you and Tommy? Good trip home?'

'Absolutely, although you know how it is – once you've done that first day back at work, you forget you were even on holiday.' I reached for another piece of bread, wondering if I could chew it without him hearing.

'Tell me about it. Ainsley left a right mess here. You're so lucky you're out of it.' Had he forgotten that it was his fault that I was, as he'd put it, out of it? 'Hey, I was wondering, did you want to catch up sometime?' he asked.

My stomach tipped and turned – not a good thing to do considering the garlicky, fishy dip. 'I don't think that's a good idea,' I said slowly.

'Where's the harm? We're two friends catching up for a drink or a bite of lunch?'

'No, I don't think so, Luke.' As if it would strengthen my resolve, I sat straighter in my chair.

'You're right of course,' he said after a brief pause. 'To be honest, though, I'm struggling at work and was hoping I could talk things through with you. You could always see through the politics.' He hesitated again. 'I wouldn't blame you if you said no, though. It must've been tough when you lost your job, but that was nearly two years ago ...'

He let the words trail off, the implication being that surely I wasn't going to hold that against him, not after all this time.

'Besides,' he continued, 'you're doing well for yourself now.'

I was, and I was also over him. Wasn't I? There was only one way to find out, though. 'Okay,' I said. 'I'll meet you, but not for a drink.' I certainly didn't trust that little minx Temptation not to cause trouble if dark corners and alcohol were involved.

'Great. Tomorrow?' He named a small restaurant on Hardware Lane, and I agreed and regretted it the second I hung up. Tomorrow would, I resolved, be the first and last time I'd meet him. I could walk away whenever I wanted.

CHAPTER TEN

There were two texts from Luke when I woke the following morning. One from last night:

Hey Al, great to chat today and looking forward to seeing you. x

And one received this morning:

Just confirming you're still right for lunch today.

I fired off a quick reply in the affirmative before making myself some toast and tea, my stomach too unsettled for anything else. It had even been too unsettled for me to have anything more than a bowl of soup for dinner last night. I took some deep breaths to coach it into submission. Agreeing to see Luke was a mistake. While rationally, there was nothing wrong with hearing what he had to say – and there was no rule that said we couldn't move on and be friends again – it was still wrong. He was married, and I wasn't interested. There was, in fact, no reason at all for my belly to be behaving as it was. Another few deep breaths. That's it, Alice. No more. There, it was gone.

My website was down again this morning. I'd

tried calling the support desk before my first client of the day but got their voicemail. I briefly considered phoning Tommy to ask if he could log in and look at it, but shaking my head, I pushed that thought aside quickly. He'd help, but I didn't want to take advantage of his kindness or send him the wrong message.

When I finally did talk to website support, the technician prattled on about things I didn't understand.

'I'm sorry, Sonny, but did you say something about a zombie apocalypse?'

He laughed. 'No, Alice, I said that whoever was targeting your website is using a series of zombie machines to launch spam attacks, and that's what's bringing the site down – it's your security doing its job.'

'Okay, I still don't understand, and I don't have time for this now. Can you kick it in the guts or whatever you do to get it going again? This has been happening way too often, and my business relies on my website being available for bookings.'

'Sure, I understand. Give me ten minutes and we'll have you operational again.'

'Before you go, I'm wondering, is there any reason I have to tell you the site is offline? I thought that's what I paid you guys for.'

'We're monitoring the servers,' he said for the fourth (or was it fifth?) time in the last week, 'not your physical website.'

I sighed heavily. 'In other words, if I didn't check

it, I might never know it was offline.'

'I'm sure you would,' he said helpfully. 'One of your clients would tell you.'

'Thanks for that,' I muttered before hanging up. Perhaps it was time to shop around for a new support provider. Mac said he was something in IT. Maybe he knew of someone? I filed that thought away for later and dialled into my next meeting.

I didn't allow myself to think about Luke again until I was on the tram and on my way into the city.

My last appointment had gone over time, so I'd run out of time to overthink what I was wearing. I'd ended up leaving on the cargo pants and long-sleeved T-shirt I'd worn for my clients and added a pair of white trainers and a yellow linen scarf and grabbed a denim jacket as I rushed out the door. It's not as if this was a date, I reasoned, but two ex-colleagues getting together to discuss work.

Even as I told myself that, I knew it for the lie that it was and groaned inwardly. What was I doing? I was so good at handing out advice to my clients, so why couldn't I follow it for myself?

Take this morning's first client, Lisa, for example. The dream client who wanted to learn about herself so she could avoid mistakes she'd made in the past — although first, we'd had to discuss the concept that imperfection was okay.

'I always give more in my relationships than I get back,' she told me. 'With David, I lost all my friends and, in the end, felt like I had nothing except my job.'

We talked about how she could manage this next time and how the challenge could be turned into a strength. We discussed the importance of 'me' time and scheduling activities with friends. We talked about how it was okay to step back and let her partner do things for her sometimes and how it was nice to appreciate those gestures for what they were without looking for perfection in their execution.

Now, as I walked up the street towards the restaurant, I wondered for the first time in a long time whether I would have followed any advice I'd been given before jumping into whatever it was with Luke and had to concede that it wouldn't have changed a thing. That was always going to happen, and it was always going to hurt. And here I was going back there.

Impulsively, I called Callie. 'Please don't tell me you're backing out tomorrow morning?' she said.

'Of course not. I'm looking forward to finding the perfect dress for you.'

'Liar,' she accused, chuckling. 'What's up?' When I hesitated, she said, 'Where are you, Ally?'

'I'm in a laneway off Little Bourke Street, trying to decide whether I'm going to walk around the corner into Hardware Lane—' I took a deep breath. 'Where I'm supposed to be meeting Luke for lunch.'

Callie's indrawn breath was loud and clear. 'Oh, Ally. Why?'

Even though she couldn't see me, I shrugged. 'I'm not sure why I said yes. I should've blocked his number rather than just deleted it. I should've said no.' I pressed myself back into the wall of the narrow lane. 'He said he needed my help with some issues he's having at work,' I added.

'And you couldn't say no,' she guessed.

'Yeah. Something like that.'

'Okay,' she said. 'Here's what's going to happen. You're going to meet him, hear what he has to say, and walk out of there. Then you're going to block his number. Under no circumstances are you going to listen to anything else he has to say.'

I almost giggled at the firm tone in her voice. 'You sound like you're channelling Tiff,' I said.

'If she was here, she'd say the same,' Cal said. 'She'd say a whole lot more than that, so be grateful you've got me, not her. And remember your rules.'

'I didn't create one specifically for Luke.'

A burst of laughter came down the phone. 'You've got a few minutes to do it now.'

I nodded. 'Okay.'

'And Al? Be careful.'

'He can't hurt me anymore,' I said.

'Can't he?'

'No,' I said firmly. 'I won't let him.' And at that

moment, I believed it too.

Luke was already at the restaurant and seated at a table outside, talking on his phone.

'Babe, don't be sad,' Luke said to his phone. 'I'll try not to be too late.' He rolled his eyes and mouthed hello to me. 'It's my job, Sash.' His jaw tightened, and exasperation was creeping into his voice. He shook his head at me, his eyebrows raised, and held the phone away from his ear, moving his fingers and thumb together in a talking sign. 'Yep, whatever … listen, Sasha, I have to go; I'm due to meet some clients for lunch.'

My eyes widened at his words, and any danger I thought my heart might've possibly still been in disappeared in an instant. I caught a waiter's eye, pointed at a wine on the menu and smiled my thanks. What was I doing here?

'Don't do this now, Sasha; you know I don't have time to talk. I'll see you when I get home.' I might not have warmed to Sasha, but I couldn't help but feel sympathy for her.

Luke exhaled in an overly dramatic sigh and turned off his phone, leaving it on the table next to his cutlery. Settling back into his seat, he looked across at me, grinned ruefully, took a mouthful of the beer on the table in front of him, and sighed again.

'You're probably wondering what that was all

about?' he asked.

'No, it's none of my business. But you lied to her, and I didn't enjoy hearing that.' The words had fallen from his tongue so easily that I wondered how often he'd done the same during their relationship.

'What was I supposed to say? That I was meeting you? Then she'd think I was doing something I shouldn't be.'

'If you have to lie, doesn't it follow that you are doing something she'd think you shouldn't be doing?' I countered, wondering whether Luke had exaggerated that little performance on the phone for my benefit.

'Shit, Al, don't you go all logical on me. I'm relying on you to lighten my load, not add to it.'

I raised my eyebrows but said nothing as the waiter arrived with my wine.

'Anyway, I don't want to talk about that now.' He held up his glass and smiled the smile that used to give me goosebumps but now left me cold. 'What will we drink to?'

'Achieving your targets?' I suggested.

'Surely we can find something more interesting to toast to than that?'

I lifted one shoulder. 'Maybe we can talk about the weather,' I suggested. 'I love this time of the year. There's nothing more beautiful than when the plane trees at the top end of Collins Street lose their leaves and the colour changes in the parks. It almost makes you wish you were a kid again and feel them crunch under your shoes and run through kicking them in the air.'

'Babe, with my luck, my leaves wouldn't crunch; they'd stick to the bottom of my shoe so I'd go arse first into the pavement – and any pile I kicked would have dog shit in it!'

I couldn't help but laugh at his expression and was still laughing when I looked around to see Mac standing there. But it was a different Mac to the one I was used to. This Mac was dressed for the office in a well-cut navy suit and open-neck white shirt. He looked … different … powerful even … and even more shaggable than usual. At first, he grinned, and then, upon noticing Luke, his expression changed to something else – something cold I couldn't read. A chill ran up my spine.

'Hey you,' I said when he walked the few steps to where we sat.

'Hey yourself.' The sexy-Mac smile was back, and I thought I must've imagined the momentary weirdness. 'What brings you into the city on a workday? Deadline avoidance again?'

'No, meeting a friend for lunch.' I dipped my head towards Luke. 'Luke, this is Mac, my sort of neighbour. Luke's an old colleague from Sydney,' I explained to Mac, not daring to meet his eyes in case that strange coldness was there again.

Luke had stood to shake Mac's hand. Although Luke was stockier and his shoulders broader, he seemed diminished against Mac's still presence. Luke must've realised it too and quickly sat back down.

'What is a sort of neighbour?' Luke asked.

Mac grinned at me as he answered Luke, and again the nerves up my spine ran wild, but this time they were far from cold. 'Oh, we live a few houses apart and have breakfast together most weekends.'

I choked on a mouthful of wine.

'Our dogs have sleepovers at each other's house from time to time, too,' he continued, a look of pure innocence on his face. 'Anyway, it's been nice meeting you, Luke.' To me, he said, 'Are we on for tomorrow morning?'

'I can't,' I said. 'I'm meeting Cal, and we're going wedding dress shopping.' I wrinkled my nose.

He laughed. 'Rather you than me, dear. You can tell me all about it later. While I think of it, are you okay to have Kevin for a few days next week?'

'Sure. You travelling again?'

He nodded. 'Sydney.'

'No problems, but can you please have Stella next weekend? I'm heading up to the Sunny Coast to see Mum and Dad.'

'It's a deal.' He bent down and kissed my cheek, something he'd never done before, and held up a hand in farewell. I stopped myself from raising my own to rest where his lips had been.

'Interesting dude,' said Luke.

I nodded mutely, my attention still on Mac, who was greeting a woman in the adjacent café with a lingering kiss on the lips. She was tall, slim and dressed for the office. A wave of silvery blonde hair floated down her back, and in her heels, she was almost at eye level with him. She kissed him back, then gently wiped away the traces of her lipstick from the corner of his mouth with her thumb before brushing at some imaginary lint from the shoulder of his jacket. This, I decided, must be Bree.

'Al!' Luke's voice brought me back to the table. 'I was just saying that I'm sure I've either met him before or seen him somewhere.' He frowned as he thought about it. 'What's his surname?'

'I have no idea.' Mac had put his arm around Bree and led her to a table.

'What's he do?' Luke asked.

'I have no idea,' I said again vaguely. Mac and the woman I'd decided must be Bree were now seated. He leant in to hear something she'd said and laughed at whatever it was. 'Something in IT, I think. We don't discuss his work.'

'Surely you must do,' said Luke. 'What else do you talk about in those breakfasts every weekend?'

I dragged my attention back to Luke. 'Sorry?'

'He said you guys have breakfast together every

weekend.' Was he pouting?

I sighed inwardly. 'I know how he made it sound, but we walk the dogs and have brekky afterwards. Not,' I added, 'that it's any of your business.'

He let out a short laugh. 'Ouch! I was more wondering what Tommy thinks about it.'

No, you weren't. 'Tommy knows about my friendship with Mac.'

'And he's fine with it?'

Where was he going with this? 'That's between us,' I finally said.

'Fair enough. Did you tell Tommy you were meeting me today?'

'No,' I admitted. 'I didn't.'

'Why was that?' I bristled at the knowing look in his eyes.

'We don't live in each other's pockets,' I said. 'But if he'd asked, I would've told him.' I refused to think about why I hadn't told him we'd broken up. 'Perhaps we'd better order lunch; you'll be needing to get back to the office soon.'

'Nah, I've got plenty of time,' he said, picking up the menu.

'Do you? Things must've changed from when Tiff was there.'

He shrugged. 'Speaking of Tiff, where's she working now? I wouldn't mind picking her brain.'

I raised my eyebrows at his effrontery, but he'd

buried his head in the menu.

'She's changed careers,' I said. 'And even if she hadn't, I doubt she'd want to help you.'

He shrugged again as if it had been worth a try, but he'd gotten the answer he expected.

'Are you struggling?' I guessed, knowing how hard that would be for him to admit.

'A little, maybe.' He looked up briefly and met my eyes, a wry half smile on his face. 'Ainsley left everything in a mess.'

'What were you expecting?'

'I'd heard rumours that Tiff had been the one who was doing most of the work or making sure the work got done while Ainsley took the credit.' He leant forward and said, 'Word is, Ainsley had no idea she was for the chop.'

'I think I know a little of how she feels,' I said pointedly. 'So if that's the case, I'm sorry for her.'

'You feel sorry for her? After what she did to you!'

'What *did* she do to me, Luke? As far as I figure it, she'd been told that I was a troublemaker but was performing too well to get rid of in the usual ways. You're the one who told her about us – she simply used it—'

'To further her own career,' he interrupted.

'True, but you gave her that ammunition. You'd already accepted my job before I knew I no longer had one.' I shook my head, biting at my bottom lip. 'Ainsley had very little to do with why I left Sydney, and we both know that. Besides, just because it happened to me is no reason for me to wish the same for her. In a way, she did me a favour – and Tiff a favour too.' How had I not realised how unkind he was? 'So yes, I do feel sorry for her, and I don't like gossip, so if that's what you brought me here for, I might as well leave now.'

He flushed a little under my stare, but by the time bowls of pasta had been placed in front of us, he'd recovered.

'There was something else I wanted to talk to you about,' he said, his eyes darting around the tables beside us as if in fear of being overheard.

'Yeeees?' I said slowly, dunking a ravioli into its sauce.

'I think I've made a mistake.' He lifted his eyes from his pasta to meet mine briefly before dropping them again.

'In moving here or in accepting Ainsley's job?'

'No, I made a mistake in marrying Sasha.'

His gaze was now holding mine, and with my heart feeling as though it was freefalling through my body, I couldn't look away. My fork dropped into my plate, the ravioli bouncing onto the table and into my lap. It was enough to snap me out of the spell as I used my serviette to wipe at the buttery smear on my clothes.

'I don't know what I was thinking,' he said, taking my silence on the subject as a signal to continue. 'I know I told you Sasha and I were over, and we were, but the holiday was booked, and Sash had these plans … We'd been together for so long it seemed cruel not to say yes when she suggested we get married.'

I gave up trying to clean my T-shirt. 'What about me? Was it cruel to spin me along the way you did? Was it cruel not telling me you had no intentions of leaving her? If you had, I would have …'

'You would have what? Stayed with Hayden?' His tone was derisive.

'No,' I conceded. 'But I wouldn't have let things go as far as they did between us if I'd known you were still with Sasha.'

'Wouldn't you?' His eyes bored into mine, accusing and daring, and I was the one to look away first.

I didn't know how to answer. I like to think I wouldn't have kissed him, but would I have stopped our flirtation? I couldn't honestly say that I would have. Temptation had such a firm grip on my hormones in those days.

'I knew you hadn't taken me seriously,' he said. 'I told myself that mine was the only heart at risk of breaking,' he added with a dramatic sigh that almost made me laugh out loud for the first time in this conversation.

He reached across the table for my hand. 'I haven't been able to stop thinking about you, Al. I especially haven't been able to stop thinking about what might have been. You and I are unfinished business. So when I saw you sitting by that pool in Ubud, I wasn't surprised. I always knew we'd get another chance.' He smiled then, the same smile that once would have had me hurling myself into his arms. Now, though, what little I'd eaten of my lunch was threatening to make a reappearance.

I dragged my hand from his and sat back in my chair, willing my heartbeat to slow so my brain could catch up with what was happening.

No,' I said, shaking my head. 'No, no, no, no.'

'It's okay, Al; I've got it all worked out. We don't need to tell anyone yet, but let's see how it goes.'

Luke's words swirled, but their meaning took time to filter into my brain. I had to stop this; the longer I let him talk, the more convinced he'd be that he had me.

'No!' I said, louder this time, locking eyes with his. 'You can't be saying this, Luke. You're married; you made a promise.'

'But that's what I'm trying to tell you.' His smile was full of confidence. 'I don't think I was thinking straight when I made it. I didn't mean it.'

'Then you shouldn't have said it.' I pushed my uneaten lunch away.

'Is it Tommy? Is that why you're hesitating? He's a nice guy, but you and I both know he's not for you.' His tone was wheedling, and something in my head clicked. Luke's enthusiasm for me had waned almost as soon as I told him I'd split from Hayden. Maybe he enjoyed thinking he could have someone who 'belonged' to someone else. I didn't think I'd pitied anyone more than I pitied Sasha in that instant – or disliked myself for how I behaved back then.

'Tommy is a far better man than you'll ever be,' I said, meaning every word.

'Is it that Mac dude, then? I saw the way he looked at you.' I didn't know what he thought he'd seen, but I'd heard enough.

'No, Luke, it's you,' I said, pushing my chair out from the table. 'Whether you meant the words you said to Sasha or not, the fact is, you made a promise to her. And even if you hadn't, I'm not interested – not anymore. I can't believe I ever was.' I picked up my bag and dug out my wallet, throwing some notes onto the table. 'Go home to your wife and please don't call me again.'

As I stormed away, the breeze lifted my hair, and I had the strangest feeling that a weight had been lifted from my shoulders. Stopping around the corner, I leant back against the wall and tipped my head to the sky, inhaling deeply. Then I pulled my phone out of my bag and blocked his number. It was over.

CHAPTER ELEVEN

My euphoria at finally having closure over Luke lasted until I got home, after which I spent the next few hours rehashing the whole debacle and beating myself up over my part in it.

I'd met Hayden at precisely the time we should've met. I was twenty-eight and thought I should have some sort of life plan because, after all, that's what you do when you're twenty-eight, but until then, the furthest I'd planned was what I'd be wearing on Saturday night.

The life plan had, of course, been Tiff's idea, as these things tended to be.

'You need a five-year plan,' she'd told me. She and Callie had come up from Melbourne to see me. We'd been out for dinner and were back at my lower north shore apartment drinking wine and exchanging deep and meaningfuls. 'That sounds awfully adult,' I'd said.

'I hate to break it to you, Al, but we're going to be thirty soon.'

I'd grimaced, laughed and poured us another

wine, but Tiff said, 'I'm serious, Al. I know you have this idea that you'll always fall on your feet, but you need to make sure the ground is stable.'

Through my wine-addled brain, I wondered briefly where the metaphors were coming from and screwed up my nose. I'd always ended up where I needed to end up, so I didn't see why that needed to change.

Tiff, however, hadn't finished with me. 'You're earning good money, Al, and you've still got that inheritance from your grandmother sitting in the bank doing nothing, so you have a deposit already. It's more sensible than paying rent and moving every year.' She'd recently purchased her apartment in South Yarra so was keen for me to join the mortgage belt too.

'What about Cal?' I asked petulantly. 'Why doesn't she need to have a five-year plan too?'

'I do,' said Callie, looking up from her phone. She was dating Jamie by then and still in the throes of new love and was constantly checking her phone for messages from him. 'But mine is more of a bucket list, I suppose. Besides, within five years, I'll be married to Jamie and maybe pregnant with our second child.' I glanced across at Tiff and raised my eyebrows. 'I'd like to have the first by the time I'm thirty,' she added gravely and, reaching for her glass, downed the contents. I poured her another, leaving a little trail of drops where my aim wasn't as good as it should've been.

'What about you, Al? Have you thought about marriage?' Tiff asked, her eyes on Cal. The concern in them surprised me. Well, well, well, Tiff didn't approve of Jamie. I raised my eyebrows in silent question. She answered with a slight lift of her shoulder and mouthed 'later'.

'I haven't thought about it,' I said, carefully lowering myself back to the floor and managing not to spill a drop of my wine. 'Probably. Although I've been single for so long, I'm not sure I'd know how to be in a relationship anymore.'

Callie choked on her wine, and Tiff burst out laughing. 'Relationships? You? Six months is a long time for you, and you can't very well call that a relationship,' Tiff said.

'Look who's talking,' I pointed out.

'True, but I don't pretend to be looking for anything other than stress relief and recreation.'

It was Callie's turn to sigh. 'You know I hate it when you talk like that,' she chided.

'Sorry, sweetie,' Tiff said, not sorry at all.

'It's a commitment thing with me,' I said. 'And that's not fair to whoever I'm with, so I end it before they get attached.'

'And before you do, too,' pointed out Callie.

'I guess. I'm waiting for that bolt of lightning – the love at first sight thing,' I admitted, hiding my face in my wine glass.

Tiff snorted a disbelieving laugh. 'You don't honestly believe in that, do you?'

'Of course she does,' said Callie indignantly.

'Yeah,' I said. 'I truly do. Mum and Dad knew they'd be together forever the first time they met – apparently, Dad told her at the end of the first date that he would marry her. Mum said the same thing happened with her parents, and even though they had a little break before they eventually got married, Laura said she fell in love with Mick right from the start.' Callie had put her phone down and was sprawled on the floor, her elbow propping her up, her chin cupped in her hand, a dreamy look on her face as she listened to me. 'That's what I want, and I don't want to settle for anything less.'

While I'd never said the words aloud before, I knew them to be true. I wanted so much to feel that rush – whatever that rush was – anything else was, quite simply, disappointing.

'So you see,' I said, 'I can come up with a five-year plan, but I can't plan on that sort of love happening, and if it did?' I shrugged. 'The plan would get thrown out the window, so there'd be no point in making it in the first place.'

Tiff made a little steeple with her forefingers and pressed it against her lips. 'That has,' she eventually said, 'a weird sort of common sense about it. Except for the fact that what you're looking for is Mr Big when everyone knows that Mr Big is the one you shag and move on from and Aiden is the one you settle and marry.' Tiff worked too hard to watch much television these days, but Callie and I knew her guilty pleasure was a Sunday afternoon *Sex And The City* binge session. She said she only watched it for the fashion – and the shoes – but she'd had to be on her second or third rewatch by now.

Callie and Tiff had left the next day, and when they were gone, my thoughts returned to the previous night's discussion. Maybe they were both right. Perhaps I needed to wake up and realise I was nearly thirty and it was time to get serious about my life. These days I'd recognise what was essentially a quarter-life crisis as the first Saturn return, but I didn't know so much about that then. Back then, the only thing I knew for sure was that I didn't know what I wanted to do with my life or who I wanted to be, although I knew I didn't want to be on the same path Tiff was on. To be honest, I'd only applied for the job at Chartered Pacific because Tiff worked there and I wanted to live in Sydney.

My intention had been to stay for a year, then move on to something else, but one year turned into two, then before I knew it, I'd been there for seven which is a quarter Saturn cycle and, therefore, a crossroads of sorts. If I wasn't careful, another seven years would go by, and I'd still be there. Not that I should complain; I'd done well, and due to being in the right place each time a restructure had come along and working hard, I had been promoted more quickly than I otherwise would've been.

But if I wasn't doing that, what would I do? Maybe that's what Tiff's five-year plan was about – to encourage me to think seriously about what I wanted to do and who I wanted to do it with.

With a cup of tea and a pen and paper, I'd sat down, ready to write.

My Five-Year Plan

Okay, now I had a title – which I'd underlined – it was time to think about a career.

My very average degree was in economics, but the sort of economics degree you get when you don't like economics, so anything where my degree would be useful was automatically out. What did that leave me with?

One thing that came up again and again was my obsession with horoscopes and astrology. Turning to my weekly horoscope was a highlight. Maybe I could be an astrologer, whatever it was that astrologers did. I wrote down:

Take astrology classes

Then I added:

Leave CP and write horoscopes

Buy a house in the suburbs where I can have a dog

Get a dog

Now for relationships. What I needed was a good

man, a kind man, a sensible man. The sort of man who would have a five-year plan.

I'd written it all down (plus a few other goals which I can't remember now), and the following week I met Hayden at a networking session. He was there with colleagues from the accountancy firm he worked for and had been doing some debt recovery work for CP. He was standing on his own, nursing his beer, and I took pity on him and started a conversation. It began with the usual things you talk about at these events – name, company, length of service – and ten minutes became thirty and we were still talking.

He told me about the stint he'd done in his company's Hong Kong office, and I told him about how Matt was there too and wondered whether they'd come across each other. As he described the expat lifestyle, his hazel eyes had lit up with little flecks of caramel, gold and green behind his black-rimmed glasses. I found myself wondering how curly his brown hair would be if he'd let it grow and how it would feel under my hand. When he offered to get me a fresh wine, our fingers had briefly touched, and a little trail of sensation ran up my arm, across my chest and straight into my heart. When next our eyes met, his were positively gleaming. I wouldn't have said I felt what the French called a *coup de foudre*, but it was a promising start.

He didn't laugh at me when I explained my no sex until after the third date rule, and when we finally slept together (after the fifth date), he was a generous and considerate lover. He also disclosed that he too had a five-year plan but, having had a head start on me, had already bought a house in the suburbs big enough for a dog. Granted, he'd said he'd bought it big enough for children, it was my idea to get the dog first.

Within six months, I'd moved in, and six months after that, I rescued Stella; life was good. My parents and friends liked him, although Tiff wasn't sure he was the right man for me. She'd expressed concern that it had all happened so soon after deciding I needed to think about settling, and when she asked me if I was in love, I told her I'd skipped that part and gone straight to the contented together sort of love.

'Hmmm,' she said. 'I know what you're like, Ally. Are you sure that's enough for you?'

'Yes,' I'd declared. 'This is me adulting.'

At about this time, I also enrolled in some astrology classes, and my five-year plan was looking good; then, on schedule, Hayden proposed. As far as proposals go, it wasn't a particularly romantic one, but Hayden wasn't a particularly romantic man; he was, however, a good man, a kind man, the sort of man a woman could grow old with contentedly. As Tiff had said at the time, again channelling her inner *Sex And The City* vibe, he was Aiden.

We'd been out for dinner, and he'd put his fork down, looked deeply into my eyes, taken a long breath, reached for my hand, and said, 'Alice, we've been together for four years, and I love you. Will you marry me?'

As I said later to Tiff and Callie, it was nice of him to ask, and I couldn't see a reason to say no. I'd squeezed his hand and said, 'Yes. Thank you.' Who answers a proposal like that?

The following week, Luke sauntered into the office.

Thrown onto a project together, I found the banter thrilling. After all, that's all it was … banter. Luke was engaged to Sasha and me to Hayden; we both knew it couldn't go any further. Until it did.

It happened one night when we'd both been working late getting documents ready to present to the project sponsors the following day. Luke looked up from the laptop and straight into my eyes. His were dark, his mouth set in a grim line, all laughter gone from his face. 'Al, this is no good,' he said.

I groaned and rubbed at my forehead. 'Don't say that; we don't have time to start again.'

'Not this,' he said, closing his laptop. 'The PowerPoint is fine. It's us.' My breath caught in my throat. 'I can't pretend any longer. I want you, Al, so badly that I think about you when I'm with Sasha.'

My hand flew to my chest, my heart beating against it. 'No, Luke, you can't say that.'

'I can, and I have to.' His voice had a tinge of

desperation, and this time, when I looked into his eyes, it was as if I'd toppled in and couldn't scramble back out again. My breath came faster, and the heat in my cheeks moved south. Somehow I managed to swallow.

'You can't say that,' I said again, my head shaking wildly, my words lacking conviction. The truth was, I wanted him to say it again and again. I wanted him to reach for me and kiss me – and I hated myself for it.

'Tell me you don't want me in the same way and we'll never speak of this again,' he said, the side of his mouth upturned in a knowing smile, his eyes dropping to my lips, then to my chest.

'I can't,' I admitted, dragging my eyes from his. 'We're both with other people, so this is wrong.'

I stood and shut my laptop, scattering pages of notes on the floor. As I bent to gather them, he said quietly, 'Sash and I are finished, Al. We're done.'

I'd shoved the papers and the laptop into my bag and fled. As hard as I'd tried, though, I couldn't shake the scene from my brain. What did it mean that I was thinking of another man while Hayden was beside me, inside me?

Over the next couple of weeks, while Luke said nothing more about it, the glances, the late-night texts, the sexy banter told me he hadn't forgotten either. I didn't think it was love, whatever this was, but it was like a kind of madness had descended on me, as if the years with Hayden had meant nothing. When I dreamt, I dreamt of Luke – wild, sexy dreams I'd wake from panting and worried that I'd called out the wrong name in my sleep.

I'd been withdrawing from Hayden, and every so often, I was surprised by a look of such sadness on his face that told me he knew it, too. None of this was his fault, and there was nothing I could do to make him feel better. He began calling me more frequently during the day and dropping by the office to walk to the station in the evenings. He was feeling insecure, and that knowledge only pushed me further away from him.

Finally, he was the one to call it. 'We're not going to get married, are we?' We were sitting in front of the telly after eating dinner from trays on our laps.

I thought about lying to him, saying something like, 'Of course we are; I just haven't found a date I like the look of.' But looking into his kind eyes, the colour now diluted to a dull grey-brown, a sob escaped me.

'I didn't think so,' he said. He took his glasses off and rubbed at his eyes. 'I love you, Alice. I thought you loved me.'

'I do,' I said, pushing the heel of my hands against my cheeks, my palms covering my tears.

'But not enough,' he said bleakly. He gently pulled my hands from my face and held them, waiting for my answer.

'I'm not ready,' I said. 'Maybe—'

'No, babe, there is no maybe. I'm ready now for all of it – marriage, babies, everything.' He paused before adding quietly. 'I thought you were too.'

I shrugged miserably. 'I tried to be. Perhaps if you give me time to catch up to you?'

'I don't want you to *try* to be anything, Ally. If you're not there now, you never will be.'

There were tears on both sides, but we knew it was over.

When I told Luke, he'd kissed me for the first time, and before long, we were taking every opportunity to meet. We hadn't been out together. He'd said things were awkward and complicated but assured me it was over with Sasha. Then he told me he had no choice but to go on the Asian holiday they'd planned because they couldn't get their money back.

'We've changed the booking to twin beds, though,' he'd said. 'I can't sleep with her when I feel like this about you.'

But in the weeks before he went away, he changed. He made excuses not to meet, and there were times he didn't or couldn't meet my eyes. When he left on holiday, he'd kissed me goodbye, and it felt like a forever goodbye, not an I'll-see-you-in-a-couple-of-weeks goodbye. And then, a few days later, Ainsley called me into the office, told me I was being made redundant, and then, as I was packing my desk up, she said, 'Thailand is such a romantic place for a wedding, isn't it? Have you seen the photos yet?'

The rest was history.

It had taken me nearly two years, but I was now completely over Luke, and in being over him, I was struck again with guilt at how I'd hurt Hayden.

Before changing my mind, I dialled Hayden's number, and he picked up almost immediately.

'Alice … hi … this is a surprise.' There was confusion mixed with an understandable level of trepidation in his voice. 'Is everything alright?'

'Yes. I was just sitting here and thinking and wondered how you were.' I squeezed my eyes shut as I struggled for the right words.

'Oh. Right. Well, I'm good. How are you?'

God, this was harder than I'd expected – not that I'd given any real thought to how it would be. I hadn't had time to plan the scene and think about what I'd say. 'Yeah, I'm good, Stella's good, and the business is going well.'

'It sounds like things are going well for you. How's your family? And Callie and Tiff? They must be glad to have you in Melbourne.'

Seriously, how many exes would ask after your family and friends? 'The family is good. Matt's back home in Australia now and, would you believe, engaged to Callie.'

'I bet there's a story in that!' He chuckled down the line. It was something else I'd missed about

Hayden, that warm, low chuckle of his.

I returned his laughter. 'There is.' I hesitated a beat before adding, 'I heard somewhere that you were engaged ...'

He let out a little half sigh. 'That news is out of date,' he said. Oh god, don't tell me some other bitch of a woman stood him up. Let me at her! 'We were married in February and are expecting our first child this spring.'

Excitement, pride and happiness filled his voice, and for the briefest of seconds, my throat closed and tears sprang to my eyes.

'Oh, Hayden,' I finally managed, 'I'm so happy for you. Truly, I am.' And I was.

'Thanks. We're both stoked.' Then, after a brief break, he said, 'Al, why have you rung?'

I drew in a breath. 'To apologise,' I said. 'For hurting you – you didn't deserve it, and I'm sorry.' There, it was out.

'Why now?' He sounded puzzled.

I shrugged, even though he couldn't see me through the phone. 'I've just been thinking about things – about us, life, you know ... and it seemed like the right time to call.'

'And once you'd decided to, you figured you might as well do it immediately,' he guessed.

'Something like that,' I conceded.

'Has someone broken your heart?' he asked.

'Maybe—'

'You'd know about it if they had,' he laughed ruefully.

'I didn't mean it like that. There is someone, but he doesn't feel that way about me, and it made me think about us and how I'd wished things had been different and how sorry I am that they weren't.'

'Oh Ally.' He paused, then said, 'The heart wants what the heart wants.'

His words should've been sad, but he didn't sound sad. He sounded like a friend trying to make another friend feel better.

'Besides,' he said with another of those chuckles, 'in hindsight, you did me a favour. It's like how you always used to say that even the shittiest things look almost alright from a distance. I would never have met Louisa if we hadn't split, and our baby wouldn't be on the way, so I should be thanking you.'

'That sounds like my line,' I said, eyes misty from grateful tears, or were they happy tears?

'It is your line,' he said. 'You always had a way of seeing the bright side in everything, and being with you helped me do that too. So, if you've been feeling guilty about how we parted, don't. Not anymore. I'm fine. In fact, I'm better than fine. I loved you, but don't take this the wrong way, there were times you were exhausting!' We laughed together.

'And Louisa isn't?' I wondered what she looked

like, then decided I didn't care. As long as she made Hayden happy.

'No, she isn't. She's calm and content and happy just to be. I saw her, and it was bam, she was the one. When I met you, I told myself I was ready to settle down, but when I met Louisa, she was everything all at once for me. It probably sounds ridiculous.'

'No,' I said softly. 'It doesn't sound ridiculous at all. And I'm happy for you. Hey, let me know when the baby arrives?'

'I sure will,' he said. 'Take care, Al.'

'I will,' I whispered and hung up.

I didn't know what I'd expected from the call; forgiveness, perhaps? While I'd got that, I certainly hadn't expected it to leave me feeling as empty as I did. It was how I'd felt at lunch with Callie and Matt, as though there were parts of me that would never be filled. I was happy for Hayden, I truly was, but even *I* was having problems finding a bright side to focus on right now.

CHAPTER TWELVE

I'd no sooner sat down with my pre-wedding-dress-shopping coffee before Callie asked me about Luke.

As I talked, her eyes grew wider. 'He was prepared to leave his wife for you?' She sounded horrified. 'Not,' she jumped to clarify, 'that that's a good thing. It's awful, but at least you know he loved you all along.'

I couldn't help but smile at the look on her face. It was as if she didn't know whether to sympathise with me, feel anger on my behalf or indignation at Luke's apparent willingness to walk away from his marriage.

'I think if I called his bluff, he would've lost interest very quickly,' I said. 'The more I think about it, the more I think I was drawn to him because deep down, I knew Hayden wasn't right for me.' I hesitated as I sipped at my coffee. 'I called him last night.'

Cal sat up straighter in her chair, her blue eyes wide. 'Who? Hayden?'

I nodded.

'Wow. Is that the first time since …?'

'Since I left? Yep.' I cradled my mug and stared out the café window. A group of lycra-clad cyclists had pulled up and were balancing bikes into the racks placed outside for exactly that purpose.

'Why?'

'Why did I call him? I wanted to apologise.' I paused and chuckled. 'Don't you look at me like that, Calliope Jones.'

She grinned and blushed. 'How was he?'

'Happy – he's married now, and they're expecting their first child.' My gaze travelled across to the muffins on the countertop. 'Has the wedding diet started yet, or do you think we can share one of those?' Callie raised her eyebrows to let me know my distraction didn't fool her.

Cal reached out her hand to cover mine. 'You deserve someone nice too, and you'll find him; I know you will.'

'Maybe,' I said, forcing a bright smile. I gave myself a little shake. Today wasn't about me; it was about Cal. 'What's our plan of attack?'

Cal grinned and reached deep inside her bag, bringing out an exercise book covered in glitter, the pages bulging.

I laughed out loud at the sight of it. 'Is that really the same book?'

'It sure is,' she said, those bright spots of pink remaining on her pale cheeks.

She pushed it across the table to me, and I traced the letters written in glitter pen on the cover with my finger. 'Calliope's wedding wish book,' I read out. 'You must've been, what, thirteen when you started this?' She nodded. 'I can't believe you kept it all these years.'

I flipped through it, a teenager's dream of the perfect wedding on every precious page. The images of dresses, hairstyles and flowers Cal had painstakingly cut from magazines and glued into the book took me back to afternoons after school sitting on the beanbags in Cal's bedroom or lying about on the carpet in Tiff's or mine. We'd gossip and giggle and share our dreams and our crushes. We were so certain of everything back then. So innocent, yet so sure of our version of a happy ending. I gently closed the book.

'Are you sure you're happy with a simple beach wedding, Cal?' I asked. 'Don't let Matt force you into something you don't want.'

She reached for the book and gently stroked its cover, a tender smile on her face, and placed it carefully back in her bag. 'I'm sure,' she said. 'We fell in love on that beach – twice – so I can't think of anything more perfect than being married there. As for the big wedding? I've grown out of that. All I care about now is marrying Matt and sharing that with the people I love the most. *He's* my perfect wedding.'

My eyes welled with sentimental tears, and I

blinked madly to stop them from overflowing. 'Well,' I said, reaching for her hand, 'let's find you the perfect dress to do it in.'

Cal's plan had us beginning in Fitzroy, moving through to Brunswick and visiting a couple of stores in the city before making our way down to Armadale and Prahran. It exhausted me just looking at the schedule.

'Ummm, there's no time built here for lunch,' I said. Maybe I should've had one of those muffins.

Callie frowned and said, 'Do you think I'm being too ambitious?'

'I'm sure it will be fine,' I said, willing the words to be true.

At the first store, the manager greeted us with champagne, smiles and promises of a dress the bride could say yes to. The manager's smile widened when we insisted on FaceTiming Tiff so she could be involved in proceedings. 'How lovely to involve your friend even when she's on holiday!' The smile slipped when Tiff warned her to avoid any dress that would make Cal look like a meringue or, worse, a toilet roll doll. The smile slipped even more when Tiff and I (and ultimately Callie) burst into laughter at the fluffy dress the manager had thought would be perfect.

'I don't know, Al,' mused Tiff from the pool lounge in her Balinese resort. 'Would we describe this as meringue-est?'

'Hmmm,' I said, gripping my chin as I contemplated it. 'It is a tad pavlovic.'

When we stopped laughing, Cal took another look in the full-length mirror and said more sternly to the manager than I would've believed she could, 'When I said I wanted something simple, confectionary wasn't what I had in mind.' She attempted to flatten some of the frothy layers. 'It is lovely'—she took pity on the crestfallen manager— 'but definitely not me.'

As the day (and the shops) wore on, she tried a sleek column dress that made her wiggle (and made us giggle). There was a strapless dress where the bodice (which was slashed almost to the waist and would be, Tiff decided, what Jessica Rabbit would wear if she was ever to be married) appeared to be held up by willpower alone. Another which had so much internal support it could have a life of its own outside the store, and one where the attendant laced the corset so tightly that while Cal's cups did runneth over (in what Tiff quipped was the *Bridgerton* effect), her internal organs were in grave danger of eternal damage.

From one change room, she emerged in an overly sequinned tight gown with a fishtail that required her to move in tiny, shuffling steps. From another, a vast gown that would require Tiff and me to hold it outside the bathroom if she needed the toilet during the evening (the gown and Cal would not both fit in the cubicle), and another that made Tiff and my eyes pop out at its simple sexiness.

'Wow,' I said. 'You could shimmy along the beach breathing "Diamonds Are A Girl's Best Friend" in that one.'

'It certainly puts the bomb into bombshell,' said Tiff.

Cal twirled from front to back, smoothing the fabric that clung lovingly to her curves. 'I'd need a strapless bra, but ...' She adjusted the neckline, which sat off the shoulder. 'I don't know ... I like it, but I'm worried the sleeves will annoy me.' She looked across at me, indecision in her eyes. 'What do you think? Is it too sexy?'

'It's very Marilyn,' answered Tiff, 'but no, I don't think it's too sexy.'

'Ally?'

I nodded slowly. 'I think this one is a contender.'

The attendant, who had been watching our reactions closely, sniffed suddenly and wiped at her eyes, her smile faltering. 'I'm sorry,' she said. 'It gets me like this sometimes.'

From my phone, Tiff's laugh was clear. 'The tears are wasted. We won't be saying yes to this dress no matter how many times you wipe your eyes. It is, however, a definite maybe.'

'Tiff!' scolded Callie. To the attendant, she smiled and said, 'I'm sorry about my friend, but yes, this is a maybe. I love it, but I'm not convinced it's the best option for a beach wedding. Thank you so much for insisting I try it, though. I'll have to think about it.'

Mollified, the attendant said, 'You're welcome. I would say, though, that's the only one we have in your size, and you said the wedding was soon …'

To me, Tiff said, 'Apparently, they do that when the bride is dithering and the dress is over budget.'

I giggled and hoped the poor girl hadn't heard.

'I wish I was there,' said Tiff.

'No you don't,' I scoffed. 'You'd hate it.'

'Maybe, but I still wish I was there.'

Changed again and outside the store, Cal's smile was no longer as bright. 'There's only one more shop on my list, Ally. What happens if we can't find anything in there? I don't have time to get anything made.'

I hooked my arm through hers, patted her hand and led her to the tram for the short ride up Chapel Street. We'd both decided we were too footsore to contemplate the short walk from Armadale into Prahran. 'All isn't lost, sweetie. You'll be on the Sunny Coast next week, and you said your mum was coming up?'

'Yes, Mum and Clio are coming up to help me with a few things.'

'There you go. There's bound to be some stores you can look in up there, and your plan C is to do a run down to Brisbane for the day. And even then, we've only touched the surface of the bridal stores here in Melbourne. Besides,' I said with more optimism than

I felt, 'we might find something in this last place. My hopes are high.' As I said it, my stomach rumbled.

'Oh Ally, I'm so sorry! We haven't even stopped for lunch,' cried Cal.

'It's okay,' I lied. We'd stopped for more coffee and a takeaway pastry, but it was nowhere near enough. 'Anyway, we're here now, so chin up – we'll find it. I feel it in my bones.'

My bones were wrong, and I didn't need Callie to tell me so. The disappointment on her face as she flipped through the lookbook she was presented with when we sat down on plush sofas said it all.

'Oh Ally,' she said. 'None of these are me. And look at the price tags! Who spends that on a dress they're only going to wear once? This is hopeless.' Her voice trembled, and her eyes filled with tears.

I gently took the book from her hands, shut it, and handed it back to the attendant with a smile. 'Thank you,' I said. 'I think we'll come back another time.'

Taking Callie's hands, I pulled her up beside me and, with my arm around her shoulder, walked her out of the store. 'You know what you need?' I asked.

'What?' she asked miserably.

'A good rummage through the bazaar. It's just around the corner, and it'll make us both feel better,' I said. 'Then we can drop in for dumplings on the way home.'

She nodded but didn't appear to be convinced by

my upbeat tone.

It had been ages since we'd visited Chapel Street Bazaar and, as always, we loitered in the doorway before deciding which stall we'd visit first. I disappeared towards the vintage china while Cal seemed taken with some planters. Fifteen minutes later, I stepped out of a change room with a pair of wide-legged reworked two-toned denim jeans over my arm to see Cal almost running to meet me with an excited flush to her cheeks.

She grabbed hold of my arm. 'Come quickly,' she said. 'I've found it.'

I hesitated for a second or two, wondering what *it* could be before understanding dawned on me. 'The dress? You've found a dress?'

She nodded furiously, and there was a sparkle in her eye. 'And it's in my size, but I didn't want to try it on until you and Tiff were here.'

Callie led me to a stall in the far corner of the vast space where a sales assistant with pink-dipped hair and a floral, midriff-baring bustier worn with paisley-printed flared pants was wrestling a dress off a mannequin. 'You found your friend then,' she said.

'Yes,' said Cal breathlessly, 'but now we need to FaceTime our other friend so she can see it too.'

The girl, obviously used to everything, merely shrugged her shoulders, handed Cal the dress and pointed her towards the fitting room. I called Tiff.

'Where on earth are you?' she asked as she took in my position on a velvet chaise lounge with racks of leather jackets in the background.

'The bazaar,' I said.

'Seriously?'

'Uh huh.'

'How's Callie going?' she asked. 'I got the impression she was a bit down after that last shop. That dress was nice, but not for a beach wedding.'

'I think it was a case of so close but not quite. Then we visited one around the corner where the cheapest dress was over five grand, and the saleswoman looked down her nose at us. So we came in here to cheer ourselves up.'

Anything else I would've said stayed unsaid as Cal whipped open the curtains of the change room. 'Oh my!' I exclaimed.

'What's going on?' asked Tiff. 'Turn the phone and show me.'

I turned the screen so Tiff could see Callie. 'Holy fuck!' she said.

Even the sales assistant was lost for words.

'What do you think?' Callie twirled, checking out the dress from every angle.

The short-sleeved, tightly fitted cream lace bodice plunged into a vee showing a hint of creamy bosom. A line of tiny pearl buttons led the eye down, with a midi-length swing skirt in cream silk flaring wide from a sashed waistband. It was perfect.

I swallowed hard, unable to answer her.

'Tiff?' Cal asked, her eyes anxious, her tone wavering.

'Oh, Cal,' Tiff said, her voice breaking. 'It's so you.'

The assistant swung into action. 'If you wear your hair up simply'—she gathered Cal's blonde tresses to form a high ponytail— 'like this, with a centre part, it would be perfect. Are you wearing a veil?'

Cal turned to me, her eyes shining. 'Do you think I should?'

I shook my head. 'I don't think you need one,' I said. Callie twirled again, and even in the cluttered shop, I had an image of how she'd look walking across the sand towards Matt.

'So you think I should get it?' Cal asked.

'Absolutely,' I said.

'Say yes,' said Tiff.

'That's what got me into this mess in the first place,' Callie said, her smile as bright as that disco ball had been glittering on the night she and Matt had found each other again.

Impulsively I hugged her, the phone (and Tiff) still in my hand. 'I'm so happy for you, darling,' I squeaked, my cheek against her hair.

'I wish I was there,' came the voice from somewhere near my belly.

'So do we,' Cal and I said together.

•

Callie had been energised after our success with the dress and had chattered happily through the dumplings and wine we'd had to celebrate.

'Now that's done, the hard work starts,' she said, rummaging in her tote bag for her trusty journal and a pen.

'You mean that wasn't hard work?' I quipped, only half joking. I popped a xiao long bao into my mouth, briefly closing my eyes to savour the porky-soupy bomb.

'Ha ha. Now we need to find something for you and Tiff to wear—'

'Didn't you say that was up to us?' I asked, reaching across with my chopsticks for a slice of delicately poached chicken in Chinese wine.

'Yes, but I still need it on my list.' She frowned, her middle finger resting on the furrow between her eyebrows. 'It's the logistics that are going to do my head in. Matt's booked the reception, the celebrant and the photographer, but we need to meet with all those people and decide on so much. Then there's the flowers and the cake to think about.' She listed each item as she spoke. 'We'll tick most of these off when we're in Mooloolaba the week after next.' Tapping the pen against her notebook, the thoughts flickered across her face. 'Thankfully, we don't need to worry about cars. We've booked a unit across the road from the beach for the night before the wedding, so the three of us can get ready from there.'

'What about the wedding night?'

'Matt said he's arranged somewhere special.' She blushed and I tried not to think about what else he'd said or done to cause it.

'Tiff said she and Jake will fly into Brisbane and spend a few days with her father before driving up,' I said. 'They've booked somewhere on the Esplanade too. I'll have to let Mac know the date, and hopefully, he can have Stella while I'm gone. Otherwise, I'll be driving up and bringing her with me.' I contemplated another soupy dumpling. 'Are you eating, Cal?'

Her eyebrows rose as if she'd just realised food was on the table. 'Yes, I'd better before you demolish the lot.' She giggled and carefully picked up a xiao long bao with her chopsticks, dunked it in vinegar, placed it on the spoon and draped finely sliced ginger over the top before popping it into her mouth.

'I'll check with Mum and Dad,' I said, 'but suppose I'll stay with them for the few days before and after. I'm not sure who else will be there. I don't think Laura and Mick have room for anyone.'

'We'll stay at your parent's place before the wedding,' Callie said. 'In Matt's old room in the granny flat in the backyard.'

'What about Matt's groomsmen?'

'I think Todd and Andi are booking somewhere. As for Alex, Matt's only spoken to him briefly and hasn't given him the details yet – dates, location, that sort of thing. Your parents said if he's not bringing anyone, he can probably stay with them too – in Laura's old room.'

'Okay,' I nodded. 'That makes sense. Have you met him yet?'

'Alex? No. We're having dinner next Thursday night. We'll organise a catch-up with us all – including Todd, the other groomsman, who I have met, and his partner Andi – when we're back from the Sunny Coast.'

'Does Alex have a plus one?' I asked. If he did, I was probably the only one attending solo.

'I don't think so. Matt said he's just as bad as you are when it comes to commitment, although he was burnt a few years back by someone who turned out to be after his money. He runs his own business and is quite successful.' She smiled archly. 'Maybe he'd be a good catch for you.'

I choked as the chilli sauce from my wonton went down the wrong way. 'Hardly. I suspect he might be out of my league. Your brother's still single, isn't he?' I wobbled my head a little to go with the cheeky smile.

'Angus is too young for you,' she mock-warned. 'Besides, he's heading back to Scotland almost straight after the wedding.' Cal's younger brother, a biologist, worked in the north of Scotland counting puffins or something. 'I know, why don't you bring Mac as your plus one,' she said.

Ignoring the knowing look she gave me, I said, 'That would be a good idea except for two teeny points: the first being that I need him to look after Stella, and the second is he has a girlfriend.'

'Oh? You haven't mentioned that? I hoped that now you and Tommy aren't together that you and Mac might have, you know … realised you wanted to be together. But if he has a girlfriend … although didn't you say they don't tend to last?'

It was my turn to shrug. 'Not usually, but this one might be different.'

'Hmmm.' A message flashed on her phone; her eyes softened, and her mouth curled into a gentle smile.

'Matt?' I guessed.

'Yes, I should be going.'

CHAPTER THIRTEEN

I saw Callie into a taxi and began the short walk home down Chapel Street, then left into Commercial Road. As the sun was dipping, so too was the temperature, and I wished I had a jacket to wrap around me. That aside, I loved this time of the year – when the leaves changed and drifted from the trees to lie in piles waiting to be kicked and scattered. Unable to help myself, I did just that, grinning when an elderly man passing me said, 'I was wanting to do that myself.'

Mac was leaning against my front fence with Kevin when I finally arrived home.

'You're just in time,' he said. 'I was going to give you another five minutes before Kevin and I walked without you.'

My shoulders slumped. 'I'm sorry, Mac. I've been walking all day, and I'm not sure my feet can drag me any further.' Every step I took was like walking over razor blades.

He looked me up and down, and suddenly, I wondered how he saw me. I'd worn my new two-toned jeans home along with a pair of clompy white trainers I'd also found at the bazaar. The clothes I'd set out in that morning were in the shopping bags I held, and it was getting too cold for the long-sleeved T-shirt I had on. I didn't need to look at my chest to know my nipples were protesting against the late afternoon air. I held both bags in one hand and wrapped my arm around my body. I'd tied my hair back loosely, but pieces of it were escaping around my face and whatever make-up I'd left the house with this morning had now worn off or been cried off in happy tears. Bree, I was sure, would still have looked perfect. Her jeans wouldn't be reworked but would be designer branded and cling to her as if made for her. Her hair wouldn't be wild, and her make-up would be that type of natural that takes forever (and a million products) to apply.

It must've shown on my face as Mac said, 'Hey, it's okay.' He narrowed his gaze. 'You do look knackered.'

'Gee, thanks for that,' I said, unlocking the front door to let us in. Kevin, released from his lead, bounded down the hall to sit at the back door and touch noses with Stella through the glass.

Mac leant against the kitchen bench, Kevin's leash dangling from his hands. 'How about I take Stella out and you have a bath or something?' A worried look crossed his face. Again, Bree stuck her head into my thoughts before I could get carried away with them.

'Thanks, Mac. I'd appreciate it.' I let Stella in and

happily submitted to the usual oh-my-god-Mum-I'm-so-glad-you're-home-you've-been-gone-forever doggy cuddle.

'You know where her lead is,' I said. 'Take the spare key in case I'm still in the bath when you get back.'

He smiled cheekily, his eyes crinkling at the edges. 'Is that an invitation?'

You wish, whispered Temptation.

'Whatever.' I shook my head as if him joining me in the bath was the last thing I'd think about. 'I'd be too tired to do anything about it anyway.'

He shrugged. 'Pity.' He yawned and raised his arms above his head in a luxurious stretch. As he did, his T-shirt rode up, exposing his flat belly and the top band of his undies. For a beat or two, I couldn't look away from it, warmth prickling across my skin at the sight of that track of tawny hair that ran down to—.

Maybe not that tired, muttered Temptation.

I forced myself to turn away, cooling my face in the fridge as I reached for the bottle of wine to pour a glass to take into the bathroom with me.

When I emerged, my face – and various other parts of me still warm – he was grinning as if he knew the direction my thoughts had taken.

'Okay, you two,' he said to the dogs. 'Do you want to go—' He didn't get to finish the sentence before both dogs were jumping around him excitedly.

'I'll leave you to it,' I said and headed down the hall to the bathroom. Stella was so focused on Mac that she didn't even notice I'd gone.

By the time I'd finished running the bath, my little house was quiet. Sinking into the water, I swear I heard my feet sigh in relief. I took a sip of my pinot gris, inhaled deeply and lay back, allowing my senses to be soothed and warmed by the fragrance of rose yet simultaneously freshened by the almost peppery citrus that filled my nose. Bliss.

I took another sip of fruity Kiwi nectar and closed my eyes.

Maybe I should ask Mac if he wanted to be my plus one for the wedding – just as friends, of course; after all, he had Bree waiting for him at home. He could only say no.

For a few minutes, I let my mind drift into a fantasy where Mac was waiting on the beach with the other wedding guests. Matt was already there, Todd and Alex, shadowy forms beside him. It was a picture-perfect winter day: blue skies, mild temperatures, small and evenly formed waves rolling in with a welcoming hello. A pair of pelicans fly across, gliding barely centimetres over the water before lifting on a current and heading further down the beach, over the spit and beyond to the river and the fishing fleet.

July is the beginning of the humpback migration

season, so I contemplated adding the blow of a distant whale into the picture but decided that would be a step too far – besides, we tended not to see them from the beach until their return trip when they swam closer to the shore.

Callie looked an absolute picture, softly pretty in her vintage dress and clutching a simple posy of white and green (the flowers weren't the point of the fantasy). Tiff and I were wearing the colours of the ocean. Both in midi-length dresses, hers was an ink-blue slip dress, and I was wearing an emerald green halter neck with an asymmetrical hem that had a ruffle on the bottom that swished when I swirled.

We walked arm in arm along the sand to where everyone was waiting, Matt and Jake following Callie and Tiff with their eyes. Mac had been talking to someone, maybe Clio's husband (that part of the fantasy wasn't important either), but then his eyes caught mine, and a grin beamed across his face. 'You look beautiful,' he mouthed to me. 'Thanks,' I mouthed back. Later, at the reception, we danced, and he held me close, murmuring in my ear that he loved me and hadn't known it until that moment. He pulled me closer, his nose brushing against mine, his breath dancing with mine. I closed my eyes and waited for the kiss. He tasted of red wine and—.

'Are you asleep in there?' Mac banged on the bathroom door, the dogs clattering down the timber hallway.

I came out of my fantasy with a splutter, spilling water and bubbles over the side of the bath and into my wine glass. 'No,' I yelled back. 'Getting out now.'

Drying myself quickly, I wrapped my hair in a towel and dressed for comfort in a soft pair of navy track pants and an old green and white striped rugby jumper. When I emerged, he'd made himself comfortable at the kitchen bench, an open bottle of beer in front of him and a fresh glass of wine poured for me.

'I didn't think you'd mind,' he said, seeing the direction of my glance.

'Of course not,' I said. 'I used to get it in for Tommy, but now, well …' I shrugged, the towel around my hair wobbling precariously. I pulled the towel off, hung my head and allowed my hair to fall forward. I scrunched it with my fists and straightened with a jerk so my hair flew back over my head to fall down my back in its usual unruly fashion.

Mac was watching me with amusement in his eyes. 'That's it?' he said. 'Hair done?'

'Uh huh.' I almost added something like, 'I bet Bree takes a bit longer with her hair,' but decided it would sound snippy, so I reached for the wine he'd poured me instead and collapsed onto the sofa with a loud sigh. Mac swivelled around on his stool to face me.

'Tough day?'

'I love Callie dearly, but shopping's not really my thing.' I took another sip.

'With the exception of vintage shopping, of course.' Mac grinned, his head tilting towards the hat and scarf I'd bought last week, now hanging on a set of hooks with others I'd bought on previous outings.

'Naturally. But if you think shopping is bad, shopping for wedding dresses takes it to a whole new level of hell.' I rolled my eyes. 'Men are so lucky.'

'How's that? A mate of mine has asked me to be his best man so it would be great to know what I'm in for.'

'Oh really? When?'

Mac shrugged. 'No idea. He caught me in the middle of something else so still needs to give me the details, but I'll do it of course. So tell me, how are we lucky?'

'You don't have any of the dress angst. All you do is rock on into a suit hire place, buy a decent pair of shoes and make sure you're wearing matching socks and'—I clicked my fingers— 'job done. In the case of my brother's groomsmen, they don't even need to worry about the shoes.'

'Why is that?'

'Beach wedding, my friend. Although, on the upside, it means we get to be barefoot for the ceremony too, so I suppose it's not all bad.' I patted the cushion beside me, and Stella bounded up, resting her head on my lap. 'Also, we found a dress for Callie on the first day of looking, and it was off the rack, so no alterations required. Now *that* was a win.'

Mac slid off the barstool to sit in the sofa chair opposite me, placing his beer on a coaster on the coffee table. 'I thought women were supposed to turn into bridezillas at the thought of a wedding.'

'I don't know about that. Even though Callie's been dreaming about her wedding day since she was a little girl, she's remarkably calm about it – even with the short time frame. Although that facade cracked a little towards the end of the day when she didn't think she'd find anything, but even then, she was fine. When it's Tiff's turn, heaven help everyone!'

'What about you? When it's your turn?' He idly scratched at Kevin's ears.

'My turn?'

'Yes. Surely you've thought about it?'

His eyes held mine for a beat longer than needed, and my tummy flip-flopped in response. 'No.' I made myself shrug. 'Not seriously. I'd have to make a commitment for that, and it seems that's not something I'm very good at.'

A little smile played around his lips as though I'd said something funny. 'I don't know about that,' he said. 'You've been best friends with Callie and Tiff for how long?'

'Since primary school,' I said.

'And we've been friends for almost two years, and in all that time, you've never backflipped on an arrangement.'

'I didn't walk with you today,' I pointed out.

'True, but we hadn't arranged that we would. There have been mornings when I know you've been hungover or exhausted after being awake all night chasing deadlines, and afternoons when I know you wanted to rug up and stay inside, and yet you've never let me down. I've let you down; I know I have, but you've never stood me up.' His gaze narrowed on me, and I squirmed enough in my seat that Stella lifted her head. 'There's no one I trust more than you to look after Kevin when I'm away.' His mouth was in a serious straight line as he added, 'I can't think of anyone I know who is as loyal and committed to their friends as you are. I feel honoured to be one of them.'

His sincerity was almost my undoing, and heat rushed to my cheeks and burned behind my eyes. 'In relationships, though, I'm truly awful. Take Tommy, for example.'

'What about Tommy? As far as I can tell, that one lasted about nine months longer than it probably should have.'

'What do you mean?' I asked indignantly. 'We were only together for ten months. Besides, you only met him a couple of times and only for a few minutes on each occasion.'

He lifted one shoulder. 'It was enough to know he was wrong for you.'

'But—'

He waved my protests away. 'You needed to get over whoever it was you were running away from when you arrived here, and Tommy was good for that.'

I stared at him, my eyes wide. 'How did you know? You never said …'

'No, well, you don't, do you? You let things run their course. I could see that you wanted Tommy to be the one and were trying very hard to make it so. Who was I to rain on that parade?' He drained the rest of his beer. 'Another?' he asked, indicating my now empty wine glass. 'I thought we might order in some pizzas.'

His rapid change of subject threw me. 'Sure,' I said.

'Is that a yes to the wine or the pizzas or both?' He stood to walk across to the fridge, Kevin following in case something interesting was about to happen.

'Both,' I said, lighting the candle that sat on my coffee table. 'You're not busy tonight?' Surely, being a Saturday night, he'd be keen to see Bree.

'You mean why aren't I out with Bree tonight?' he guessed.

I wrinkled my nose and suppressed a grin. Was I that transparent? 'Yeah.'

'No, not tonight.'

While he busied himself getting us both drinks and had his back to me, I said, 'Was that Bree you were with at lunch yesterday?'

'It was,' he said. I waited for him to elaborate, but he didn't.

'She looks nice.' So lame, Alice!

He handed me my glass and raised his eyebrows at my comment. 'I'm glad you think so.'

'Is she the one?' I persisted, cringing as I waited for his answer.

He paused for a second, his eyes raised to the ceiling in thought. Finally, he said, 'No, she's not.'

'Do you believe in that sort of thing, though?' When he frowned, I elaborated, 'The whole concept that there is someone who is "the one".'

He nodded slowly, 'Yes, I do. Now, I'm going to order pizza, then you're going to tell me about that guy you were with yesterday.'

I blinked twice and swallowed hard, but he'd already turned to get his phone.

'The usual?' he asked. 'Extra chilli on the bacon and egg and yes to olives and anchovies on the supreme?'

'Yes,' I squeaked.

I waited as Mac finished ordering, hoping he'd forgotten his previous subject.

'Okay,' he said, settling back in his chair, beer replenished. 'Who was he? An old boyfriend, or a new one?'

'Just someone I used to know.' I dismissed Luke's importance with a wave of my hand.

'Really?'

His eyes turned the same icy blue they'd been yesterday when he'd seen me lunching with Luke, and I crumbled. 'No, he wasn't just someone I used to know,' I said. 'I used to work with him back in Sydney.'

'Is he the one who …?' He took a mouthful of beer, his gaze flicking away from mine.

'Who what?'

'That you were running from when you came down here?' His voice sounded gruff.

I nodded, tracing the condensation on the side of my glass. 'Yeah.'

'Tell me,' he said quietly.

So I did. I told him about Hayden, and I told him about Luke. I told him how I'd believed what Luke had said to me and how I'd lost my job.

'When I think of how I behaved with him, I cringe. Looking back, I think I knew it wasn't love but some ridiculous crush. I was completely uncaring of any consequences – until they came back to bite me in a big way. I behaved appallingly, and the worst was I'd convinced myself that I was being open and honest and that was so much better than the opposite. What I should've done, of course, was never put myself in the situation in the first place.' I hadn't looked at Mac's face during the telling, but now I did, and I couldn't read the expression I found there.

'Have you been beating yourself up about it ever since?' he asked quietly.

I nodded. Uncrossing my legs, I got up from the lounge and retrieved the bottle of wine from the kitchen counter. 'Do you want a glass of red now?' I asked.

'Thanks.'

I swapped the white for a new bottle. He waited until I'd poured glasses for us both before asking, 'The other day at lunch, was that the first time you'd seen him since?'

'No. I ran into him in Bali the other week. Tommy and I had dinner with him and Sasha, his wife. He called me on Thursday afternoon and said he wanted to see me, to pick my brains about work. He and Sasha have moved here. He's taken the management role in Tiff's old office.' It sounded lame. Why would he need my help? 'When I got there, though, he wanted to start everything back up again. He said he'd made a mistake in getting married—'

'He's not wrong there,' muttered Mac. In a louder, derisive voice, he added, 'Let me guess, he hadn't been able to stop thinking about you?'

I nodded. 'Yeah, something like that. The thing is, it all left me so cold and, in that moment, all I felt was shame for how I'd acted in the past and sympathy for Sasha. She knows what he's like – I know she does. It was easy to see by the way she kept watching him with me in Ubud. Anyway, I got up and left and now have blocked his number.'

He let out a little breath that sounded like relief. 'Is he the reason you split with Tommy?'

'No, well maybe, but not how you think. I'll admit that when I first saw him in Bali, it all came flooding back, the way these things do. Tommy knew, and his insecurity made me realise how he felt about me and how I didn't feel the same way about him.'

Whatever Mac would've said to that was interrupted as the doorbell rang, announcing the arrival of our pizzas.

Once we were settled back on the lounge, the pizzas and the red wine on the coffee table, I said, 'You're probably disappointed in me now.'

When he'd finished chewing, he shook his head and said, 'No, Ally, I'm not disappointed. As I said the other day, you're not a cruel person, and it would've been cruel to let Tommy continue to think there was a chance. I do have one question, though, were you in love with Hayden?'

I peeled an olive off my pizza slice and chewed it thoughtfully. 'I loved him, but I wasn't in love with him. We'd been together for a while when he asked me to marry him, and on paper, it should've worked.' I let out a little rueful laugh. 'He's married now and with a baby on the way.'

'How do you know?'

'I called him last night, to apologise. He was so nice about it and told me that when he met me, he thought he was ready to settle down, and that's how our relationship progressed, but when he met Louisa, it was bam. She was everything all at once, he said.' My voice sounded wistful. 'It's all worked out well for him, and I'm happy it has.'

'But?' he prompted.

I shrugged and reached for another slice of pizza. 'I'm just wondering why I can't get it right. Tommy and Hayden were both perfect on paper, so what's wrong with me that I couldn't make it work? I want the bam that Hayden was talking about. That feeling when you meet the right person, and you *know* that they're the right person.' I snuck a look at him, and the intensity on his face took my breath away. He'd stopped chewing; his jaw was set, his eyes inky blue, the light from the candle flickering in them. 'Like my brother and Cal.'

'What if the bam doesn't last?' he asked softly.

'I'm realistic enough to know it won't – that it will change and grow and soften and do all those things that a proper bam should do. The thing is, I thought I could settle without it, but I can't, Mac, and it scares me that I'll never find someone who feels it for me at the same time I feel it for them.'

I reached over and poured more wine. The buzz

was loosening my tongue. Man, was I going to regret all of this tomorrow.

'Anyway,' I said. 'Enough about me and relationships; what are you looking for?'

He sipped at his wine before answering. 'The same.'

My eyes widened. 'But I thought—'

'That I was happy fooling around?' I nodded. He continued, 'Maybe. I was burnt once – it was a few years ago now. She wanted … well, she didn't want what I wanted, as it turned out. After a few years of hard slog, my business had started doing well—'

'I didn't know you had your own business,' I said.

'I don't suppose it's ever come up,' he said. 'Anyway, Katya – Kat – liked the trimmings of success more than me in the end and left me for someone who was doing better than me.'

'I see,' I said, hating her already.

'She did me a favour, though, by pushing me to take the business to the next level.' He laughed shortly. 'I probably should ring and thank her.'

'Did you love her?' I asked.

He tipped his head back, his nose screwed up. 'I thought I did. In hindsight, I think I was dazzled. We never got beyond that to the everyday, so no, I didn't love her. She taught me a lesson, though.' He returned his gaze to mine. 'Have you ever felt it? The bam?'

I nodded, a lump in my throat. 'Yeah, but he didn't feel the same way. You?'

'The same.' Something in his eyes made all the butterflies in my belly take flight. 'I had a call from an old friend last week, someone I've known for years. He's been living away and has been back for a couple of months, but for whatever reason, we haven't caught up.' He paused and sipped his wine. 'He told me he's engaged – a complete lightning bolt from the blue. He said he saw her, and that was it. We didn't have long to talk, but it made me think … you know?'

'Yeah,' I said quietly, 'I know.' Then, before I could stop, I said, 'Will you come to my brother's wedding with me? It's on the Sunshine Coast in July – I already told you that, though, didn't I?' When he said nothing, I jumped to fill the space. 'It's okay, you don't have to; I mean, we'd have to drive up with the dogs, and you'd need some time off, so I totally understand, and well, forget I asked. It was a stupid idea.'

He cocked an eyebrow, his mouth curved in amusement. 'Are you quite finished telling me why you think I should say no?'

I nodded.

'Good, because you haven't given me the chance to say that yes, I'd like to go with you. I haven't been to the Sunny Coast in years and need a proper break from work.'

'Oh. Okay, well, that's good then.' My brain couldn't seem to come up with anything better to say.

'You do want me to come, don't you?' He sounded

uncertain, unlike his usual confident self.

'Yes. Of course. I mean, yes, please.' As I stumbled over my words, our eyes met, and I'm not sure who started it, but we were both laughing.

'There's one condition, though,' he said. 'We take a few days to drive up, and I get to choose the road trip music.' He smiled that cheeky smile, the one I could never resist. 'Think about it, Ally, the two of us and the dogs … It will be fun.'

I thought on that for a second, my heart skipping a beat, then another. It would be fun – it would also be a kind of hell. Mac and I in a car together for a few days – how on earth was I going to get through that without giving away my feelings for him? But then again, how could I miss the opportunity to spend time with him?

I nodded slowly, feeling my smile widening. 'Yeah,' I said. 'Let's do it.'

He reached for me, his arm wrapping around my shoulder and hugging me briefly to his side. If I could have, I would've snuggled in, but it was over too quickly. He planted a hard, quick kiss on my cheek, and I had to stop myself from holding it there with my hand. 'It's been years since I did a road trip,' he said. 'How cool will it be?'

My mind returned to the last road trip I took, the one where Stella and I drove down from Sydney with all my worldly belongings in the back of my car, my heart bruised and battered after Luke had messed with it. While I had my redundancy payout and a small inheritance from my grandmother to fall back on, my head was full of worries about where I'd live and what I'd do to make a living. I'd pushed them aside and tried to convince myself that it would all be an adventure, and I'd then spent the rest of the drive concocting my 'if I ever saw Luke again' fantasy.

This trip would be very different, and every nerve in my body quickened at the thought of it. 'Very cool indeed,' I replied. I tried to be nonchalant, but the hope that flared in my heart came out as a smile I couldn't stop.

CHAPTER FOURTEEN

On Friday morning at the airport, I told Callie about Mac coming with me to the wedding. She threw her arms around me and hugged me as if it was the best news she'd heard. 'I'm so pleased, Ally,' she said.

Once I extricated myself, I said, 'We're just friends, remember.' I didn't know if I was reminding her or myself.

'I know, but maybe … Things can happen at weddings, you know, and he could be the one for you.'

'You've never even met him,' I said, laughing.

'I know, but it's in your voice.'

'What's in her voice?' asked Matt, who'd returned with the over-priced airport coffees he'd gone in search of.

'The way she feels about her friend Mac,' said Callie. 'He's coming to the wedding.'

'Is he now?' Matt narrowed his eyes. 'Isn't he the one who was going to be looking after Stella?'

'Yes, so we'll be bringing the dogs and turning it into a road trip. The dogs can stay at Mum and Dad's, and I told him there wouldn't be room there for him there, so he'll find somewhere to stay.' My eyes slid away from Matt's in case he read more in them than I wanted him to. Mac and I had drunk another bottle of wine on Saturday night as we'd planned our road trip and talked some more about it while walking the dogs on Sunday afternoon. I hadn't seen him since. He'd been away until Wednesday and had messaged me yesterday to say he'd pick Stella up after work.

'It sounds like you've got it all worked out,' he said. 'Cal will be disappointed, though; she'd already decided that Alex would be perfect for you,' he said with a mischievous grin.

'I nearly forgot!' Cal clapped her hands together. 'You'll never guess who Matt's mysterious Alex is—'

'I never said he was mysterious,' said Matt. 'It's just that he's busy and I'm busy, so you haven't met him before last night.'

Cal gave a little shake of her head. 'Whatever. Anyway, Alex turns out to be my boss!'

My brow furrowed. 'Hang on; I thought your boss was a woman, Marion someone or other?' Cal worked in human resources for a philanthropic company that specialised in resource sharing for start-up businesses.

'Yes, Marion is the program director, but Helium is part of a company called DotPoint, which is owned by Matt's friend Alex. I've met him before, at my interview and again at the Christmas party. How coincidental is that?'

'Very coincidental indeed,' I said, grinning at Cal's enthusiasm.

'That means there'll be two people from DotPoint there,' she said. 'I've also asked Emily from work.'

I frowned. 'Isn't she the one you thought was involved with Jamie?'

Cal had rung in a tizz a few months back when a new member on the web development and social media team turned out to be the same woman she'd seen with Jamie one night and who she and Tiff had come across in a coffee shop the day she'd decided to finish with Jamie for good.

'Yes, we've become friends, and Matt and I have met her and her partner for dinner a few times. If I hadn't seen her in that coffee shop that day, I might've gone to Phuket with Jamie, and Matt and I wouldn't be together today.'

'Well, whatever or whoever made you see sense that day, I'm glad for it,' I said. I took a sip of my coffee and grimaced at the bitterness.

'Anyway, I'm not sure that Alex is for you after all,' she said.

'Why's that?' I asked.

'I'm interested to hear this too,' said Matt. 'You were all for the plan until last night.'

'Yes, but when I was telling him about Alice and'—she sent a look of apology in my direction—

'what she does for a living, he went a bit strange. Didn't you notice?' She directed the question to Matt.

'I can't say I did, but I'd be surprised if he judged her for it. Alex isn't normally like that.'

Callie shrugged. 'I wouldn't have thought so either. Maybe I imagined it.' She brightened. 'Not that it matters – you'll have Mac.'

If only that were true.

While Matt and Callie met with the events manager at the surf club, Laura and I, Newton, and baby Matthew – the three eldest were at school – went for a walk along the boardwalk. Laura pushed the pram, and Newton tore ahead on his scooter, stopping every so often when he realised how far he'd gone, only to scoot back and repeat the process.

'How's Mick's business going?' I asked. Mick, a builder, specialised in renovations of what were known as Queenslanders – raised timber homes designed to maximise breeze and keep the heat out.

'Better than we could have expected. He has plenty of work. He's even got a crew working a job up at Maryborough. It means he has to drive a couple of hours north each week to check the site, but we make it work. There are some gorgeous old houses up there just waiting for a refresh.'

'That must take the pressure off money-wise,' I said.

'It does, but he's away from home more than ever, which puts the pressure back on me with the kids.' She shrugged lightly. 'Not that I have anything else to do.'

My head jerked up at the tone of her voice, and it surprised me to see a bitter twist in her mouth that was gone almost as quickly as it was there.

'Don't listen to me,' she said. 'I'm fine, I'm just ...'

'Bored?'

She nodded. 'Although how can you be bored when you're this busy?' She laughed ruefully.

'It's okay to be, you know,' I said.

Up ahead, Newton had fallen off his scooter. I was about to rush forward to pick him up, but he brushed his hands down his trousers, flashed me a cheeky grin, picked up the scooter and took off again. The resilience of childhood.

Seemingly keen to change the subject she said, 'Is everything definitely finished with Tommy? He seemed lovely. I know Mum thought he was, although Dad never had much to say.' Laura sniggered and gave me a sideways glance. 'But that could be because he never likes to get too attached to any of your boyfriends.'

'Oh, ha, ha.' Laura might've said it with a laugh in her voice, but it was a little too close to what I'd been thinking, and it struck a nerve.

I thought about making the glib reply that she'd expect me to make but was honest instead. 'Yeah, it's finished.' I hesitated briefly, then said, 'I wanted so much for him to be the one, you know.' I suddenly had problems squeezing the words past the lump in my throat. 'Like you and Mick, and Matt and Callie. Matt was so sure right from the start.'

'And you wanted the same?' she asked softly.

I nodded, my eyes on the path. 'Yeah, that's exactly what I wanted. It's what I've always wanted, but every time I've felt the fireworks, it's been for the wrong man …'

'Aaah. The married one.' I flicked a glance at her, and she lifted a hand from the pram. 'No judgement,' she said.

'He wasn't married then,' I said. I bit at my top lip. 'I saw him again … in Bali and again last week.'

Laura steered the pram off the path to a picnic table near some play equipment. 'Newton,' she called. 'Do you want to play while Mummy and Alice sit down?'

With a squeal of delight, he tossed his scooter in our direction and ran off to the slide.

'You're not—' Laura said, the disapproval in her eyes making me feel like a teenager again.

'No! I won't be seeing him again.' I looked across at her, forcing a wry smile. 'I didn't sleep with him, not then and certainly not now. He wanted to – he says he still does. The girls think we had an affair, but we didn't. It was this almost thing.' I grimaced.

'Sometimes I think an almost lover is worse than a real lover,' Laura said, the intensity in her tone causing me to frown. 'Did you think it was love?'

I shook my head. 'No, I can't say I ever did. Not honestly, and that was how I knew that Hayden and I would never work.'

'If you could be tempted by someone you weren't even in love with?' When I nodded, she added, 'So why meet him?'

'Because he said he wanted some advice about a work thing. He's been appointed into Tiff's old job and is having a few problems with the politics and thought I might be able to help.'

'You? Help with office politics?' The look of disbelief on her face made me smile.

'I know. But I went anyway.'

'And?'

'Nothing. I felt nothing for him.' I hesitated before adding, 'The worst thing was, someone saw us.' If I closed my eyes, I could still see the disappointment in Mac's and feel the way my stomach had fallen all the way down into my boots.

'Who?' Laura's gaze seared into mine.

'My friend Mac,' I said in a small voice.

'The almost neighbour whose dog you look after?'

I nodded.

'And that matters because …?' Her voice trailed off, and her eyes opened wide, a knowing smile on her lips. 'I see.'

'What?' I demanded, already knowing the answer

but wanting to hear her say it anyway.

'That's why Tommy didn't work?' she guessed. 'Because Mac's the one.'

I nodded miserably. 'He has a girlfriend and even if he didn't, he doesn't feel the same way about me, and we're mates, which means we can't be together.'

'That's ridiculous—' she began.

I shook my head. 'It's not. I need him in my life, and that's the rule: you never shag a friend because when you break-up, you lose a friend as well, and that's harder, I think.' I raised a shoulder. 'But I'll probably lose him anyway.'

In the pram, Matthew let out a wail. Laura stood to lift the back so he could look around.

'Just like Matt knew with Cal and you knew with Mick, I knew with Mac the very first time I met him. The difference is we can never be together, and that's so not fair.' Saying the words out loud for the first time made me feel lighter, even as it made them more real.

'And back then?'

'I'd only just moved down from Sydney, and I'd lost everything, Laur. I didn't trust myself to know whether it was day or night, let alone trust my hormones or my heart, both of which had gotten me into so much trouble in the past. By the time I knew it was the real thing, we were too far into the friend zone.'

'Oh Ally.' Laura reached an arm around me and squeezed me to her side. 'I'm so sorry.'

'Yeah, me too.' I hesitated. 'I asked him to come to the wedding with me.'

'And …?'

I couldn't help the smile that spread across my face. 'He said yes. And we're bringing the dogs, so that means a road trip.'

'Which means some time together in a forced proximity,' Laura guessed.

'Yep. By the end of this trip, I'll know whether he'll ever be interested in me or whether it's a complete lost cause.'

Matthew made another squark, and Laura handed him a rattle to placate his restlessness. 'Matt and Callie should be finished by now, so let's get back.' She called for Newton. 'And on the way, you can tell me all about this Mac. That's not really his name, is it?'

I grinned. 'I'd love to talk about him but, to be honest, I don't know much about him, not even what his real name is or what he does. He says it's something in IT sales, and I know he travels quite a bit, but we don't talk about work. We talk about everything else, and I mean *everything*.'

It felt so good to talk about Mac as we walked back to the car park. It was as if, for those few stolen minutes, I could do so freely. To admit to someone else how I felt about him, and for that short time, I could pretend that maybe, in another world, we could be together.

CHAPTER FIFTEEN

After Laura left to pick the boys up from school, and with Matt and Callie still off doing wedding-related things, I spent the rest of the afternoon at home catching up on life with my parents before we all trooped down to the beach for sausage sandwiches and to watch the sunset.

Although we were well and truly into autumn and the evenings were getting cooler, it was still pleasant down on the beach. While Dad, Mick and Matt supervised the cooking of the sausages and the older kids played on the sand where we could keep an eye on them, Callie caught Mum, Laura and me up on what they'd achieved that day.

'I still can't believe Matt thought you could get this organised in less than three months,' said Laura, scooping baby Matthew out of the pram and placing him into my outstretched arms.

'It was a shock to me too, but things are falling into place,' she said. 'The celebrant is handling the legalities, and we'll be meeting with her over the next couple of days. We arranged the menu today, and Mum and Clio will be up tomorrow to visit some florists with me. The surf club will organise the music for us and have given us the name of some cake designers. The only thing I now need to worry about is what Ally and Tiff will be wearing.'

'Look at you ticking boxes.' I laughed, struggling to hold the squirming baby in my arms. 'He seems to want to get down,' I said to Laura.

'It's fine,' she said. 'Let him down.'

I carefully lowered Matthew to the grass, and off he went in that slightly drunken nappy heavy toddle of the new walker, his little face plastered with a content smile.

'We haven't spoken about your bridal shower or hen's night yet,' I said. 'Tiff and I were wondering when the best time for that would be.' Matthew had made his way over to the barbecue and was pulling at the bottom of Mick's shorts. He placed his beer on the edge of the barbecue and picked his son up.

'I've been thinking about that. Tiff won't be back until just before the wedding, and I don't want to do anything without her. I don't need a shower – I mean, they've lost their relevance now, right? And Matt and I were thinking we'd all go out together rather than doing a hen or a stag night. There's that great hotel down at The Wharf backing onto the river. We thought we'd book some tables down there.'

'It certainly takes the pressure off us, but what about the strippers and the bad behaviour?' I teased.

'That can wait for when it's yours or Tiff's turn,' she said, a cheeky grin on her face.

Matt wandered across from the barbecue and kissed Cal's temple. She reached for one of his hands and raised it to her heart, tipping her head back so he could kiss her lips. Watching them, the same hollowness I'd experienced on the day of their engagement returned, and I automatically reached for a cracker to dip into hummus. They were so easy together. So completely sure of their love for each other and the rightness of being together. Each of them had found their person; their days of wondering and wandering were gone.

Mum rose from her chair and took a plate over to where the other men stood, and Laura began buttering slices of bread for the kids. Mick brought Matthew back and sat him in his pram before walking to the edge of the picnic space and yelling down to the boys on the sand. 'Come on, kids, dinner's ready.'

It had all happened seamlessly; everyone knew their places and roles. I was the only one who didn't seem to have one.

The rest of the weekend flew by. Mum, Dad, and I rose early on Saturday and drove down to the farmer's market at Kawana Waters for the week's fruit and vegetables. It was a mild and sunny morning, and despite the hour, everyone was in good spirits. I laughed as my parents bantered with particular stallholders in a routine that probably took place every Saturday morning. Aside from the fabulous weather, Mooloolaba Beach and, of course, my family, one of the other things I missed about home in South-East Queensland was the freshness of the fruit and vegetables. There was something wonderful about eating a tomato that hadn't been near cold storage or lettuce leaves that tasted as though they'd been flown in by fairies. It's why I tried to grow a few of my vegetables, but it would never be enough to feed myself. While I bought most of my fresh food from Prahran Market – an easy walk from my house – I made a mental note to make sure I visited the farmer's market in Melbourne more often.

Other than that, I spent Saturday on the beach, walking along it, or reading. As a result, by the time I boarded my flight home on Sunday afternoon, I felt as rested as if I'd been away for a week rather than a few days.

Mac had texted to see what time I'd be home and sent me a photo of the two dogs in the park, but even so, my insides set off on a rollercoaster ride at the surprise of seeing him waiting for me at the airport.

He pecked my cheek and took my carry-on bag from me. 'Do you have checked luggage?' he asked.

I shook my head, still too bemused by his appearance for words to come out in the correct order.

'Good flight?'

I nodded.

'Good weekend?'

I nodded again.

'Good weather?'

'Yes, great. What's wrong, Mac?'

'Nothing.' His pace became faster, and I quickened mine to keep up. 'I just thought it would be a nice surprise to pick you up – save you from having to find an Uber.'

'Thank you. It was thoughtful of you.'

He led the way out of the terminal and to the car park. Once in his car, he asked about my parents, Laura and the kids, and how I'd spent my time.

Finally, I said, 'Mac, is Stella alright?'

'She's fine. Why?'

I snuck a glance at him. It was dark out and had started raining, and in the light from the dashboard, a little pulse was beating in his jaw as he concentrated on the road.

'Something's wrong,' I said.

His eyes flicked to me briefly, but before he could say anything, my phone pinged with a text. It was Callie.

Everything's fine, but can you call me when you land, please?

It was so like Cal to preface her message with a reassurance, but what could be so important?

'Is that Cal?' he asked.

'Yes.' I frowned in the darkness. 'But how would you know?'

'Lucky guess?' His voice sounded a little high-pitched. 'Can you not ring her back yet, please?'

'Mac, I think you'd better tell me what's going on.'

He swallowed and tightened his grip on the wheel.

'Whatever it is you need to tell me, just say it,' I warned, my mind busy with all the plausible reasons Cal could need to talk to me urgently and why he would know what it was about. My heart skipped a beat, then another. 'What's going on, Mac?'

He turned down the volume on the radio and drew in a deep breath. 'You know how I told you I've been asked to be the best man at my mate's wedding?'

I nodded. 'Yes, but you didn't have the details.'

'I do now,' he said dryly. 'It's in July.'

'That's nice, but what does that have to do with …?' The penny dropped. 'Oh, I get it – it's on the same weekend as Matt and Callie's? And you can't come to theirs with me.' Disappointment hit me like a blow to my belly.

'Yes and no …' His voice faltered. 'It's the same day as Matt and Callie's, but I can still go with you.'

What was he saying?

'I'm Matt's best man.'

His eyes didn't move from the road, and the sound of the windscreen wipers filled the car.

'But … Matt's best man is named Alex, who, it turns out, owns the company Callie works for,' I stammered. 'And Todd, who Tiff knows.'

'Yes.'

'He's never mentioned you.' I turned in my seat to face him. 'That must be why Cal needs to talk to me – she needs another bridesmaid,' I mused. 'That's not a problem; she can always ask Clio again …'

'Ally, she doesn't need another bridesmaid. I'm Alex.' We'd stopped at a set of traffic lights, and his eyes met mine, the streetlights turning the planes of his face into hard angles. 'My full name is Alex McInnes, but my close friends and family call me Mac.'

'Why didn't you say you knew my brother? Or my best friend?' I demanded, struggling to work out how these pieces all fitted.

'Because until last Thursday night, I didn't know I did. I've known Matt for years, but I've never met his family, and while he talked of a sister named Alice who worked with one of the banks, there are plenty of people out there with a sister named Alice. When we've caught up over the last few years, he certainly hasn't updated me on you or where you're living and what you were doing.' His chin was squared, and that tiny pulse at the edge of his jaw was still beating. 'Why would he? It's not like I ever knew you? It's not like I was ever interested in you?'

I flinched as if he'd slapped me. 'And my surname

never gave it away?' I drawled.

'It might've done ... if I'd known it!' He tightened his grip on the steering wheel. 'What was I supposed to do? Ask you out of the blue: hey Ally, I know we've known each other for ages and talked about everything there is to talk about, but what's your surname?' We came to a stop behind a build-up of traffic, and he turned his eyes to me again, holding my stare for a half beat before he gave a little shake of his head and looked away as the traffic began moving again. 'Besides, as far as I can recall, you've never mentioned his name. It's always been "my brother this" and "my brother that" and "Cal and my brother".'

He could've had a point, a small one, admittedly, but a point nevertheless. Unwilling to concede, I tried another tack. 'What about Cal? You can't tell me you didn't know Cal?'

He turned back to me, his eyes glittering. 'Of course I knew *Calliope*,' he stressed. 'I met her at her interview and at last year's Christmas party. Why would I connect her and you? As for connecting Matt with Callie, I knew he was hooked on someone, that it was serious enough for him to move back from Hong Kong, but he's only been back a few months, and we haven't been able to get our acts together.' He gave a little shrug. 'We've been mates for years but never lived in each other's pockets – not like you girls do.' We pulled into my driveway.

'But Matt hasn't referred to you as Mac …Why did you introduce yourself to me as Mac?'

He rubbed his jaw, his thumb and forefinger pulling at his chin. 'It was always my nickname as a kid; but Matt knows me from uni and we didn't become friends straight away. The same goes for Todd.' He raised his eyes and met mine, and the fight went out of me as the air sizzled between us. I fancied that if I tried hard enough, I could see the little crackles of light in the dark. 'And I knew from the start that you and I would be friends …'

I swallowed hard, pushing my heart back down from where it had jumped into my throat. 'And we are.'

'Yes.' He smiled then. 'Why are we arguing about this, Ally? I've got as much right to feel as blindsided as you do; it's just a weird set of coincidences, and besides, what does it matter?' He tilted his head to the side, his mouth curving into a wide grin. 'I think it's great that I'll be standing up for your brother and you'll be my partner in the whole thing.'

I let out a short laugh, acknowledging my overreaction. 'I hadn't thought about it that way.' I replayed Friday morning's conversation with Callie in my head. 'She said Alex, well, you, got a little strange when she mentioned I was an astrologer. That's when you knew, wasn't it?'

'It's when I was almost sure, yes. She'd made another few comments during the evening which made me think that her and Matt's Alice was also mine.' I ignored the warmth that ran through me at his words. 'But when she told me about the astrology, I was almost positive. I didn't say anything to them until I knew you were on the flight home.' He flashed me another glance, this time with a rueful smile. 'I wanted to tell you before they could.'

I should've felt grateful and pleased that he'd considered my reaction, but all that was going through my mind was how little I knew about him. Here was a man I'd spent so much time with over the past eighteen months. We'd walked, we'd talked, we'd looked after each other's dogs and had keys to each other's house, yet I never knew his real name, and I certainly had no idea that when he said he worked in IT, it meant that he owned one of the more successful firms in the country.

Cal had told me about DotPoint and how the owner had also founded Helium as a way of helping start-ups with the same vision he'd had, obtain the resources they would otherwise be unable to afford to take their business to the next level. Whenever she'd spoken of him, it had been with respect and awe. And this was the man sitting beside me in well-worn jeans, ratty sneakers and a thin wool jumper that had seen better days.

The man I'd seen having lunch with Bree was Cal's Alex. That man exuded power and charisma and a controlled, still purpose. I almost laughed out loud when I realised that the man was the one from my fantasy reunion with Luke. It wasn't my Mac, though. Or was it? I'd allowed myself to dream of the possibility of a future with Mac, but Alex? He was the same but suddenly so much different.

'What are you thinking?' Mac asked gruffly, parking in front of the garage and turning the car off.

I unclipped my seatbelt and turned to face him. 'I'm wondering whether I know you at all,' I said simply, my throat closing with tears I couldn't risk spilling over. I pushed the door open and slammed it shut, stalking to the front door and opening it without waiting for him.

He followed with my suitcase, shutting the front door softly behind him.

'Thanks,' I muttered before going to the back door and letting Stella and Kevin in, burying my face in my dog's welcome for a second before Kevin pushed in for his hello.

'I'm still the same man, Ally.' Mac stood awkwardly by the kitchen counter, his hand shoved into his pockets. 'Please talk to me.'

As the dogs transferred their affections from me to Mac, I stood and cradled my cheek in my hand for a second. Eventually, I turned to face him. 'Yes, you're right, you are. It's just … I'm having trouble matching the Mac I know to the Alex McInnes who runs a multimillion-dollar company. I know it shouldn't make a difference, but I feel …' I swallowed hard. 'I feel a little foolish.'

I strode past him to open the fridge and get a bottle of wine. I held it up in silent question. He nodded. 'Thanks.'

I poured us both a glass. 'I'm sorry, Mac, I know I'm overreacting even as I'm overreacting.' I forced a tight smile.

'I'm the one who should be apologising. I know I should've told you who I was and what I did, but when I'm with you, I'm Mac, the dog walker and neighbour. People have a habit of changing the way they are around me when they know all of the other stuff, and by the time I realised you wouldn't be one of those people, we were too far into our friendship, and I had no idea how to tell you. I didn't think it would make a difference, but now I can see that it must seem as though I'd been lying to you. It wasn't my intention.' His hands were open as though he were pleading with me to understand.

I nodded slowly with a sad smile. 'I know it wasn't,' I finally conceded. 'My brother's generally a good judge of character. Speaking of which, what did he say when he found out?'

A grin streaked across his face, almost as if he couldn't help it. 'Let's just say he flipped quickly from how cool the coincidence is to questioning my intentions regarding you.' He chuckled and shook his head. 'Then I got a lecture on how you'd been hurt in the past and I'd better not be taking any liberties with you, and he hadn't planned on that when he'd offered me a bed under your parent's roof before the wedding. He was fine once I told him we were friends and that I meant you no harm.'

I raised my eyebrows at that. 'You mean me no harm? Please tell me you didn't say that? Next, the pair of you will be heading out at dawn with duelling pistols.'

For the first time in the months I'd known him, his ears tinged pale pink, and he wouldn't meet my eyes. Mac was embarrassed – what could possibly have caused that?

He took a large mouthful of his wine. 'Things don't need to change between us, do they?'

'It depends,' I said. 'Is there anything else important about you I don't know? No wives hidden away anywhere?'

A smile curled at the end of his lips. It began tentatively, but soon, it was his usual Mac smile. The smile I loved. 'Nope, no wives and no kids – that I know about anyway. What about you? Any more fiancées you didn't quite make it down the aisle with?'

'Nope. You know it all now,' I said.

'As do you.'

This time when I met his eyes, it was different. Tummy flipping, nerve-dancingly different. Oh, I want to kiss you.

My phone ringing broke the spell (or whatever it was). Cal. 'I'd better get this,' I said.

'You had.'

'Cal, hi. Sorry, I meant to call you back, but …' Mac walked to the lounge and made himself comfy, placing his wine glass on a coaster and ruffling Stella's head.

'It's okay, Ally. I was just wondering, have you seen Mac yet?'

'I have; he drove me home from the airport. In fact, he's here now.' He looked right at home, grinned and lifted a shoulder in a half shrug.

'Oh.' Cal seemed lost for words. 'Ummm, has he said anything to you?'

'What would he need to tell me?' I asked innocently.

'Hang on; I'll put Matt on.'

'Hey Matt, long time no speak.'

'Whatever. Now, Al, a funny thing has happened.'

'Yes? What's the funny thing that's happened?'

'Well, it's like this. It turns out that your friend Mac is the same person as my friend Alex. I probably should've twigged when you spoke about a friend named Mac who lived near you, but the truth is, I didn't.'

'Probably because you were so busy being loved-up with Callie that you had no time to listen to anything I was telling you,' I said, only half joking.

'Yes, but it turns out it's the same person, and how coincidental is that? Your friend and my friend? Who'd have thought?' His laugh sounded forced.

'Who would have thought? But he's here now and already told me.'

'Oh.' It was rare for my brother to be rendered speechless. After a little while, he said, 'You two aren't … you haven't …'

'No, Matt, we're not shagging, and it wouldn't be any of your business if we were. We're friends.'

'Hmmm. That's what Cal said, but she also said she suspected you had a thing for him, and if you do, I want to warn you. I mean, he's one of my best friends, but he's not—'

'Matt! Stop right there,' I hissed, turning away from Mac. 'You're my big brother, and I adore you, but that does not give you the right to interfere in my life, understood?'

'Understood. But—'

'No, Matt. Just leave it there, and I'll see you when you're back.'

I hung up, sat my phone on the counter, took my wine to the lounge and sat beside Mac. 'Let me guess, Matt warned you about me and my nefarious ways with women?'

I pressed my lips together and nodded. 'He sure did. What I don't understand is why I haven't seen that side of you before now?' I'd forced a light, teasing tone into my voice.

He downed the rest of his wine, stood and kissed the top of my head lightly. 'That's an easy question to answer, dear,' he said, whistling for Kevin. 'You mean too much to me. Besides, now he knows your brother would kill me.'

And with that last comment, he left.

I sat there for a few more minutes, pondering what he'd meant by the last comment and that strange moment before Cal called when I was sure he wanted to kiss me as much as I wanted to kiss him.

I grabbed my phone and googled him. Alex McInnes, DotPoint.

It was no wonder Luke had thought he recognised him – he was all over the business pages and had even made it onto the cover of one of the men's magazines. Socially, he was rarely photographed with the same woman twice. While I'd known he had an active dating life – that had certainly never been a secret – knowing it and being confronted with the photographic evidence were two different things.

The women Mac went out with were carbon copies of Bree, sleek female versions of his Alex persona, expensively maintained, stiletto-wearing and red-carpet ready. He was so out of my league that we might've been in different universes. But, I consoled myself, we were friends, and he cared about me – I was sure. And that, I decided, would have to be enough for me.

CHAPTER SIXTEEN

The next few weeks passed as weeks tended to pass. Mac and I seemed to have settled into a new normal. He'd been away more often than usual and since the big reveal – as I'd taken to calling it – now spoke openly about his business when we were together, which hadn't been very often as he was setting up an office in Brisbane. 'I'm keeping the infrastructure quite flexible to keep costs down. The vision for this site is to give independent artists and retailers access to affordable web design and branding solutions, so I'm operating it similarly to Helium and will probably leverage Helium from a resources viewpoint.' For the most part, there'd been no more long, loaded looks, and I wasn't sure whether I should feel disappointment or relief at that.

In terms of work, horoscopes were written and submitted (on time), articles were written and submitted (on time), clients were seen, and radio shows were completed. However, I was rethinking my association with the latter. The segment was, apparently, as popular as it had been, but enquiries and bookings were dropping off. More importantly, it was moving away from how I had envisaged it into an almost reality TV show version of astrology. These days Joe was after sensationalism and conflict, which was great for their ratings, but not for my personal integrity. Most weeks, I was driving home with a rather bitter taste in my mouth and needed to phone some of the callers to apologise personally, which wouldn't do. It was time to wave it goodbye, so in the middle of June, that's what I did.

Walking back to my car after my last on-air appearance, Tommy was getting out of his. After that first time, he seemed to be in the car park as I was leaving each week. We'd chat, and it was all amicable, but I couldn't shake the feeling that the meetings were contrived.

This morning I sighed and plastered my usual smile as he walked towards me.

'Alice, this is a surprise,' he said (as he did every Thursday morning). 'How are you? Sami and Joe treating you well?'

'I'm fine,' I replied. 'And as for Sami and Joe, I've just done my last show with *The Toast Team*.'

The smile fell off his face, but he quickly recovered. 'Oh? Why? I thought you enjoyed it.'

'I did, well, I used to. Just lately, though?' I shrugged. 'It's run its course.' As I said the words, I inwardly cringed. It was all too similar to why I'd ended things with him.

He didn't seem to notice and pushed his hair back from where it had flopped over his eyes. 'How's Callie and Matt? Wedding plans progressing? It can't be long to go now.'

'I think they're organised, and so they should be; there are less than five weeks to go now. I'm even organised and have finally bought a dress.' Much to Cal's relief. 'I'll be heading up there a week before the wedding, and we'll do the hens and stag nights when we're there.'

He nodded. 'Sounds good and a great place to escape the cold.' He laughed an awkward laugh, and I wondered whether he was remembering last winter when we were there together. 'Is Mac looking after Stella while you're gone?'

'No,' I said. 'He has a wedding on the same weekend, so I'll be driving up with Stella.' I crossed my fingers behind my back, even though what I'd said was not technically a lie. 'We'll make a road trip of it.'

'Sounds like a plan. How's your website going now? You mentioned the other week you were having some downtime; is that still causing you problems?'

'It is, but—'

'Let me look at it for you. It sounds very much like what was going on with it last year.'

I hesitated. It was after he'd fixed some issues for me last time that led to us having coffee, then to him asking me out. I didn't want him to think the same thing could happen again.

'It's okay, Al, I don't expect anything more than friendship from you. I've accepted that we're over.' He peered out at me from under his hair. 'As a matter of fact, I probably should tell you, I'm seeing someone new, so you don't need to worry about me not being over you.'

The way he said it sounded almost like an accusation, and I cursed my own conceit.

'I'm happy for you,' I said sincerely. 'And I hope she makes you happy; you deserve it.'

'Thanks, Alice, and I hope you find someone too.' He hesitated, then added, 'Unless you already have?'

I shook my head. 'No, I'm not seeing anyone.'

He seemed surprised. 'I thought you and Mac might have …'

I shook my head again. 'No, we've always been just friends.'

'Right, well, the offer to look at your website stands.'

'Thanks, Tommy, I'll take you up on that. Do you still have my login details from last time?'

'You'd better give them to me again,' he said. 'Last time, if you remember, you gave me your laptop.'

As I was about to say I'd email them, he said, 'Just tell me now, and I'll write it down. You don't want to be emailing things like that.'

I found the details on my phone – in the app I

kept all my passwords – and he typed them into his notes. 'Done,' he said. 'I'll check it out tonight and see what's going on.'

I smiled my thanks.

'It's going to be different without you here every Thursday,' he said. 'But I'll call you once I look at your website.'

'Thanks, Tommy, I appreciate it.' I kissed his cheek lightly and, with a little wave, climbed into my car and drove away. When I looked in the rear-vision mirror, he was still watching me.

On the last Saturday in June – with four weeks until the wedding – Matt and Callie arranged dinner to introduce me to Matt's other groomsman, Todd, and his partner Andi at one of our favourite restaurants in Flinders Lane. Andi had come straight from work, as had the others, and was dressed in what should've been a sober black business suit, but the split in the back of the skirt, the red silk shirt she wore with it and the red-soled black sky-high heels, along with her dark mermaid hair gave a look of high-octane glamour.

Tiff had told me she was a lawyer and a very good one too. Beauty and brains – an intimidating combination. I figured I had two choices in the situation: allow myself to feel intimidated or toss back my hair and make the best of it. I chose the latter. I would, after all, be in her company quite a lot over the next few weeks. Besides, Tiff had been friends with her for a while, and Tiff had good judgement.

I needn't have worried though as I'd only been in her company for less than five minutes before I realised she was lovely and that she and Todd worked beautifully together.

I made a comment along those lines when we were standing at a high table in the bar waiting for Mac to arrive and for our table to be ready.

'It wasn't always like that,' she said. 'We used to argue all the time, I mean *really* argue. And that was inconvenient as our best friends were together – Brad and Abby, you've probably heard Tiff mention them?' I said that I had. 'You'll meet them at the wedding. Brad knew Matt from uni too. Anyway, Todd and I would glare at each other the whole time. He had a problem because I tended to date married men – quite by accident, mind you; they should be made to wear their rings and tell you the truth from the start – and he used to say it was my fault for being so gullible.'

'If that's the case, how did you get together?' I asked.

'Brad and Abby were on a break, and Todd and I decided it was up to us to make sure the break wasn't permanent. It started with us tolerating each other to work together, and before you knew it, we'd fallen in love.' Her eyes sought and met Todd's across the crowded room. I could feel the desire flickering between them even from here.

'And by the sounds of it, Brad and Abby made up,' I commented.

'They did and were married in Bali earlier this year.' She took a sip of her martini. 'And what about you? Do you have a partner? Or are you and Alex a couple?'

'No. As you'll see – when he finally arrives – we're just good friends.'

Andi seemed disappointed. 'That's what Matt had said, but I hoped he might've been mistaken. Brothers, you know, don't tend to know what's going on in their sister's love life, and it would be nice for Alex to have someone like you rather than some of the others he's dated.' She wrinkled her nose and rolled her eyes. 'Oh god, does that mean he'll be bringing one of them tonight? Or to the wedding? You'll be fine – you'll be at the bridal table, but I'll be left with her.'

I laughed out loud at the look of horror on her face. 'Don't worry; he says he's not bringing anyone.' I didn't even think he was seeing Bree anymore. That one appeared to have fizzled out. I'd asked him a couple of weeks ago if he was bringing her to the wedding, and he'd made a smart-arsed comment about how with some women, it wasn't a good idea to give them ideas. I'd told him not to be so unkind but, at the same time, hadn't been able to help the glow of satisfaction that ran through me. Since then, Bree hadn't been mentioned.

As I finished laughing, I looked up to see Cal and Matt walking back from the bar. Mac had joined them, sneaking in without me noticing.

Was it my imagination or had his eyes widened when he saw me? Yes, there was definite warmth in his gaze, and as it ran down my body, it sent a burst of heat whooshing through me to the parts where his eyes had lingered the longest. Andi noticed too and flashed me a 'just friends, hey?' look.

He kissed my cheek. 'Hey Ally, looking good!'

I'd made more effort tonight than usual, and both Callie and Matt had noticed it. Callie had commented on how my (new today) forest-green jersey dress brought out the green in my eyes and made my hair flame. 'That's a very sexy dress,' she said. 'I love those bat-wing sleeves and how the tie cinches your waist. You're completely covered up, but at the same time, it clings to all of you. And what have you done to your hair? It looks very smooth and bombshelly.' She grinned and added, 'You wouldn't be trying to impress anyone, would you?'

Matt's head had snapped up at that and frowned. 'Well, Ally? Are you trying to impress anyone?'

'Of course not,' I lied.

Dinner was a raucous affair with the men catching up, and Cal and I getting to know Andi better and filling her in with what Tiff was up to. We'd ordered several share plates, with bowls of rice being passed around and everyone reaching across with their chopsticks to grab morsels. It was one of my favourite restaurants, and the food was, as always, amazing, yet strangely (especially for me), I didn't feel that hungry. Something that was, I suspected, Mac's fault.

He'd sat beside me and, at some point during the meal, his calf had come to rest against mine. I shifted my leg a tiny amount, and his followed. I risked a glance to the side, but he was giving nothing away, using his chopsticks to illustrate a point he was making with Matt. I tried to concentrate on the conversation to my left – Andi was telling Cal about a winery in the Yarra Valley she and Todd had been meaning to visit – and I tried to concentrate on the food, but the only thing I was conscious of was the heat from Mac's leg and the force field of sensation that was fizzing between the two of us under the table. He seemed completely unaffected, but I was highly charged. It was as if every part of my body was full of electricity and every nerve was completely aware of him. Oh. My. God. I want him.

Once the bill was settled, while everyone was getting ready to leave, I said goodbye to Andi and Todd and excused myself to go to the bathroom. I was running cold water over my hands to cool my blood when Callie came in.

'What's wrong, Ally?' she asked, watching my face in the mirror.

'Nothing, why?'

She raised her eyebrows. 'I think you know why. You ate barely anything, and you normally love the food here. Is it Alex?'

I delayed long enough for her to put two and two together and come up with the correct answer. 'I knew it!' she said, a broad grin sweeping across her face. 'This might be the first time I've seen you two together, but it's something Tiff and I have suspected for ages.' She leant against the counter. 'Is that why you asked him to the wedding?'

'You mean before I knew he was coming anyway?' Callie nodded, and I continued, 'Yes. But things have changed since then. He's so far out of my reach. Even Andi was saying his girlfriends are usually the expensively maintained, perfectly put together types.'

'The ones that only last a few weeks, you mean?' said Callie. 'Matt told me at the same time as he told me I needed to warn you about Alex in case he thought he could treat you the same way. I told him it was different, and I'm right, aren't I? He cares about you.'

'Which is why we can never be more than friends,' I said.

'How long have you known that he's the one?'

I didn't pretend to misunderstand, and I didn't even contemplate lying to her. 'Since the day I met him.'

'Oh Ally,' she said. 'And that's why Tommy never stood a chance.'

I nodded. There was no need to say anything else.

Back at the table, the men were standing with their coats and scarves on, waiting for us. Mac's looked like it might be cashmere, and I ached to run my hand along his sleeve. He held my tan leather jacket and helped me put it on, the back of his hand grazing the side of my cheek. It was over so quickly I thought I'd imagined it, but Matt was watching me, frowning. I raised my eyebrows at him in a gesture I hoped he read either as 'nothing to see here' or 'mind your own business'.

Mac, however, had already turned and was leading the way out of the restaurant and into the frosty night. As he'd driven to work that morning, we'd already arranged that he'd drive us both home, so we said our goodbyes to the others and began walking down the lane to the car park. I shivered involuntarily and zipped my jacket shut, pushing my hands into the pockets. Mac buttoned up his overcoat but unwound his scarf and reached out for my arm to get me to stop walking. 'Here,' he said. 'You're cold.'

'So are you.'

Rather than answering me, he wound the scarf around my neck, lifting my hair and allowing it to fall through his fingers as it floated back into place. His touch sent goosebumps running along my skin, rushing from my belly to my heart, across my chest and into my throat.

'There,' he said, his hand skimming down my arm

as he released me, a half smile on his mouth, his eyes almost indigo under the streetlights. Just when I was wondering if he'd kiss me, he said, 'You look lovely tonight, Ally.'

'Thanks,' I managed. Then because I couldn't think of anything else to say, I said, 'So do you. Not lovely, of course, but good.'

He grinned and threw his arm around my shoulder as we started walking again. 'Not lovely, but good? Is that the best you can do?'

I shrugged, loving the feel of his warmth beside me, loving the woody, leathery smell of his cologne in the soft wool of the scarf, loving being with him. 'Hey, it's a compliment, be grateful.'

He chuckled, the sound rumbling through his body. 'Tell me, how long did it take you to smooth your hair?'

'God, don't ask. Let's just say it's why I don't do it very often.'

'I'm glad,' he said. 'Not that I don't think it looks fabulous – because it does – but because I've gotten quite attached to that crazy red, curly mane of yours.' As he said it, he squeezed me closer to his side for the briefest of seconds before releasing me as we reached the car park.

I smiled into the darkness but held his words tightly to my heart.

The drive home was mostly silent, punctuated

only by comments on the food or something someone had said.

When he pulled into the driveway, I said, 'Did you want to come in for coffee?' I asked it casually, the way I would've asked it after a Saturday afternoon walk, but this time I held my breath as he appeared to be considering his answer.

'Nah, thanks, it's late. Are you around tomorrow afternoon?'

I gave a slight nod.

'Great. Will see you then.'

Before I could stop myself, I leant across and kissed his cheek. For one brief, reckless second, I wondered what he'd do if my lips had strayed closer to his. Temptation was yelling, but I ignored her, slid out of the car and said, 'Goodnight then.'

'Sleep well, dear,' he said, waiting until I'd unlocked the front door before reversing.

As I watched him pull into the drive a few houses down, I shivered and realised I still had his scarf around my neck. I burrowed into its soft folds and brought it up to my nose, allowing that heady, spicy, woody scent that was Mac to fill my senses. How on earth would I survive a week on the road with him?

CHAPTER SEVENTEEN

Tommy phoned on Wednesday to tell me he'd investigated the issues with my website and thought someone was specifically targeting it.

'It might be easier if I explain it over coffee,' he said.

I'd inwardly sighed but agreed. He was, after all, helping me out.

We met the following morning at the coffee shop around the corner from the radio station. It was the one everyone who worked there went to, and I hoped no one would be there this morning.

He was already there when I arrived (right on time) and kissed my cheek in a cheery this-is-the-way-friends-greet-each-other hello. He'd also already bought my coffee and one of the croissants I used to treat myself.

'How are you doing?' he asked when I sat down.

'Good,' I said. 'And you?'

'Great. Keeping busy, especially now that football season is well underway.'

'The same soccer team as last year?' I didn't seem

to know what else to say. 'You said you were seeing someone; how's that going?'

His expression brightened. 'She's lovely, and we're happy.'

'I'm glad.'

'And you? Have you seen anything of Luke?' His fringe flopped over his eyes so that I couldn't read any message in them.

'No. Why would I have?'

'No reason; I just got the impression he might've wanted to catch up with you again.'

I shook my head. 'No. I won't be seeing Luke.' Since I'd blocked his number, I'd received the occasional flirty email from Luke but hadn't replied to any of them and had blocked these too.

'And Mac? How's he?' He'd pushed his hair back and his expression was guileless.

'Yeah, he's good.' I pulled the end from the croissant and nibbled at the soft, buttery insides. 'You said you found something on my website.'

'Yes.' His smile disappeared and was replaced by the serious business face I'd seen him wear in the office. 'Someone is trying to get past the security, and judging by some of the messages that have been left, I suspect it's someone you know.'

'What?' My breath caught. 'How do you know?'

His cheeks coloured slightly, and he said, 'The messages have been quite explicit.'

'Like what?'

His cheeks grew redder. 'Comments about you being a homewrecker, for starters. I deleted everything, Ally; I couldn't read some of them, let alone repeat them.'

'Someone I know, you say?' I asked, my voice catching.

He nodded. 'I think so. Do you think it could be someone who knows about you and Luke?'

I touched lightly at my throat, feeling my breath coming faster. 'But there's nothing to know.'

He shrugged one shoulder, his spaniel eyes full of pity. 'I know you said nothing had happened between you, but someone obviously believes there was, and whoever it is, is trying to access the back end of the site and post on your home page.'

'Oh my god! Seriously?' This was so much worse than I'd thought.

'So far, the security is holding, but that's what's bringing your site down, then it stays down for several hours before it can be reset. Whoever it is, though, always seems to know when it's back up.' He hesitated. 'Do you think it could be Sasha – or someone she knows?'

I shook my head emphatically. 'No.'

'But you have seen him, haven't you? Since Bali?'

'Yes, but how do you know that?' I asked suspiciously.

'I don't,' he said. 'I just assumed he would've looked you up once he knew you were here.'

'Right.' I wasn't sure I believed him. 'So what do I need to do to stop this from happening?'

'We can strengthen your security some more, and I'd recommend that.'

'Will it keep whoever it is out?'

He half shrugged. 'It depends on whether they're better than I am.'

I laughed at his confidence. 'Okay, can you get me a quote for the software and the work? And don't argue,' I said when he was about to open his mouth. 'I know it can be expensive, and I appreciate you doing it, but I'd like to pay you for it.'

He nodded. 'Sure. I'll get you a quote and get back to you.'

When I got home that afternoon, I drew the curtains and felt stupid. No one was watching me … it was all in my imagination. And if I told myself that often enough, I might even believe it.

With the wedding the following weekend, on Sunday morning, Mac and I packed the dogs and ourselves into his car to begin the drive north. Melbourne to the Sunshine Coast wasn't far short of two thousand kilometres, so we'd broken it down into four driving days to arrive on the Sunny Coast on the Wednesday before the wedding. Matt and Cal had flown up yesterday, and

Tiff and Jake would arrive on Wednesday too. We'd planned on getting together on Wednesday evening, then on Friday night Cal and Matt had arranged a combined hen's and stag's night with anyone who was arriving early invited to attend.

As for Mac and me, we'd be stopping in Canberra for our first night before heading east, spending the second on the coast in Port Macquarie and the third in Kingscliff, near the Queensland border and the town where his parents had retired.

While I was hesitant at the thought of meeting Mac's parents, I comforted myself with the fact that the following day he'd be meeting mine. I was, however, more concerned about spending those nights – at both his parent's house and mine – under the same roof as him. Knowing there would probably be only a thin wall between us, I doubted I'd get much sleep.

Mac didn't seem to have any of the same worries and kept up his usual stream of banter as we left the city behind, and it wasn't long before we were both singing along loudly (and, in my case, at least, badly) to his playlist of classic rock.

We pulled in at Benalla for coffee and sausage rolls, giving the dogs and us a chance to stretch our legs. In Holbrook, we stopped in a park with a decommissioned submarine, donned our beanies, scarves and jackets, and had our picnic lunch. I'd packed flasks of homemade ham and lentil soup, which we ate with sandwiches and a slice of lemon drizzle cake to finish.

When we hopped back into the car for the final few hours through to Canberra, Mac left the music off. 'I've never asked you before,' he said, 'but what made you get into business as an astrologer?'

'Ummm …'

'If you don't want to tell me, that's okay,' he said.

'No, it's not that; it's more that I'm deciding where to start.'

'At the beginning?' he suggested with a cheeky grin.

'Why not? Well, I've always been interested in it, but more in the Sun sign aspect: I'm Sagittarius, so these are the characteristics I might have and the people I might go well with. That sort of thing. When I was a kid, I used to joke that that was what I would do when I grew up – write horoscopes.'

'What about Callie and Tiff? What did they want to do?'

'Callie, god love her, wanted to be a mother but figured she'd study literature or teach until that day came, and Tiff was going to be a photographer.'

He chuckled and said, 'Well, Tiff got there.'

'She did. Anyway, I'd put it to one side for years and took it up again about five years ago and got hooked on the whole possibility of it. Not so much the forecasting side, but the maximising potential side – how if you know your own inherent strengths, weaknesses, motivations and challenge points, you can choose to make the most of the opportunities you have, or not.' I shrugged to emphasise the last point. 'I'd written a few freelance articles and done some ghostwriting of horoscopes in the few years before I left Chartered Pacific, so when I got retrenched and moved out of Sydney, I thought, why not now?'

'You told me you lost your job because of Luke?'

'Yeah, but they did me a favour. I'd still be there and wishing that I wasn't. The truth is, I never felt as though what I was doing was meaningful, yet I'd lie awake on a Sunday night with my stomach in knots worrying about something going wrong that would matter for about five seconds in the scheme of things. I tried in my own way to give it some meaning. I'd argue over policies and procedures that were unfair or unjust and stand up for what I thought was right even if it didn't do me any favours with the executive.' I flashed him a sideways grin. 'Don't get me started on aligning performance appraisals to bell curves.'

'I'll remember that.'

'I wasn't popular with management, but their problem was that I was still doing my job well. Luke, though, told someone in HR about us. There are, apparently, rules in place for shagging people in your own department, and Luke officially worked for me.'

'Surely you could've fought it? You can't tell me you two were the only ones doing it.'

I smiled ruefully and shrugged, watching the country rush by. 'The thing is, we weren't even sleeping together, but Luke had implied that we were. And yes, plenty of others were doing it, but they were far more senior. If I was the gossiping type, the tales I could tell.' I laughed shortly. 'So they got rid of me but wrapped it up and called it a redundancy and got me to sign a deed of release so there'd be no comeback. Then they gave Luke my job, although strictly speaking, they'd offered it to him before getting rid of me. In any case, the experience left a bitter taste in my mouth, and I vowed I'd never again put myself through the type of stress that I'd been through with them.'

'Not all companies are like that, though,' Mac said softly.

'I know. From what Cal tells me, you have a very different model from the burn and churn that's practiced by so many.'

'I'd like to think so. Even though we need to run quite lean to be profitable and stay competitive, our people are our most important resources, so we take engagement seriously. It can be quite challenging knowing you need to employ the best people to keep your creative edge but also ensuring they're engaged with what we're doing so we can retain them. Otherwise, all we're doing is lining the pockets of the recruitment agents and …'

'And losing productivity because you're training

and retraining.'

'Pretty much,' he agreed. 'And I'd prefer investing that money by rewarding the people we have for good performance than spending it on recruiters and psychometric testing for people who, for whatever reason – often no fault of their own – don't fit the role and leave in the first six to twelve months.'

'I remember it being like that at CP. Sometimes it felt you were constantly training people who'd been sold a role that wasn't for them. In the meantime, though, whoever was training – and it was usually the best people – wouldn't achieve their targets and receive their bonuses because they were slowed down training people. Which left them pissed off when someone was rewarded instead of them, simply because they were free to hit their numbers. Not only would you then lose new recruits but also top performers.'

Mac hit the top of the steering wheel. 'Exactly! In fact, it got me wondering whether what you do could help. I know we've spoken about workplace astrology before ...'

'You mean your eyes didn't glaze over?' I laughed.

'Not at all. I find it interesting. It's why I was thinking that using Sun signs, or rather the principles around those Sun signs, may be a more effective way of accurately profiling personalities and role fit. Let's face it, anyone can manipulate some of the more subjective methods of personality profiling. It doesn't take much time on the internet to work out how to answer some of those tests to get the desired outcome. But Sun signs are different. And before you tell me that people are more complicated than their Sun sign, I know that, but I'm thinking about core motivations.' He flashed me a quick look. 'See, I have been listening.'

'You have indeed.'

'In fact,' he said, warming to his subject, 'it would also be useful in terms of team management and motivation.' He shot me a quick smile. 'I think it's worth exploring in more detail. Maybe we could trial it in Helium and see how we go there? It can be something you work on with Callie once she gets back from her honeymoon, and if it's successful, we'll see what we can use in DotPoint.'

'Sounds good.'

It might've been cold outside, but the warmth of his approval flushed through me.

CHAPTER EIGHTEEN

We'd made one more stop – at Jugiong to check out a local food producer I'd heard good things about – and arrived at our hotel in Canberra at around four in the afternoon. The sun had all but given up on the day, casting a soft pink light over the Brindabella ranges. It was also cold, bitterly so. Melbourne was cold at this time of the year, but Canberra was on another level entirely.

As he got out of the car, Mac stretched his arms in the air and bent from side to side, causing his jumper to separate from his jeans and expose some tanned stomach. A slap of frigid air soothed the heat that had come to my cheeks as I busied myself with the dogs.

The interconnecting rooms we'd been allocated on the ground floor were perfect for the dogs. Each had a fully enclosed (and artificially grassed) outside space that was large enough for them to move around in but also far enough away from the rooms in the main part of the hotel so any barking wouldn't disturb the other residents. Both dogs had coats, and their portable carry cases would be fine to sleep in out there; plus, we knew we'd be able to leave them together while we had dinner in the hotel bar and they'd be perfectly happy.

After walking (and feeding) the dogs, we retreated to our rooms for showers and freshening up. I stood under the shower for some time until the chill from our evening walk had left my body and the steaming water had tinged my skin red. I dressed in jeans and an olive wool jumper, had put the barest layer of make-up on, and was debating whether to tie my hair back up or let it hang loose when a soft knock came from the door that connected our rooms.

Mac had Kevin and a bottle of red wine with him. 'I thought we could have a glass to wind down before we go for dinner,' he said. Stella and Kevin greeted each other as if it had been days rather than minutes since they saw each other.

'Great idea.' I opened the cupboard beside the TV and pulled out two wineglasses.

He poured wine into each, and we clinked. 'Cheers,' he said. Our eyes held, and my first sip of wine met a bubble of warmth that was making its way through my body. I looked for somewhere to sit down. The bed? But that seemed too weird. The one at the desk? Too uncomfortable. Mac had plonked himself into the chair beside the door that led to the dog's patio, so I sat awkwardly on the bed.

For the first time all day, we seemed to have trouble

with a conversation, and I didn't think it was just me.

'Thanks for today. It makes the driving easier when you've got a great co-pilot,' he eventually said.

I returned his smile. 'Thanks, but you know I'm happy to take my turn behind the wheel. I'm not that bad a driver.'

'I'm sure you're not. But I'm a bad passenger, and I enjoy driving. When we do it the way we did today, with decent stops and friendly conversation, it's easy.'

'We were lucky the weather was clear too,' I added, cringing inwardly at the inane comment.

'We were. I don't think we'll be as fortunate tomorrow. They forecast bad weather out of Sydney.'

'We've got to get through Sydney first.' I screwed my nose up and slumped my shoulders dramatically. 'That's a nightmare in itself.'

He chuckled. 'Yeah, not looking forward to that mess.'

More silence. There was nowhere to rest my wine glass, so I hung onto it, still perched on the bed.

'I bet you're looking forward to seeing your parents,' I said.

'I am. I haven't been home since Christmas. Have you ever been to the Tweed Coast?' I shook my head. 'You'll love it. Not that we'll have much time to look around, though. Maybe next time.'

The possibility of a next time floated through my brain, and I pushed it aside before it could settle in and become a real hope. 'You have a sister, don't you?'

'Yeah, Ruby. She lives in London with her husband and daughters. She was over for Christmas last year too; it was great to see them. Mum thought all her Christmases had come at once. She made such a fuss of the girls. Now she looks at me with disappointment because I haven't given her grandkids she can actually see from time to time, but I remind her that even if I had, she still wouldn't see them often.' He grinned to himself.

'It's hard being so far away sometimes, isn't it?' I said. 'I'm glad I have you to look after Stella or I wouldn't get home as often as I do.'

He tapped at the side of his wineglass then said, 'Have you ever thought about moving back there? To Brisbane?'

I shook my head. 'I've never thought about it, although Brisbane summers do my head in. Obviously, I can work from wherever, but I love Melbourne, and it's where Tiff and Callie are.' And it's where you are too.

'But Tiff's not there anymore, is she? And Matt and Callie haven't decided where they'll settle.' His eyes darkened and held mine in a way that was difficult to look away from. The room suddenly seemed tiny. 'What would you do if they moved away? Brisbane's more affordable for them.'

Matt and Callie move away? Where had he got that idea from?

'They've said nothing to me about it,' I said, quelling the ripple of panic that ran through me.

'I don't think they've decided,' he said quickly, 'and maybe I misheard them.'

I wasn't so sure. 'What about you?' I asked. 'Would you ever leave Melbourne?'

He shifted his gaze from mine and stretched out in the chair, his legs crossed at the ankle. 'Maybe,' he said. 'It's always been the plan to settle in Brisbane, when I do finally settle,' he said.

My heart dropped at the possibility of him moving on – without me. 'At least that way, your parents would get to see their grandkids.'

He turned his head and looked at me again, the intensity back in his stare. My breath came faster, and I wanted nothing more at that minute than to have him rise from his seat and walk the few paces to where I sat, take the wineglass from my hand and push me back on the bed to start making those grandchildren.

'That's always been the plan,' he finally said, not moving a muscle. Damn.

I wanted to ask if he had anyone in mind to put that plan into action, and by the way he was staring at me, the tension fizzing between us, he was obviously waiting for me to say something too. A little knowing smile played around his mouth as if he knew what was going on in my brain. I shook my head slightly and downed the rest of my wine.

'I don't know about you, but I'm getting hungry,' I said, rising to put the empty wineglass on the bench.

'Yeah, so am I,' he said. My breath caught in my throat as our eyes met again. Get a grip, Alice.

I dug out a couple of dog treats from my bag and called for the dogs lying near the patio door. Mac stood, putting his wineglass next to mine. There wasn't room in the space between the bed and the bench for both of us and, for a brief, tantalising moment, our bodies were within touching distance. My heart fluttered as I searched his face for a sign that he was feeling this too.

'I'd better put the dogs out,' I said, feet remaining planted.

'Yeah, you'd better,' he said, his eyes still holding mine. My breath caught as I saw all I was feeling – both desire and apprehension – reflected in his.

He swallowed hard, one hand coming up to rest lightly on my shoulder; whether to push me towards the door or pull me towards him, I didn't know. Stella broke the spell by insinuating herself between us, eager for her treat. He smiled ruefully (apologetically?) and stepped to the side, allowing me to pass. 'I'll go next door and get a jacket,' he said.

I nodded. 'I'll settle these two,' I said.

While the dogs had been fed after their walk, I made sure they still had enough water, patted them and closed the door against the chill that had rushed in.

Pausing at the mirror, I debated again whether to

put my hair up or down.

'It looks fine out,' he said, coming back into the room, his hand lifting a curly strand and letting it fall. 'Crazy fine and very you.'

I took a deep breath. 'Let's get dinner,' I said.

'I think that would be a good idea.'

The hotel restaurant was also a casual bar and quite noisy. Televisions were placed on walls in three corners – two were in the bar displaying betting odds and race results, another replaying the afternoon's AFL game from Melbourne, and one in the restaurant with the volume up broadcasting a rugby league game.

Mac ordered food for us at the bar, and we found a table as far away from the television – and the resident football fans – as we could. Judging by the cheers, I guessed the home team must've been winning.

Our conversation over dinner (steak and chips with salad for him, chicken parmigiana and chips with salad for me) was so light and easy I could've almost imagined the loaded atmosphere that had been in the hotel room.

After dinner, we took our drinks into the common lounge area, where a welcoming fire was burning. I sank into one of the plaid couches while Mac wandered around the room, taking in the vintage mirrors, elegant sconces, and portraits of spaniels and horses. The decor was very much Art Deco and from the late 1920s when the hotel was built.

'I read somewhere that this is one of the oldest hotels in Canberra,' Mac commented.

'Hmmm,' I said absently, more interested in the way his chunky knit jumper shaped his shoulders and the way his jeans hugged his bum than in the history of Canberra.

He turned and grinned, walking over to join me, choosing the other end of my couch, the end closest to the fire, rather than the chair opposite. Placing his drink on the table, he rested one ankle on the opposite knee and half turned to face me.

The soft light from the fire cast a glow around him and picked up the tawny tints in his brown hair. I drank in the sight of him, from the wavy hair I so desperately wanted to run my fingers through to his extraordinary eyes, so deeply blue I could lose myself in their depths. To the planes of his face, the trace of stubble along his jaw and above his top lip that would feel so good against my softer skin. To his mouth, the bottom lip a little fuller than the top. I ached to reach out and trace my thumb across it and then my tongue. If I closed my eyes, I could imagine how his lips would feel, how he'd taste. My heart leapt into my throat, and a chaos of butterflies exploded in my belly. Oh god, I was in trouble.

'Hey,' he murmured. 'What are you thinking?'

I shook my head. Temptation whispered in one ear, *tell him*, while Reason said, *remember the rules.*

'Ally?'

Tell him, said Temptation. *What have you got to lose?*

Plenty, reminded Reason. *He's your friend. Do you want to risk losing him?*

You won't lose him, said Temptation. *He wants it too – he's just waiting for you.*

I'm not so sure about that. Look what happened last time she listened to you.

That was different. Mac is different from Luke.

What makes you so certain of that?

I know these things. Go on, tell him.

I swallowed and said, 'What are you thinking?'

'Do you really want to know?'

I bit my bottom lip and nodded.

'Say it,' he encouraged gruffly.

'I really want to know,' I said quietly.

'Well,' he said slowly, drawing out the word, the flicker of the fire reflected in his eyes. I held my breath, waiting for what came next. 'Do you remember when you asked me to sleep with you?'

I cringed inside, my face hot as I remembered. It was the morning after Tiff had announced Project Yes. Mac and I were out for breakfast with the dogs at our favourite place in Richmond and I'd made the mistake of telling him all about it. He found it hilarious.

'Tiff's decided it's time Cal and I got back on the horse – you know, started dating again,' I said.

'What do you think about that?' he'd asked.

'I don't know if I can be bothered, but she's probably right. She says I'm hungry all the time because I'm horny and if I don't scratch that itch, I'll end up fat.'

Mac had attempted to keep the smile from his face but failed dismally. 'And are you?'

'Horny, hungry and itchy?' I paused as I considered the idea. 'Yes, I think I probably am.'

The laughter had burst out of him just as he was reaching across to spear a piece of hotcake from my plate. 'I'm sorry,' he said. 'I shouldn't laugh, but you've got to admit it, Al, it is pretty funny.'

I grinned too. 'Yes, I guess it is. I suppose I'll have to shave my legs as well. This whole dating thing involves a surprising amount of maintenance.'

'Did I need to know that?'

'Probably not. While we're on the subject, though, I don't suppose that you would consider—?'

The water Mac was sipping must have gone down the wrong way because it came back out in a surprised splutter. 'Are you asking me to help you out? With your itchiness?'

'Why not? I'd shave my legs.'

He was silent for a second as if he was giving the idea some genuine consideration. While he did, I tried my hardest not to look into his eyes in case mine gave me away. 'You know what?' he finally said. 'As tempting as that offer is, I'm going to decline it. I seem to remember one of your rules was not sleeping with anyone you were already friends with. I think you commented that once you do, there's no going back.'

Oh well, it had been worth a shot. 'Yes, you're right; when it comes to sex with friends, there's no going back.'

'And while the idea of it certainly has merit,' he sounded strained, awkward even, 'if it meant losing you as a friend'—he shook his head— 'I couldn't risk that. After all,' he added with a smile that seemed forced, 'who would look after Kevin for me?'

He didn't seem able to look at me, and I couldn't look at him, and the only way I could think to come back from the ridiculous situation was to act as if I hadn't cared either way. 'No worries,' I said. 'I might ring that cute IT guy at the station. He's been helping me with my website and that's still not performing as it should be lately, so two birds and all of that.' I shrugged and forced a grin.

Mac shook his head and gave a short laugh. 'Of course you will.'

'Besides,' I added thoughtfully, 'I've already seen what he looks like in daylight, so the three dates rule is already by default down to two.'

'How does that one work again?'

'It's simple – you can't sleep with someone until after the third date, and at least one of those meetings has to be in daylight.'

'Presumably to deal with beer goggles?'

'Yes, it's amazing how people can change their appearance so markedly after that first bottle of wine. It also gets you past the first date best behaviour thing and yet isn't so far into the game that you're attached before you realise their charm is only an act. In my experience, very few men can keep up the act much past three dates.'

Mac laughed. 'Listen to you, the expert,' he'd said, and just like that, we were back to normal, all awkwardness gone.

In retrospect, I was glad he'd said no. I'd seen how quickly he grew bored and, as he'd said, our friendship was too valuable. To both of us.

The next day, I went to the radio station, and before I had a chance to ask Tommy out, he asked me. His timing couldn't have been any better.

Mac had never mentioned it again, and I certainly wasn't likely to. I'd almost convinced myself that I'd imagined the whole embarrassing scene. Obviously, I hadn't.

With cheeks burning, I said, 'I don't think I actually asked you to sleep with me.' The little smile playing around his lips was playing havoc with my hormones. 'Anyway, what does that have to do with now?'

He shrugged. The apparent lightness of the action was a contrast to the intensity in his eyes. He swallowed and caught his lower lip with his teeth. 'I was wondering whether I'd made a mistake in turning you down,' he finally said.

'Only now?' I whispered. If I closed my eyes, I was sure I'd be able to taste his lips, red wine mingling with woodsmoke.

'No, Ally, not only now,' he said throatily. 'Your turn.' When my eyes widened in confusion, he added, 'It's your turn to tell me what you were thinking.'

'I was thinking how much I wanted to kiss you,' I said simply.

He closed his eyes briefly, and when he opened them, he was smiling. 'I hoped that was what you'd say.'

As he moved to close the gap between us, my phone, which had been sitting on the coffee table, rang. Reluctantly, I cast a glance at it – Tommy. Mac had seen the name too and pulled back. 'What's he ringing you for?' he asked. I couldn't tell whether it was impatience, frustration or something else entirely in his voice.

I smiled apologetically and picked up my phone.

'Hi Tommy, what's wrong?'

Mac smiled ruefully, picked up his wine and walked across to the fire, far enough away to give me some space to take the call but close enough that he'd be able to hear the conversation.

'I'm sorry to call so late, Alice; where are you?'

'In Canberra, on my way to the wedding.'

'That's right, you said you were driving up.'

'What's wrong?' I asked again.

'I've been checking your site, and I've taken it offline.'

I stood and walked to the other side of the room, anger bubbling inside me. 'You've what?'

'I've taken it offline,' he repeated calmly.

'Why would you take it upon yourself to bring my website down?' I spat out through clenched teeth. From his position near the fire, Mac raised his eyebrows.

Doing my best to ignore him, I concentrated on what Tommy was saying. 'Whoever has it in for you has been leaving comments on several of your blog posts, and they're not pretty.'

'Like what?' A wave of something that could only be foreboding washed through me.

'You don't need to know.' The way he said it told me *he* needed me to know.

'Tell me, Tommy,' I said firmly.

He healed loudly. 'Okay, but only because you've insisted … One comment is about how you pretend to help other people with their relationships, yet you can't manage your own. Another says you're unfit to advise your clients when you cheat on your boyfriend with a married man, and there's another hinting at you juggling three men.'

'Three?' My heart was in my throat, and I rubbed at my forehead as if that could make any of this easier to understand.

'There are no specifics, but I'm assuming they

mean Mac.' His pause was loaded as if waiting for me to confirm or deny the claim.

'Mac?' At the sound of his name, Mac turned away from the fire and raised his eyebrows again in a silent question.

'Unless there's anyone else you're regularly seeing?'

Ignoring his question, my mind raced to keep up with what he was saying. 'How do you know the comments are from the same person?'

'Because even though they have different names attached to them, they're all coming from the same IP address.' He said it as if I should've already known the answer.

'Right. So it must be someone in IT then?'

'Not necessarily,' said Tommy. 'If it is, it's clumsy. If it were me, I'd ensure different IP addresses were used.'

'Okay, okay …' I said slowly, pushing away the anger in order to think clearly. 'How do we get rid of them?'

'Thankfully, when we updated your security last year, we also changed your comment policy to ensure that any comments by a new person needed to be approved before they could be published. I also put in some other safeguards, but all you need to know is that I've been able to catch them.' As I sighed in relief, he added, 'I'm surprised you didn't see them in your comments pending queue.'

'I've been on the road all day and haven't had a chance to check on my website.' I pinched at my chin as I wondered how long it had been since I'd checked that pending queue.

'Okay, well, no need to worry; I've sorted it before it can do you any damage.'

'Thank you, Tommy, I appreciate it. Thanks also for phoning to let me know.' Mac had finished his wine and was now talking to an older couple exiting the restaurant. Something he said made the woman laugh and touch her hair. He could charm anyone.

'Al, I was thinking …' Tommy said as I was about to wish him goodnight and hang up. 'Mac's in IT, isn't he? Does he know about you and Luke?' My tummy dipped, and I glanced to where Mac was still chatting with the other couple. As if feeling my glance on him, he turned, his smile turning to a frown when he saw the look on my face.

'No,' I said, 'it's not him. You said the comments were all put up today?'

'Yes,' said Tommy.

'It's not him,' I said again. Not only was the idea unthinkable, but he'd been with me all day, beside me in a car and definitely not on my website attempting to leave comments he had to know would upset me.

'How can you be sure?'

'I just am,' I said firmly. What about this afternoon when he was in his room? I shook my head to dislodge the thought before it could make itself comfortable. 'Anyway, I have a long day tomorrow, so I'd better go,' I said. 'But thanks again, I appreciate it.'

'No problems, Alice. You know I'm here for you. I'll email you my recommendations tomorrow morning.'

I thanked him again and hung up, pushing the phone into the back pocket of my jeans, and stood there a few seconds more, my fingers steepled against my lips as I fought to think past the worries that were now clouding my brain.

'All good?' Mac joined me, his hand resting lightly on my arm.

I thought about nodding and saying everything was fine but grimaced and shook my head. 'No, there are some problems with my website. Tommy's looking into it for me.' I forced a smile. 'But it's a long story that I need to get my head around.'

'No problems, we'll have plenty of time tomorrow for you to tell me,' he said. 'But now I think we both need some sleep.'

I searched his face for an indication that I hadn't imagined those moments before Tommy rang. He'd been going to kiss me, but now? There was nothing there.

We walked down the corridors back to our rooms in silence. At my door, I pulled the room key card from my wallet and said, 'Did you want to come in for another drink?'

'Yes,' he said, 'but I won't.' He lifted my hand to his mouth and kissed it. He took the room card from my other hand and used it to open the door. 'Sleep well, Ally,' he said, kissing me gently but way too quickly on the mouth.

'You too,' I said breathlessly, wanting to drag him inside with me. 'Do you want me to send Kevin into your room?'

He shook his head. 'No, *he* can have a sleepover.' He grinned again. 'Now, get inside before I change my mind.'

'Night, Mac,' I said softly and closed the door on him, leaning against it until I heard him finally move away and his door close.

After checking on the dogs, who settled again quickly after greeting me, I undressed and climbed into bed, allowing myself to luxuriate in the memory of that quick kiss. As I drifted off to sleep, Reason whispered in my ear, *how do you think you're going to deal with this in the sober light of tomorrow?*

Temptation, that capricious minx, was nowhere to be found.

CHAPTER NINETEEN

I'd just finished dressing the following morning when Mac knocked at my door.

'I come bearing coffee and pastries,' he said. He was dressed in different jeans, last night's woolly jumper, a thick jacket and a scarf.

'Oh, you beautiful man. Thank you!' I took them out of his hands as Kevin and then Stella jumped all over him as he attempted to shrug out of his jacket and unwind his scarf.

'If I knew coffee and pastries would get you this excited, I would've bought them for you more often.' He chuckled, squatting down to wrestle with Kevin.

'Oh, ha, ha.' I tore open the paper bag and used it as a plate for the croissants and cinnamon rolls. 'How cold is it out there? I poked my head out to let the dogs in and thought twice about going outside.'

He looked up at me and grinned, Kevin still in a headlock. 'Yeah, it's icy. There was a thick frost overnight – the windscreen will need a credit card to get through it, although one guy I spoke to said the best way to get rid of windscreen ice is to pee on it.'

'Eeeeeuw.' I lifted the lid on my coffee and inhaled. 'Well, I need to go out and clean up after the dogs.'

'I tell you what, you do that, and I'll venture out and take them for a quick walk before we hit the road.' He let go of Kevin and picked up one of the cinnamon rolls, taking a bite into it and leaving little flaky bits of pastry on his chin. I itched to brush them off – or better still, kiss them off.

'Deal,' I said, pulling apart a croissant.

I sat on the bed to eat my pastry and, after a second's deliberation, he sat beside me.

'Are we okay?' he asked.

I nodded. 'Why wouldn't we be?' In my dreams, we'd kissed, my eyes closed as his lips touched mine, but when I opened them, Tommy was standing there watching us, my laptop in his hand.

Mac reached across and lightly flicked some croissant crumbs off my lip. The resultant increase in my heartbeat had nothing to do with the caffeine.

'I didn't imagine it, did I?' he asked softly. 'Last night, there was a moment, wasn't there? Before Tommy rang.'

'No,' I whispered, swaying towards him. 'You didn't imagine it.'

'Good.' He closed his eyes briefly, and when he opened them, he was smiling, but still, neither of us moved to close the gap. I reached across and ran my thumb lightly along his bottom lip, my nail flicking across his teeth. He caught my hand in his and used it to draw me closer, his lips hovering over mine, our breath mingling until finally, I couldn't wait any longer and pressed forward, capturing his bottom lip between mine. I pulled back, searching his face, my hand stroking his cheek. His eyes flicked from mine to my mouth, then, with a muffled groan, pulled me towards him and kissed me properly, his tongue dancing with mine. He tasted of buttery pastry, and the smoke from last night's fire lingered on his jumper, and I could've kissed him all day.

He pulled back, resting his forehead against mine. 'Wow,' he murmured.

'Wow,' I echoed, pulling his lips back to mine.

'What does this mean? This thing?' I asked when he lifted his head.

'I don't know, Ally, but if it's okay with you, I'd like to explore it further.'

His eyes were intense, searching mine. In their depths I saw both fear and certainty. I gave a slight nod. 'Yeah, me too,' I said, then paused. 'I'm scared, though … of losing you.'

'Me too, of losing you. But I want to kiss you more than I'm scared.'

I caught my breath, his honesty stirring me to the core, and kissed him again, pulling back before we could take it further. 'We need to finish breakfast, deal with the dogs, pack up and hit the road,' I said.

'We do.'

He made no attempt to move, so I stood and said, 'Mac!'

'Okay, okay.' A sexy grin settled on his lips. He took another bite of the cinnamon bun and kissed me quickly, his lips sticky with cinnamon and butter and sugar. Decadent.

'Go,' I urged, handing him the leads, both dogs leaping around in excitement.

When he and the dogs had left, I sat back on the bed for an instant, long enough to get my thoughts in order. What I'd said to Mac was the truth that had kept me awake for hours last night. If things went wrong between us, I'd lose him, which would break my heart. That's why I had those rules in place. I knew what Mac was like, and even though I'd never met any of the women he dated, I'd seen how quickly he grew bored with them and knew that was what Matt had been trying to warn me about. I was different to them, though, wasn't I? Or was that what each of them had told themselves as well? But who was I to talk? My track record with commitment wasn't great either.

The way I figured it, I was buggered whichever way I went and had been from the start. He was always going to break my heart at some point, but now that we'd kissed? It would be so much worse, but was that enough to keep me from going to the next level with him? I didn't think I'd be able to help myself.

As if he could read my mind, a text came through from Tommy.

Good morning. I've brought your website back up again, and all looks fine. On another note, have you thought any more about whether Mac could be behind your problems? I didn't know until I saw him in this month's IT Professional mag that he was Alex McInnes from DotPoint, so he'd definitely have the skills, but from the look of this photo, he's otherwise occupied. Anyway, I'll leave that with you.

I opened the link he'd attached – what appeared to be a monthly newsletter for IT professionals – and there was Mac attending something or another with Bree on his arm, looking glamourous in a white body con dress, her lips red, her hair sleek and shiny. Glancing at the mirror opposite the bed, I bunched my unruly curls into a fresh ponytail. I was nothing like Bree – or any of the other girls he'd been photographed with.

But you're his best friend, whispered Temptation, *and that makes you different.*

Perhaps, said Reason, *but it also means it will hurt more if it ends. Are you sure he's not still seeing Bree?*

Ignoring the voices in my head, I sent a quick text to Tommy: *Was there a timestamp on the comments?*

It was something I should've thought to ask last night. If the comments had been timestamped, it would be easy to prove that Mac wasn't behind it, not that I believed he could be. But then he'd also told me he was no longer with Bree, and this photo proved otherwise. But had he actually told me outright that he was no longer with Bree? Surely he wouldn't be talking about exploring something with me if he had been? Would he?

Clicking on the link again, I searched for a date, something to tell me when this photo had been taken, something to prove that he wasn't still seeing Bree. Finding nothing I clicked back to the messenger app.

The three dots showed on the message pane … then they disappeared. Why hadn't he completed his reply?

Sighing heavily, I stood and picked up a plastic bag. I needed to finish packing, but first, there was dog shit to clean up.

We hadn't been on the road for long when Mac said, 'Does Tommy call often?'

His jaw was set, his eyes on the road.

'No. Last night was the first time for ages.'

A fine mist rose from the paddocks, and a mob of kangaroos grazed in the distance. From the way his eyes flicked briefly to them, he was watching for any foolhardy enough to try and cross the highway.

'Are you going to tell me what that call was about last night?' When I hesitated, he said, 'Tell me to mind my own business if you like, but it seemed to upset you.'

I cursed Tommy for placing the kernel of doubt in my mind; of course Mac wasn't involved. 'I've had some problems with my website over the last couple of months, and Tommy is looking into it. Last night he had to bring my website down.'

He glanced quickly across at me. 'Tell me more.'

Mac listened carefully and asked me to go through the history with him: when I'd first begun noticing the issues, what my service provider had said about it and what actions had been taken. When I finished going through it, his mouth was in a straight line, his chin firm and his hands clenched on the steering wheel.

'Before we came away, I felt as though I was being watched,' I said, remembering that afternoon I kept the curtains drawn. 'I know it's ridiculous, but it was as though someone had been through my stuff, even though I knew no one had been in the house, but that's how it felt.'

'It's not ridiculous,' he assured me. 'Have you ever given the password for your website to anyone?'

I nodded. 'Yes, to Tommy when he offered to look into it.' I frowned as I remembered part of the conversation. 'That's weird. He asked me if my password had changed, but I'm sure I didn't give it to him initially.'

'How did he check it out then? The first time? What prompted that?'

'My provider had told me I needed to up the

security on the site and had quoted a ridiculous amount of money to do so. When I was telling Tommy about it – this was before we were dating – he said he could check to see what programs I was currently running.'

'How did he do that?'

'I gave him my laptop for half an hour while I was doing something else.' Mac lifted his head; his mouth opened as if a thought had occurred to him, then closed again as if he'd decided to keep it to himself for now. 'You think Tommy has something to do with this?' I guessed.

Avoiding the question, he said, 'What did he say after he'd looked at it?'

'Just that he felt my provider was trying to scare me into spending money I didn't need to spend and that he could put the same software in place for me without the cost.' At the time, I'd been so grateful to him – which was partly why I'd said yes when he asked me out, even though I'd told Mac I'd been ready to ask him out myself.

'I see. And did you have any problems after that?'

'No. It only began again a couple of months ago.' I didn't need to see Mac's raised eyebrows behind his sunglasses to know what he was thinking. 'Right after we broke up.'

Mac nodded, and I exhaled heavily, slumping into the seat. 'What do I do?'

'Changing your password would be the first thing,'

he said seriously. 'Then phone your provider and get the software they recommended installed. Finally, over the next day or so, I'll get someone on my security team to look at it for you.'

'How can they do that?' We wouldn't be back in Melbourne for another week at least.

'They can use some remote access software and have a good look around.' He paused; the muscles in his forearm tense. I ached to reach out and touch him, to give him the comfort of knowing I was okay, even as I sensed it was him who wanted to provide comfort to me. After another minute, he asked, 'He hinted I could be behind it, didn't he?'

I hesitated briefly before nodding once. Mac was my friend, and I couldn't lie to him, not even to make him feel better. 'Yes. Last night he suggested that you'd know how to leave the comments that had been left, although he added that if it was someone who knew their way around IT security, they'd been clumsy.' I forced a smile to lighten the mood, but Mac didn't return it, his mouth still set in a hard, straight line.

'How did he know I'd have the skills? I didn't realise you were still speaking to him.' His words sounded awfully like an accusation, and I bristled at the innuendo.

'No, I haven't spoken to him about you since we've broken up. He subscribes to some IT newsletter that had a picture of you at some event. He sent it to me.' I tried to make my words sound casual as if I didn't care who he'd been photographed with.

His head flicked quickly to me, then back to the road. A little pulse beat in his jaw. 'And what do you think?'

'Do you even need to ask that question?' I demanded, my guilt at the knowledge that I had doubted him, albeit briefly. Behind his sunglasses, his eyebrows rose at my defensive tone. 'Sorry, of course you need to ask. I think he suggested it to put the idea into my head, and maybe if I didn't know the comments about us were lies, I might've believed him.'

'It's okay, Ally,' he said, reaching out to squeeze my arm briefly, a faint smile on his lips. 'We'll sort this out. What has he said the next steps are?'

I sighed with relief. 'He's going to email me a report and recommendations of what I need to do to amp up the security. In fact, he might've already done that.' Reaching for my phone, I opened my emails. 'Nope, not yet, although there's one from Callie with a spreadsheet of what everyone is supposed to be doing on Thursday and Friday before the wedding. She's asked that I pass it on to you in case my brother forgets to send it.'

Mac chuckled. 'Matt might've sprung this wedding on everyone, but Callie has taken that and organised the hell out of it. Maybe I should consider her when the next project manager role becomes vacant.'

'I'll tell her you said that.' I typed out my response and only had to wait a minute or so before her reply came through. 'She said I'm to tell you not to be such a smart arse, and she likes her own job, thank you very much.'

The laughter that ensued lightened the atmosphere in the car, but afterwards, neither of us had much to say.

The rain started when we were about thirty minutes south of Sydney and didn't let up for the rest of the day. While we still stopped as often as we could – both for our comfort and that of our canine companions – we were limited to roadside service centres.

We had a slow trip through Sydney due to roadworks and an accident, more roadworks on the freeway near Gosford, and yet more around Taree. With the difficult conditions, Mac had to concentrate harder than he'd had to yesterday, so the mood and the conversation in the car was more subdued – more music, less talk.

By the time we arrived at our accommodation in Port Macquarie, it was late afternoon and already dark. We were tired, the dogs were restless, and the rain was relentless.

'Christ, it's cold,' complained Mac when we got out of the car at the motel. 'I'll go and check us in if you want to stay here with the dogs,' he said, grabbing his rain jacket and holding it over his head. 'Back in a sec.'

I settled the dogs and got back into the car, where it was at least warm and dry. It took him longer than I'd expected, and I was starting to wonder what was wrong when he climbed back into the car with a half-sheepish, half-annoyed look on his face.

'What's up?' I asked.

'You're not going to believe this,' he said, scratching at the back of his head, 'but there's only one room available.'

'Sorry? We booked two, I'm sure of it.' I'd been looking forward to a warm shower – the idea of getting back in the car and driving somewhere else filled me with no joy – and I wasn't the one who'd been driving all day. 'Hang on, let me find the paperwork.'

As I bent to pick up my handbag, he put his hand on my arm to stop me. 'Don't bother, Ally; I had the confirmation on my phone, and it says we've booked two rooms.'

'Then …? I don't see the problem.'

'The problem is they only have two dog-friendly rooms, and they've given the other one to someone who arrived yesterday. It's their problem, and they've admitted that, but it leaves us down a room.'

'Maybe we can have the dogs in one room and have another normal room,' I suggested, my brain whirling between a weird sort of panic and hope.

He searched my face and said, 'I suggested that, but they have some of their rooms closed for renovation – it's the off-season for them apparently – and are otherwise fully booked. I'm sorry, but we'll have to take the room they have or start looking for somewhere else, and'—he cast his eyes to the roof of the car where the rain seemed to have gathered even more velocity— 'other than going out for takeaway I don't fancy getting back in the car and looking for somewhere else to stay.'

He looked tired. It was in the shadows under his eyes and the weary way he rubbed at the back of his neck. Even his voice sounded exhausted. I felt selfish for being churlish.

'It's okay, Ally,' he said. 'There are two double beds in the room. I'm sure I can keep my hands off you for one more night.' He turned away and muttered something else under his breath.

'What was that?'

'Nothing.' He shook his head. 'I'm tired and cold and … I'm sorry … I'm just—'

I placed my hand on his leg, feeling it tense under my hand. 'Don't apologise. You've been driving all day, and I'm sure I can keep my hands off you, too.' I forced a smile. 'Let's get inside, and I'll take these two out to stretch their legs.'

He smiled tightly, and I got the impression that I'd said something wrong. Rather than say anything, though, he nodded. 'Okay. If you're sure.'

'I am. And I'll also check in with the office about whether there's anyone who can deliver food so we don't need to go out again.'

The room was clean, dry and blessedly warm. While there was no attached yard the dogs could run in, the floor of the room was tiled, and it was large enough that we could throw down their bed cushions on the floor and still have room to walk around. There was a kitchenette with a microwave, toaster and jug, and a sliding glass door led to the garden that we could let the dogs out into as long as we kept an eye on them and cleaned up after them. Aside from a narrow two-seater couch, there was a small round pine table with four chairs tucked into the corner. There were also, as Mac had said, two beds. While a bedside table separated them, I wondered if I'd sleep at all with him so close to me. When I snuck a glance at him, he was looking at them too, a strained look on his face – probably wishing he could collapse into one and go to sleep now.

'You get warm and dry,' I said. 'I'll be back soon.'

'I'll come too,' he said. 'We may as well both be wet.'

I shook my head. 'No, Mac, you've been driving all day. Besides, this way you can have first shower so I won't be sitting around in wet clothes waiting for you to get out.'

The hotel receptionist said the dogs could run in the vacant block beside the motel, so after donning my rain jacket and pulling up the hood, that's where we went. As I watched them chasing each other around the sodden grass, their feet landing in puddles with little splashes that both pooches, judging from the wagging tails and tonguey grins, seemed to find joyful, I wondered again about Mac's mood and told myself he was simply tired. He'd be fine after a shower, a beer and something to eat. As for the bed situation, well, we were two mature adults with self-control. Nothing would happen.

But what if we want it to? whispered Temptation.

I shook her out of my head and whistled for the dogs.

CHAPTER TWENTY

Luckily we had a pile of towels in the car just in case the dogs got wet, so I could towel dry them off before we went back inside and laid more along the tiled floor near the sliding door that led to the garden. The shower was running when we got back but stopped soon after. 'Just me,' I called, even though he probably wasn't expecting it to be anyone else.

He'd been out to the car and brought the esky inside and had put a couple of beers in the mini fridge. The half a bottle of red wine left over from last night was sitting on the table. I looked longingly at it. Shower first.

As if he'd read my mind, the bathroom door opened, and Mac emerged, dressed for a night in, in soft track pants and a baggy long-sleeved T-shirt. Sexy his outfit might not have been, but the way he was still towelling his hair made all my hormones jump to attention.

'Aaah, eau de wet dog,' he chuckled. 'There'll be no escaping that smell tonight.'

'There certainly won't. I've dried them off as best I can, and they've got some towels to roll around on …' I shrugged. 'Now that you're out, I might have a shower too.'

'You do look a bit like Stella when she's all wet and rumpled,' he said, smiling to let me know it wasn't a criticism.

I laughed, relieved his mood seemed to have passed, but the heat rushed to my face when his eyes were drawn to my damp shirt and the nipples that were very much asking to be noticed under it. I tried to cross my arms across my chest casually but knew from his grin that he'd noticed. I turned away and gathered fresh underwear, track pants and baggy top, pushing the clean bra back into my arms when it threatened to fall on the floor, and scuttled into the bathroom. I swear he laughed as I shut the door.

I'd been so cold and wet my skin tingled when the hot water hit it. As I soaped my body, I imagined that he'd come in to join me and that it was his hands roaming my body, around my breasts, across my belly, between my … Enough. I turned the hot water off and withstood the blast of cold required to chase the images away.

When I emerged, he was sitting at the table, a half-drunk beer and an open packet of crisps in front of him.

'I thought you'd got lost in there,' he said.

I blushed again at the thoughts that had kept me in there for so long.

'Feeling better?' he asked.

'Much. And you?'

'The same. Ally, I'm sorry about—'

I shook my head. 'Don't, Mac. Whatever you were about to apologise for, don't. It's all good. At least it will be once I have a glass of wine.'

He smiled but said nothing more about it. With his eyes on me, I poured my wine, closing my eyes briefly as the first mouthful warmed me from the inside. When I opened them again and turned to face him, there was an expression on his face I'd never seen before, something unreadable that made my heart skip. It was, however, gone as quickly as it had been there.

I took my wine and sat on the couch, grimacing as I sank deeply into it. Mac laughed. 'Why do you think I'm sitting here? I sat into that thing and figured I'd need to climb out of it.'

He stood and took my wine, placed it on the table and offered me his hand to pull myself up. I sprang up too fast and landed against his chest. Before my body could get any ideas about the closeness, I picked up my wine glass and retreated to the edge of the bed.

'Are we going to be like this all night, Ally?' he asked, taking his seat again at the table.

'Like what?' I pretended not to know what he was talking about.

'Like this, afraid to touch, afraid to say something in case it's misconstrued.' He shook his head and smiled ruefully. 'That's not us.'

'No, it's not,' I admitted.

'I know this is less than ideal, being in this room smelling of wet dog with a lounge that should've probably been replaced twenty years ago, but it's just one night. You don't need to worry. As I said before, I'm sure I can keep my hands off you for one more night.' He reached behind his head and pushed his fingers into the base of the neck as if to loosen them after the hours behind the wheel.

'So you said.' Before I could change my mind, I got up and placed my glass on the table. Walking behind him, I eased his fingers away and replaced them with my own. 'The problem is, I don't know that I can keep my hands off you,' I said, massaging his neck and shoulders through his top, feeling the muscles tense in surprise, then release under my hands.

He tipped his head back and closed his eyes. 'Oh, that's good,' he groaned.

'Mac,' I said hesitantly. 'Just then, and before in the car, you said "one more night". What did you mean by that?'

His eyes snapped open. At first, I thought he wasn't going to answer me, then he took a deep breath and said, 'Exactly that. I feel as though I've been trying to keep my hands off you since the day I met you.'

My hands stilled on his shoulders. He tilted his head to the side and rested it against one of my hands. Our eyes met in the long mirror hanging on the wall behind the table. 'I don't understand.'

He reached for one of my hands and grabbed it, kissed my palm and held it against his chest where his heart beat against it. 'At first, it was fine; I knew you were running from someone, then you began dating Tommy, and we were well and truly in the friend's zone. Over the last few months, it's been harder to hide, and I reminded myself that you have rules about this sort of thing ... but there have been times lately where I wondered whether you might be feeling the same way about me.' He tilted his head again, staring at the ceiling, this time resting it against me. 'I want you, Ally, so so much, and I'm sorry I was short with you before, but the idea of sleeping in a bed so close to you and not being able to touch you ...' He shook his head, my breasts cushioning it. 'It was bad enough last night having that door between us. I'll do it, though – if you ask me to.'

Our eyes met again in the mirror; this time, I read the expression in his. It was uncertainty, and it was also the same yearning desire I felt for him, and the rush of it drowned out any protests Reason might've wanted to make. Without answering, I bent and kissed his neck, nuzzling my way up to his ear. He turned in the chair, and somehow I ended up sitting across his lap, kissing him with all the longing I'd been hiding, in a way I'd never kissed anyone before, being kissed in a way I'd never been kissed before. 'I want you too,' I said against his mouth, moaning softly as his hand travelled under my top to find my breast, his thumb rubbing my nipple.

'I had to stop myself from coming in when you were in the shower,' he muttered, raining soft kisses down my neck.

'I was imagining that you had,' I said throatily, my eyes closed, my world reduced to him.

He pulled away, panting. 'Oh Ally, if you want to stop this from going any further, don't say things like that.'

'Who said I wanted to stop?' I pushed myself off his lap and stood, holding my hand out to him. As I did, my phone, which I'd left on the table, rang. His eyes went to it. 'Ignore it,' I said.

He looked at the name on the screen. 'It's your brother. Maybe you should take it.'

With a reluctant sigh, I let go of his hand and picked the phone up.

'Hey Matt, is everything okay?'

'Yep. The weather's not great, but it's forecast to clear up from tomorrow,' he said.

'I'm glad, but what are you calling for?' Mac had stood too and straightened his clothes, his track pants unable to hide the evidence of his desire. My mouth went dry at the sight of him. He shrugged ruefully and walked across to the fridge to get another beer.

'Alice?' Matt was saying. 'Are you listening to me?'

'No, sorry. I was distracted; I'm trying to keep an eye on … Stella.' I opened my hands in a "what can I say?" motion when Mac grinned at the lie.

'Why? What's she doing?' Matt had always known I was a lousy liar.

'Nothing. I mean … what are you calling for, Matt?'

'I'd heard the weather was pretty bad down south and wanted to make sure you guys were making decent time still.' Who was the liar now?

There was something else in his voice. Something big brother-ish and exceedingly annoying. 'It was a bad driving day, but we're in Port Macquarie now. We're staying in Kingscliff tomorrow.'

'With Mac's family?'

'Yes, you knew that,' I said defensively.

'No, I didn't – Callie only told me today. You can't stay with his family,' he said. 'It implies something.'

'Why not? He's staying with mine.'

'That's different – he's staying with mine. I asked him first.'

'Seriously? Oh my god, you're so immature,' I said. The discussion sounded like the arguments we had as children.

'I just don't think you should get involved with him. I don't want to see you get hurt.'

I stalked across to the sliding doors, stepping over where the dogs lay, wiping at the condensation and peering out into the dark.

'I don't see that it's any of your business!' I rested my forehead against the cold glass, not wanting to turn to see if Mac was listening to the conversation.

'Look,' Matt said, more calmly, 'Mac's my friend, and he's been a good friend, but I know what's he's like with women. I get that you guys have been friends for a while, but if you sleep with him and it ends badly, which these things do with him – and also with you – you'll be left without a good friend.' When I didn't say anything, he added, 'You haven't slept with him yet, have you?'

'No,' I finally said. 'But I intend to.' Before he could retort, I added. 'I'm hanging up now. Give my love to Callie.'

I slid the phone back into my pocket and stayed where I was a few seconds more, my fingers pressing into my temple, my breathing slowly coming back to normal.

Finally, I turned around. Mac was leaning back against the kitchenette counter. 'He was warning you again about me, wasn't he?'

I nodded.

He shrugged, a cheeky grin on his face. 'That's okay; if you were my sister and I had a friend like me, I'd warn you too.'

'He said I was just as bad as you are – and he's probably right.' I let out a short laugh. 'He asked if I'd slept with you yet.'

'What did you say?' Was it my imagination or was he holding his breath, waiting for my answer?

'That I intended to.'

He nodded once and picked up his keys. 'I'll find us some food before I drink any more of this beer.' He crossed the floor to where I stood and kissed me hard. 'Whatever you decide will be okay with me.'

'I know what I want, Mac,' I said.

'I'm giving you the space to make sure you do,' he said.

As I watched him open the door and walk out into the cold, wet night, I wondered whether we'd be able to get back to where we were before Matt phoned.

While Mac was gone, I finished the glass of wine I'd poured earlier, checked in on my emails, answered a few queries, booked some readings for the end of August and proofread an article that had been sent back to me. While I'd cleared the deck workwise before leaving Melbourne, it paid to keep on top of emails. Before I logged off, though, I updated the password on my website, wondering how long it would take Tommy to notice that I'd done it and to realise what that meant.

From time to time, one or both dogs would get up, stretch and pad around the room, nudge my elbow with a nose, and lay their head against my leg. It was quite comforting in a weird way, the three of us wrapped up in here, warm and dry – even though the room was completely devoid of personality and now reeking of wet dog. I was glad we had the towels so, at least when we left, so too would the odour. Hopefully.

When Mac returned, it was with bags of delicious-smelling plastic containers. 'There wasn't much open,' he said, taking off his wet weather gear and hanging it from a hook behind the front door. 'At least not where I was. So I went with Chinese – it seemed like a safe bet.'

'Sounds good,' I said, taking out some plates and cutlery and setting the little round table. 'Wine?'

'No thanks, I'll have that beer I opened before. While you're doing that, I'll feed the dogs.'

Although the room was small, we got our meal ready without getting in each other's way, even though we were tiptoeing around each other.

As we ate, we chatted about the drive tomorrow and where we could stop along the way.

'It's only just over four hundred kilometres,' said Mac. 'About four and a half hours driving time depending on roadworks and the traffic through Coffs Harbour and Ballina. If this rain clears, I thought we might stop at Byron Bay or Bangalow for lunch and aim to be at Mum and Dad's by three-ish.'

'It's been years since I was in Byron, so fish and chips by the beach sounds like a good idea.'

As if even she knew how inane the conversation was, Stella stood at the back door and looked pointedly outside. When I didn't get up immediately, she barked.

'That's me told,' I said. 'I'll take the dogs out.' I opened the door enough to look outside. 'It's stopped raining ... for now, at least.'

'You'll still need a jacket,' Mac said. 'I'll clean this up while you're gone.'

I could've groaned at the awkwardness of it but pulled my jacket on and went out with the two dogs.

Because they'd had a good run earlier, both seemed keen to do their business and come in out of the cold for the night – as was I.

Once back inside and the dogs settled on their beds, I turned to Mac, who had finished putting away the dinner things.

'Mac ...'

'Ally ...'

We both spoke at the same time.

'You go first,' he said.

I debated making some vague comment about how awkward we both had been, how we didn't need to be so damned polite, then decided that we'd always been honest with each other, and why should that change now? Not that I was going to be *completely* honest, of course – I certainly wasn't going to tell him I loved him – just honest enough. But first, I needed to know about Bree.

'You know how I said Tommy sent me through a link with your photo?' He nodded, his brow furrowed as if wondering where the conversation was going. 'Well, what I didn't say was that it was a photo of you with Bree.'

'Aaah.' A wide smile took the place of his confused frown. 'And you're wondering if I'm still with her?' I nodded. 'I'm not. Regardless of whatever Tommy has hinted, that day you saw me with her was the day I ended it.'

I almost sobbed with relief. 'Here's the thing,' I started, pausing to make sure the words I needed to say came out in the proper order. 'When you told me this afternoon that you'd been, well, thinking about me differently, I didn't tell you, but I've wanted you like that too. Not just yesterday and today and the last few weeks or months, but for ages.' I smiled a nervous smile. 'I don't know what this is between us, and I don't want to give it a label – at least not yet – and my brother might be right; it could end in tears. But even if it does, I don't want to regret not knowing, and I don't want to regret not trying.'

I lifted my top over my head, pushed my track pants over my hips and kicked them away, all the while watching his face for a reaction. As I reached behind to unclip my bra, he stopped me. 'Don't,' he said gruffly.

My heart flipped and braced for rejection; I held my breath and forced myself to hold his stare.

He took a step towards me and trailed his finger down my sternum. 'I want to do that.' His voice was hoarse, suggestive. 'I've been dreaming of doing that.' And just like that, I started breathing again.

CHAPTER TWENTY-ONE

Our coming together had been as easy as the rest of our relationship had been. We stroked and nibbled and kissed and giggled, and my groan of frustration when he pulled away to deal with protection turned to sheer joy when he entered me for the first time.

Afterwards, I would've wriggled from his arms, but he held me close. 'I just want to hold you,' he said, and I was more than happy to stay exactly where I was. As I drifted to sleep with his arms still around me, I thought I heard him whisper, 'I've waited so long to hold you.'

The following morning, Stella woke me up by jumping against the bed. Mac leant across and kissed me, his face and lips cold, his stubble rough. 'Have you been out?' I murmured, stretching languorously.

'I have. I had another way in mind for waking you, but the dogs couldn't wait,' he said throatily when the sheet slipped to show one escapee boob.

'Mmmm, I would've liked that,' I said, reaching for his head to kiss him properly. 'I don't suppose we can now?'

'I wish.' He lowered his head and caught my nipple in his mouth. I moaned and arched into him. 'But somehow, I think these dogs won't let us.'

As if they could understand us, they began to play wrestle on the towels.

'I'd better get up,' I said, making no move to do so.

'You had,' he said, 'but one more kiss first.'

As if mirroring our mood, the rain had cleared overnight, and the sun shone as we left town for the drive north. Even with a few stops, we made good time and pulled up in the McInnes driveway mid-afternoon. Mac's parents must've been waiting for us and were quickly out the front door to greet us.

Cheryl McInnes was a slightly built woman with short, grey curly hair that used to be blonde. When she smiled her greeting, it was with Mac's bright blue eyes and with Mac's open grin. It was, however, from his father that Mac got his height and build. Russ was a tall man, still as broad across the shoulders as his son and, like his son, with the lean strength of someone who moves a lot. His parents, Mac had told me this morning, were keen walkers and were often on the water paddling their kayaks.

They greeted me with warmth and pleasure, yet I detected an underlying hesitancy under Cheryl's hello and wondered how many of Mac's girlfriends he'd previously introduced them to. As far as they were concerned, however, I was just a friend – we were just friends. Even after last night, I wasn't sure whether that had changed. Were we now friends who had extremely good sex, or were we more than that? I'd told Mac we didn't need a label, but maybe I did.

As Mac and Russ unpacked the car, Cheryl and I took the dogs into the backyard and let them loose to tear around and sniff everything that was new to be sniffed and to acquaint themselves with Buster, the McInnes' chocolate labrador.

Leaving them to it, Cheryl led me inside. 'Mac made such a fuss about how you two were just friends, so I've put you in separate bedrooms,' she said.

Feeling my cheeks colour, I nodded and said, 'That's fine. Thank you.'

She looked me up and down and smiled. 'Although, and I hope you don't mind me saying so, given we've only just met, but the way my son was just looking at you, I'm not sure you're just friends anymore. Am I right?'

My cheeks were on fire and I couldn't find the words to answer her.

'Don't worry, Alice,' she said. 'I'm not going to give you the third degree, but you are the first woman Alex has brought home to meet us.'

My head snapped up. 'Oh, but I thought …' What had I thought?

'Anyway,' she said, 'we can talk later. I'll let you get

settled in. Come through to the kitchen when you're ready, and I'll put the kettle on. We thought we'd have a barbecue on the deck for dinner.' She suddenly looked concerned. 'You're not vegan or free from, are you?'

'Free from?'

'Gluten-free, dairy-free, meat-free or any of those others,' she clarified. 'Not that it would be a problem if you were; it's just that Alex hadn't mentioned it.'

I shook my head. 'No, I eat pretty much anything.'

'Good,' she sounded relieved. 'Well, I'll leave you to it.'

As she left the room, Mac walked into it, kissing his mother on the top of her head as she passed. 'It's good to see you, Mum,' he said.

Cheryl rubbed affectionately at his arm. 'It's good to see you too.' With a pointed look in my direction, she added, 'Both of you.'

As she left, Mac closed the door and took me in his arms. 'I've missed you,' he said, nuzzling behind my ear.

'What do you mean? We've been together all day.'

'Yes, but I've missed holding you,' he said, the look in his eyes filling me with warmth.

'In that case, I've missed being held. I've also missed being kissed,' I added cheekily.

'I'd better rectify that miserable situation then,' he said, lowering his head to devour me thoroughly.

'Mmmm, that's better,' I said when finally he pulled back, both of us breathing more heavily.

'I could think of ways it could be even better, but my mother has given us separate bedrooms,' he said with disappointment.

'At your instruction, I believe,' I teased.

'I should've had more faith in myself,' he said.

'Sorry?' I had no idea what he meant.

'Well,' he said sheepishly, 'I'd hoped that this might happen – forced proximity and all that …'

'Yeah,' I admitted, 'so did I.'

That admission earned me another kiss.

'You know we'll have separate bedrooms at my parent's too,' I said.

He groaned dramatically. 'If that's the case, I vote for leaving the dogs with your parents after the wedding and you and I going somewhere we can be alone properly for a few days.'

'I'd like that,' I murmured.

'Leave it with me,' he said. 'But we'd better get out of here before Mum sends in a search party.'

'I think she knows,' I said.

'That we're together? I'm not surprised; very little gets by her.' He kissed me again, quickly, and opened the bedroom door. As I followed him through it, I couldn't help the rush of hope that coursed through me at his words. Reason, though, had other ideas. Mac had said we were together, but were we together as in *together*, or were we just together for now and as long as his interest held? His mother might've said he'd never brought anyone else home, but given that he lived in Melbourne and they lived up here, that wasn't surprising. We were only here now because we were passing through. While Reason told me not to get too excited about it, I chose to ignore the advice. Whatever this was, I intended to make the most of it and enjoy every minute we had together.

Later that afternoon, as Mac and his father caught up, I helped Cheryl in the kitchen to prepare some salads for dinner.

'We'll keep it quite simple,' she said. 'Alex's favourites – butterflied lamb with garlic and rosemary, a potato salad, beetroot and feta, and a garden salad. Plus, I've made his favourite dessert – a strawberry cloud cake.' She opened the freezer and showed me the cake that was inside. High and pink, it was not what I expected. Although, I had to admit, he rarely had anything sweet when we ate together. Usually it was breakfast or takeaway pizza. The only time we'd sat in a restaurant and had a proper meal was the other week with Matt, Callie, Todd and Andi. Who was I to say what he liked or didn't like?

'It looks so pretty,' I said. 'What's in it?'

'Aside from the biscuit base, a punnet of strawberries, two egg whites, some sugar and a dash of lemon juice.' At my look of disbelief, she chuckled. 'Truly, that's all.'

I opened the freezer door again. The cake stood tall and pink and proud – as if a cheesecake had made love to strawberry ice cream.

'I know,' she said, 'it shouldn't make sense, but it does. To me, it's a sign that as unlikely as some situations appear, magic can happen.'

Her words sounded light yet also seemed heavy with a meaning I couldn't grasp.

'I met your brother once,' she said, changing tack. 'Years ago when we were still living in Brisbane. He and Alex were like two peas in a pod in those days. Alex said he's spent most of the last ten years in Asia.'

'Yes, he was based in Hong Kong for some time.'

'And he's marrying your best friend. Alex was saying it was quite a sudden thing.'

'Completely,' I said, feeling on safer ground. 'They'd known each other when we were all younger, of course, before Matt started university, but hadn't seen each other since. Then they met again last winter at my brother-in-law's fortieth birthday party and clicked immediately. Matt moved back to Australia earlier this year but surprised us all with the speed of his proposal – not that it should have been a surprise; once he decides on a course of action, that's pretty much it. Does this onion need slicing?'

Cheryl passed me over a red onion. 'Into half moons, please. I'll pop it into a little bit of vinegar before we serve it – it softens the flavour. Your brother sounds very much like Alex.'

'Maybe,' I conceded. 'I wonder, though, whether Matt and Cal would've worked if they'd met at any other time. They might still have fallen in love, but if Matt hadn't been ready to commit, Cal's heart would have been broken.'

I concentrated on slicing the onion while keeping my fingers intact, yet I could feel Cheryl's eyes on me.

'Would that have stopped her?' she asked gently. I thought she meant to ask if that would stop me.

'No,' I said simply. 'Even though it's the biggest risk of all to take, you take it, don't you?'

I placed the onions into the bowl with vinegar. 'Yes, you do,' said Cheryl, passing me across a punnet of cherry tomatoes to slice. 'Russ and I were like you and Alex – great friends. What he didn't know was that I'd always loved him but didn't want to tell him in case I lost him as a friend. What I didn't know was that he felt the same.'

'How did you get together?'

'You might laugh at this, but it was at a wedding. His best friend was marrying my best friend … then less than twelve months later, we were standing up there saying our forever vows with Alex already on the way.' She poured a little olive oil into the base of a bowl, added a splash of the vinegar the onions were resting in (now almost as pink as the cloud cake in the freezer), and tossed some green leaves through it. 'In hindsight, I couldn't imagine not marrying my best friend. It makes it easier when the kids have left home to know that we're enough together without them. Having said that, though, it would be nice if they weren't quite so far away,' she said with a half smile and raised her eyebrow. 'We'll be glad when Alex finally moves back to Brisbane.'

My breath caught in my throat at her words. Alex moving?

My distress must have shown because Cheryl put her hand to her mouth. 'Oh, I'm sorry. Have I spoken out of turn? I assumed you knew, and with your family on the Sunshine Coast too …'

I shook my head briefly. 'It's fine,' I said. 'He had mentioned it; I just didn't realise it was so far down the track.'

'I don't know that it is,' said Cheryl, recovering quickly. 'It's something he's spoken about, that's all.'

Yes, that had to be it. Otherwise, he would've told me, wouldn't he?

'I'm not wrong about one thing, though, am I?' she said. 'You are in love with my son?'

I nodded. 'Yes, I am.'

She brightened. 'That's alright then. I'm sure it will all work out.' She covered the salad bowl with something that looked like a shower cap. 'I'm trying to cut down on plastic,' she said. 'Okay, let's take this wine out onto the deck and join the boys.'

While we hadn't discussed how we'd behave in front of his parents, Mac didn't hide it either. He often laid a hand on my arm or my leg to illustrate a point and draped his arm around me from time to time, his smile both a memory of the previous evening and a promise for when we could be alone.

The conversation was easy, the food simple yet tasty, and the cloud cake fluffily miraculous. When Mac kissed me goodnight at my bedroom door, I tasted the strawberry sweetness on his lips and wanted so much more of him.

'I could get very used to this,' he said, resting his forehead against mine, both of us panting our need. 'Kissing you, being with you.'

Unable to answer without giving myself away, I reached for his head to bring his lips back to mine.

I hadn't thought I'd sleep knowing Mac was on the other side of the thin wall, but it surprised me when I opened my eyes to find it was morning and I'd barely stirred. Cheryl and Russ were heading down for an early morning paddle, so Mac and I took advantage of their absence for some exercise of our own. Later we all went for breakfast at the beach, the weather mild enough to leave our jackets home.

When we left to begin the drive up to Mooloolaba, Russ said, 'It's a pity you couldn't stay longer and have a bit more of a look around.'

While I smiled and made no comment, Mac said, 'There's plenty I'd like to show Ally. Maybe we'll stay an extra night on the way back down.'

I shot him a quick look. We hadn't discussed when we'd be leaving the Sunshine Coast yet or the route we'd take back down.

Cheryl gave me a quick hug. 'Fabulous. We'll see you both again in another week or so.'

'You will,' said Mac. 'I'll let you know once we work out what we're doing.'

In the car, he said, 'That's okay, isn't it?'

'What?'

'Staying an extra night in Kingscliff. You didn't say much, so I wondered … If it's not okay, I can call and …'

I rested a hand on his leg. 'That's fine. Your parents are lovely, and I can't believe how well I slept last night.'

'We'll need to rectify that situation next time,' he said with a wicked grin. 'Mum and Dad will be fine with you sharing my room.'

'I mightn't be, though,' I said, blushing.

'If you're not, then we won't,' he said. 'I don't want you to feel uncomfortable.'

'I didn't mean that.' I struggled for the words to clarify the reason for my hesitancy. 'It's just they're so lovely, and I don't want them to hope and …'

He frowned. 'What do you mean?'

I inhaled deeply. 'Your mother mentioned you were considering a move to Brisbane. Actually, she made it sound as though you were doing more than considering it.'

'I see,' he said slowly. 'And you're wondering why I haven't said anything to you?'

I nodded. 'Not that you have to, of course. I mean, it's none of my business.'

He flicked me a quick sideways glance. 'It's not yet a done deal,' he finally said. 'I said the other day that it's always been my plan to go back, and a few months ago, I began looking at real estate – at about the same time as I began work on the office up here. Things have changed since then, though,' he said. 'I'm not in as much of a hurry to move.'

There was something in his voice I didn't understand. Did he mean us and this thing between us? 'You said yesterday that Matt and Callie are considering it too. Have you spoken to him about it?'

'Sort of. It's probably one of the reasons he's worried about you getting too involved with me.'

I let out a short, derisive laugh. 'One of the reasons. Matt forgets that he and Callie wouldn't be getting married now if I issued the same warnings to him about breaking her heart as he's issued to me.'

Mac chuckled. 'I don't know about that, Ally. Matt wouldn't have allowed her to get away regardless of what you had to say about it. I haven't met your older sister, but what I know so far about the Delaneys is that they're pretty formidable when it comes to going after what they want.' I was about to open my mouth to argue with him, but he said, 'Don't think I haven't noticed how you've grown your business in the time you've been in Melbourne. From what I can tell, you arrived in Melbourne broken and quickly picked yourself up and got on with it. I remember the first time I met you; you laughed at Kevin as if you hadn't laughed in a long time. It struck me that you'd decided to laugh – that Luke might have hurt you, but you weren't going to let that stop you. Since then, you've pitched articles, grown your client base and even got up at sparrows fart for a year to do that radio program. You're making a success of what you do, and I truly think there's something in this workplace astrology idea we've been talking about. So tell me, if someone had told you that you wouldn't be able to make a living doing what you do, would that have stopped you from trying?'

I shook my head, unable to speak – not that I would have known what to say. The backs of my eyes were tingling, and my throat was full.

'Exactly,' he said. 'Matt's the same and, I daresay, once I get to know your sister, I'll find that she also has that Delaney spirit.'

He might have said more, but my phone pinged with a text from Callie.

How far away are you? I can't wait to see you.

'Is everything okay?' asked Mac.

'Yep, Callie's just getting impatient.'

We've cleared Brissie and North Lakes. Not long now. What's for lunch?

Callie responded with a row of laughing faces. It would be good for the three of us – Tiff, Callie and myself – to be back together, but how would I handle the Mac element? I snuck a glance at him. Would he want to make our relationship public, or wasn't there a relationship to be made public? Were we just friends with fabulous benefits or was this something more?

'I've been thinking,' I said hesitantly.

'Did it hurt?'

'Ha, ha. Seriously, Mac, I've been thinking maybe we shouldn't, well, flaunt this thing between us just yet.'

He frowned – or was he squinting into the sun? I couldn't tell.

'It's just until …' I screwed my eyes shut and wrinkled my nose as I chose my words.

'Until after the wedding?' he finished.

'Yeah. Just until then.' At least that way, if things didn't go as I wanted them to, no one would know, and Matt wouldn't need to jump in and defend my honour.

He nodded but didn't reply immediately. Eventually, he said, 'But I can still kiss you as long as no one is around?'

'Yes please.'

He chuckled. 'I'll be guided by you,' he finally said. 'It's your family and your friends.'

While I was grateful he was prepared to go along with me, it disappointed me that he gave in so easily.

I didn't have long to think about it, though, as my phone pinged again. As I picked it up, I chuckled. 'I wonder what Callie's forgotten to tell me.'

My laugh died when the sender's name appeared on the screen, an icy chill working through my body, pushing my heart into my throat.

'What is it?' asked Mac, noting my mood change.

'It's Tommy. He wants to know why he can't get into my website and why I didn't tell him I was travelling with you.' I turned panicked eyes to Mac. 'How does he know? How can he know?' My hand flew to my chest, my heart pounding against it. When Mac didn't answer, I asked my question again.

'Hey,' he soothed, placing a hand briefly on my thigh. 'Let's think this through logically. Read me his text.'

I opened the message again. '"Hi Alice, what's going on? I've just gone to check your website, and the password isn't working. Did you change it? I thought we trusted each other and now I find that you've been lying to me about Mac. Did you always intend to take him instead of me? How long has that been going on – or have you cheated on Luke and me with him?" Then he calls me a nasty name and says, "The joke is that he's cheating on you with at least one other woman. You'd better be careful, Alice … or maybe it's him I should be warning."' Turning back to Mac, I said, 'What do you think it means?'

'Aside from the fact that he's a dick?' He huffed out a sigh. 'What contact have you had with Luke?'

I searched his face for a sign that part of him believed the things Tommy had accused me of. Finding nothing there but concern, I said, 'None. After I saw him at lunch that day, I blocked his number, but he emailed me a couple of times afterward – nothing untoward, but I ignored them.' I sighed and tapped my fingers against my temple as I realised what he was really asking. 'You think Tommy's had access to my emails as well?'

He gave a half shrug and said, 'He didn't know that I was with you until now, and I know you mentioned me in the email you sent Callie the other day … Had you mentioned it before that?'

I shook my head. 'Not via email, no. That time was the first.' My stomach was churning in a combination of horror, disbelief and fear. 'He's had access to my emails, hasn't he? That's how he knew about Project Yes and when to ask me out, and that's how he knew about the Bali conference and—'

'Ally!' Mac's voice was firm. 'Let's assume he has had access – there's nothing you can do about that now, but you need to change your password to your email immediately.' It was a glimpse of Boardroom

Mac – businesslike and practical.

If what we suspected was true, I should be angry with Tommy, furious even, but while I was all those things, I also felt sad for him. Mostly though, I was mad at myself for my behaviour. Not only had I, the one with a hefty personal rulebook, broken every rule in the IT security rulebook, but I'd also encouraged Tommy into thinking there could be more to our relationship than there ever would be. I'd known how he felt about me, and I'd pushed that to one side while I concentrated on trying to feel the same, all while knowing full well that I never would. Hayden had let me off lightly when I'd done it to him, and I'd thought Tommy had too. This was Karma reminding me of the consequences of my behaviour.

'You're quiet; what are you thinking?'

I lifted one shoulder. 'I got into a mess with Luke because I believed what he'd said to me. Now I'm in a mess with Tommy because I believed him when he said he was fine about us finishing. In both cases, I believed them because it suited me to do so.' I let out a short, rueful laugh. 'I'm the one who led him on and hurt him.'

'Don't make excuses for Tommy's behaviour,' warned Mac. '*If* we're right, what he's done is the equivalent to stalking you, and that's never okay – regardless of whatever you're beating yourself up about right now. You are not responsible for his actions.'

When I wasn't convinced, he added, 'Are we clear?'

I mock saluted and told him he was right, even though part of me still felt culpable.

'Are we clear?' he asked again. 'I'm serious, Ally. Don't go feeling sorry for him; this is his problem, not yours, and he knows that you'd be feeling bad for him and will do anything for you to reach out and let him back into your life. That's a cruel way to manipulate anyone – and particularly you.'

I nodded, the lump in my throat too big for the words to pass.

'This afternoon, we'll speak to my security guys and see what's going on, then we'll close this down. You know you'd have grounds for making a formal complaint? He could lose his job over this?'

I nodded grimly. Mac had said before that he admired my way of going after what I wanted, but I had no idea how to deal with this.

'It's okay, sweetheart,' he said gently. 'I'm here, and we'll deal with it together. And for the record? I've never cheated on anyone in my life, and I'm certainly not seeing anyone else now – nor,' he added, 'do I intend to.'

Even though his smile was forced and manufactured to make me feel better, the firmness in Mac's jaw and the bunching of his fist on the steering wheel told me what he'd do to Tommy if he had the opportunity.

CHAPTER TWENTY-TWO

Callie and Matt came out to meet us as soon as we pulled into the driveway. While Matt welcomed Mac with an enthusiastic handshake and man hug, he still frowned each time he looked at the pair of us. Callie noticed it and mock punched him. 'Enough,' she said. 'Sorry Alex, Matt seems to have forgotten you're friends.'

Matt coloured, protesting that he was allowed to look after his baby sister if he wanted to, at which I mock punched him – in the same spot Callie had. Although mine might not have been as much of a mock punch as he rubbed his arm and looked balefully at me for a few minutes.

Mum and Dad either didn't notice Matt's pointed comments and repeated frowns – or pretended not to notice – and I made a concerted effort not to look at Mac as often as I would have liked, so there was no doubt that everyone believed we truly were just friends.

At least that's what I thought until later in the afternoon; Mac was catching up on some work calls and emails, and Mum was showing me around the garden. As usual, there was no beating around the bush with Mum. 'Alex seems nice,' she said, pointing out the cherry tomatoes (which had no right to be fruiting in July) and the butternut squash.

'Yes, he is. He's a good friend.'

'Does he know you're in love with him?'

How did my mother know everything? 'No. At least, I don't think so.'

'And he's the one?'

I nodded, no longer able to hide the truth. 'Yes. From the first time I met him.'

'I see.' As always, there was a wealth of meaning in those two words. 'Why doesn't Matt approve?'

'Because they've been friends for a long time, and he and Matt have had …' I struggled with the right words for my mother.

'Adventures?' she guessed.

'That's a perfect word for it, Mum, yes.'

'Well,' she sighed. 'That's ridiculous. Plenty of men go through that until they find their person. Has Matt forgotten what he was like?'

'Apparently not,' I said with a rueful grin. 'And therein lies the problem.'

Mum let out a laugh, almost as if she didn't want to laugh but hadn't been able to help it. 'And what do you think about it?'

'I don't know how he feels about me, but I know how I want him to feel about me.' I shrugged. 'I also know that once you find the right person, it's all a clean slate – you just need to look at Matt to see that.'

'I agree. Don't listen to your brother – you know your own mind. Just don't hide how you feel from Alex for too long. You need to know one way or another, and you've never been the type to wait patiently.'

'What are you trying to say, Mum?' I chuckled.

'You know exactly what I'm saying,' she replied, with a stern face that she couldn't hold.

'Ally,' called Mac from the deck. 'Can I borrow you for a minute?'

From the sound of his voice, it was time to find out whether our suspicions regarding Tommy were correct, so I simply nodded in his direction.

Mum must've seen the look on both our faces and said, 'Is everything okay?'

I couldn't see any point in hiding what was going on. 'Not really. Someone has been attempting to sabotage my website, and all indications are that it's Tommy. Mac is getting his security team to look into it for me.'

'I see. Well, that is disappointing.' I couldn't read her expression.

'I know I shouldn't have let him believe we had a future, but—'

Mum shook her head. 'Stop right there, Alice Delaney. You're not responsible for his feelings or how he behaves. Take a step back and pretend it's happened to Callie or Tiff and think about how you'd react then. Would you blame them at all?'

'Of course not!'

'Well, treat yourself with the same kindness.' And then she smiled and turned back to her garden, pulling out a weed that had dared to emerge from beneath the sugar cane mulch.

By the time I returned inside and retrieved my laptop, Mac had set up on the kitchen table with Scott, a senior member of the security team, on a video call. He introduced me and gave Scott a brief rundown of the issues I'd encountered. I gave my permission for him to remotely access my laptop and watched as his cursor moved across my screen, dipping and gliding into directories, files and applications. After a few minutes, Scott confirmed my fears, patiently explaining that someone had installed some mirroring software on my email agent. I stopped listening after that. The website had been easier to infiltrate because Tommy had my password. I'd essentially handed him all he needed.

'There's been no attempt to damage your website,' Scott said.

'But what about the messages and attempts to clone my pages?' I asked. 'I was told there were some very nasty messages left for me.'

He looked bemused. 'No, I didn't find anything like that.'

'I see.' Not that I did completely understand what I was being told. Tommy had lied to me the entire time, and the outages I'd experienced had been solely due to his attempts to access my website before I'd given him my password. It really had been my security settings working as they were supposed to.

'In any case, I've updated your security settings and removed the malicious software. It's all as clean as a whistle now,' Scott said. 'But I wouldn't be going about giving your password to anyone again,' he warned. 'When you're back in town, come into the office, and we'll talk some more about permanently upgrading your security.'

Once we hung up, I closed the lid of my laptop and sank back in the kitchen chair, my gaze on the ceiling, a nasty hollow pit in my gut. I closed my eyes as if that simple action could delay the decision I needed to make and the confrontation I needed to have. One tear squeezed out past my closed eyelids, then another, and before I knew it, I was doubled over, sobbing. My tears were hot and angry, but inside I was deeply sad. Sad that I'd broken Tommy's heart, sad that he'd done this to me, sad that my trust and my instincts had been so wrong.

'Oh Ally,' Mac said, putting his arms around me.

'What the fuck have you done to her?' demanded Matt from the kitchen doorway, his fists clenched, fury on his face. Callie stood beside him, concern for me written all over hers. She placed a restraining hand on Matt's arm.

I squirmed out of Mac's embrace and wiped ineffectually at my eyes, leaving him to do the talking. 'Nothing, as it happens. She's had some bad news.' Mac leant against the table. 'I'm doing what any friend would do, comforting her.' When he raised an eyebrow in my direction, I nodded, giving him permission to tell them what had happened.

When he finished, Callie rushed over to hold me. Matt declared, 'What's his number? Let me at him!' Then he turned to Mac and asked, 'What are you doing about it?'

I shook Cal off and sprung to my feet, uncaring of my red, snotty nose and streaming eyes, and stalked over to where my brother stood. Squaring up to him, I said, 'Mac's helped me get this far, the next steps are on me, and you'—I poked Matt in the chest— 'and you'—I pointed at Mac— 'are not going to interfere any further. I will talk to Tommy and decide if I want to take this further, and you two will stay out of it.'

With hands planted firmly on my hips, I glared at my brother. 'I know you care about me, but please, this is now my problem to sort out. I got myself into it, and I'll get myself out of it.'

'Sweetie,' said Callie, unable to hide her horror over what Tommy had done, said, 'This is not your problem – it's Tommy's, and you are not to blame.

So you broke up with him? That doesn't give him the right to stalk you. You do understand that, don't you?'

I sniffed and nodded, my hands leaving my hips, my posture relaxing. 'Yeah, I do, but I can't help feeling sorry for him at the same time.'

Matt rolled his eyes. 'Not this again! Man, I thought you would've grown out of that.' To Mac, he said, 'When Ally was a kid, she used to feel sorry for everyone who was mean to her, and when Laura and I would ask why, she'd say because she was a lovely person and a good friend and they were missing out on that.'

Mac roared with laughter. 'I can well believe that.'

Callie said, 'I'm glad she hasn't grown out of that and is still the bright-sider in our little group.' To the men, she said, 'How about we leave Ally to make her phone call, hey?'

I smiled gratefully at her but added, 'Mac, can you please stay? Just in case I need you.'

He nodded simply, but Matt frowned and would've said something about why I'd asked Mac and not my brother. 'Matt, everything doesn't need to be a competition.'

He was still frowning when Callie dragged him away.

Drawing a shaky breath, I picked up my phone and called Tommy, who answered almost immediately.

'Al, I was beginning to wonder if you would ever call me back.' He sounded normal, as if he hadn't sent me a threatening text only a few hours ago, as if everything was how it used to be back when I trusted him. In fact, he sounded so normal I could almost have convinced myself that despite all the evidence to the contrary, I was imagining it all.

'I didn't want to call you until I was sure,' I said.

'Sure of what?' He sounded genuinely puzzled.

'Sure of what you've done,' I said simply.

'And what is it I'm supposed to have done? Has Mac tried to tell you lies about me?'

'Tommy, enough! The head of the security team at DotPoint has screened my laptop. They've cleaned it of everything that doesn't belong on it and upgraded the security.'

He was silent for a few seconds, and as tempted as I was to jump into the silence, I didn't.

'Right. Well, that's good then,' he finally said.

'I've also changed my passwords,' I said.

'Right,' he said again flatly. 'Probably a good idea.'

'And Tommy?'

'Yes,' he said hesitantly.

'I don't think you should try and contact me again.' Mac raised his eyebrows and shook his head in exasperation at my mildness.

'No. You're probably right,' he said. Then he added, 'I'm not going to apologise for loving you, Alice.'

'I'm not asking you to,' I said. 'But that's not the way to do it.'

'You left me no choice,' he said. 'You made me believe you loved me; then you threw me away as soon as Luke came back on the scene.'

Anger bubbled past the sadness, completely washing it away. 'I *made* you believe nothing, Tommy, and any relationship with Luke was a figment of your imagination. As for leaving you without a choice, what a load of bullshit.' I stood and began stalking around the kitchen, ignoring the little smile playing around Mac's mouth. 'And on the subject of bullshit, I don't think I've ever heard a more bullshit excuse than that one. I left you no choice? You had plenty of choices, Tommy – the best one was to accept what had happened, be glad we'd had a great time and get on with your life. Instead, you've given me ample reason to make a formal complaint against you – not just to the police but also to your employer.'

'What?' The word came out as a high-pitched squeak. 'This has got nothing to do with my employer.'

'Oh no, Tommy, that's where you're very wrong indeed.' I was on a roll, my finger waggling in the air as I played to a script I didn't even know I'd prepared. 'We've both done the training on sexual harassment in the workplace, and what you've done breaches all of that – and before you tell me I no longer work there, that makes no difference. Besides, this started while I was still working there and you wilfully put that mirroring software on my laptop using workplace resources. Plus'—my finger circled the air as I warmed to my subject— 'you can not tell me you haven't been fart-arsing around with my website and email during office hours. So yes, Tommy, this has *everything* to do with your employer.'

I drew breath and looked across at Mac, who was shaking his head, grinning, and clapping all at the same time. In the doorway, Matt and Callie were applauding too.

'What are you going to do?' he asked in a small voice.

'I haven't decided yet – I'm too angry. I know what I should do, and that's report you so you don't do what you've done to me to anyone else – that is unless you've done it to someone else in the past …'

'No, I haven't,' he stammered. 'And I'll never do it again.'

'Hmmm.' I deliberately paused for a minute as if thinking. 'As I said, I haven't decided yet – although I do know what my brother wants to do about it. Given that you also made a threat against Mac, I'll confer with him too. I've taken copies of your messages and asked security to take a copy of the logs in my laptop just in case you're tempted to follow through on any of those threats.'

'Right,' he said.

I inhaled deeply and drew myself up to my most haughty. 'I feel sorry for you, Tommy.'

'Why's that?'

'Not because I wasn't in love with you, but because I'm a good friend and now that's something you'll miss out on. Goodbye.'

As I hung up, I collapsed into a chair and heaved a heavy sigh. 'I do believe my work here is done,' I said.

Callie giggled and kissed my cheek. Matt ruffled my hair, and Mac said, 'I was expecting you to take a bow after that little performance.'

I returned their smile and allowed myself to relax. I wouldn't report Tommy, and in not doing so, I also knew I'd let him off easily – just as easily, in fact, as I'd thought *he'd* let me off. I'd also resisted the urge to ask him if he'd known about Project Yes from Tiff's emails to me before he asked me out and if he'd known about the astrology conference in Ubud before mentioning he was going diving and did I want to join him. Knowing for sure about either of those things wouldn't have done me any good.

CHAPTER TWENTY-THREE

Callie grabbed my arm as the four of us walked to the surf club that evening to meet Tiff and Jake. 'Tell me all about it,' she encouraged.

'The drive?' I asked with an innocent look on my face. 'Or Tommy?'

'No, you idiot, the sex. You have slept with him, haven't you?' As my face flamed, she giggled. 'It must've been good for you to blush.'

'Ssssh …' I said with a pointed glance at the two men walking ahead of us.

'You don't want Matt to know?' she guessed.

'Not yet. Not until I know what the deal is myself,' I said.

'But it was good?' She grinned, her eyebrows waggling.

'It was the best,' I admitted, unable to stop the smile that spread across my face at the memory.

At our giggles, Matt turned and frowned at me. 'What are you two cackling about?'

'You, my dear brother,' I said, walking through

the front door at the surf club.

The glint in Mac's eye told me he didn't believe a word of it, and when he stood beside me as we waited to sign in, his little finger reached for mine. He dropped his hand just before Matt turned back to face us, but it had been enough.

It was a fine, mild evening, and Tiff and Jake were sitting at the high tables on the deck, the sky turning the ocean all the shades of pink and lilac as the sun went down.

I don't know whether Callie noticed before I did, but we both screamed and cried at the same time, hugging Tiff, who had slid off her chair and into our arms.

'Oh my god!' said Callie.

'How long?' I asked. 'Why didn't you say?'

'I'm so happy for you,' said Callie, wiping the tears from her eyes.

When we'd finished hugging and kissing and crying, Cal and I pulled away so we could look at her properly.

'Can I touch it?' Cal asked tremulously, eyeing Tiff's baby bump.

Tiff rolled her eyes, her smile foiling her attempt to appear exasperated. 'If you must,' she said drolly.

Jake stood to one side, chatting to Matt and Mac, a grin on his face as he didn't appear to be able to take his eyes from Tiff. 'Congratulations,' I said, hugging him.

'You must both be pleased.' It was more of a question than a statement.

He pulled Tiff to his side and kissed her lips. 'It's definitely going to mean some changes, but we couldn't be happier.'

A faint tinge of pink coloured Tiff's cheeks. 'No,' she said, beaming back at him, 'we couldn't be happier.'

'So, how far are you?' Cal asked.

'Sixteen weeks,' she said. 'I hope you don't mind my baby belly in your wedding photos,' she said to Cal.

Callie squealed again and hugged the side that Jake didn't have a hold of.

I shook my head in disbelief; Tiff had gone from I don't believe in love and I'm never having children, and nothing will come between me and that senior management role to loved-up and pregnant in twelve months – and I couldn't be happier for her. She caught my eye and, as if she knew what I was thinking, she nodded and said, 'I know, right? Who would have believed it?'

'I always knew you just needed the right man,' said Callie, not even attempting to temper her joy.

'That's my darling, the eternal romantic,' said Matt, coming behind her to pull her close and kiss her throat.

I watched the loved-up couples with a lump in my throat that was mostly happiness but also a smidgeon of envy. Why couldn't this be Mac and me? I wanted so much to go to him and have his arms enclose me, for him to whisper in my ear, 'That'll be us someday.' Until that second, I didn't know just how much I wanted that, yearned for it. Children had never been part of my life plan – not like they were in Callie's, but I wanted Mac's children. Plural. I wanted to grow big with them, feel them kick and move inside me. I even wanted to feel that primal urge to push them into the world, with him beside me every step, looking at me the way Jake and my brother were now gazing at Tiff and Callie. I wanted it all. Mac might be happy as friends with benefits, but I'd never be. It was all or nothing.

I tried not to look at him, but when I did, the look on his face made me catch my breath. If I didn't know better, I would've thought it was a look that mirrored how I was feeling. As if he'd felt my eyes on his, the expression was gone in an instant – so quickly I thought I'd imagined it.

As I turned back to the little huddle around Tiff, her eyes narrowed on Mac. Extricating herself from Callie and Jake, she walked over and shook Mac's hand. 'You must be Ally's friend Mac,' she said. 'Or am I supposed to call you Alex because you're Callie's boss too, aren't you?'

Her eyes didn't leave him, and while a lesser man would've folded under her stare, Mac stood his ground. 'I'm sort of Callie's boss, but we're forgetting all about that for the moment, and yes, you can call me Mac.'

Tiff looked him up and down, pursed her lips and

nodded. 'Okay, Mac, but be warned, you harm a hair on this girl's head, and you'll have me to deal with – and I'm a whole lot scarier than Matt.'

'I have no intention of doing so, but I'll bear that in mind,' he said seriously.

Tiff was the first to drop her eyes – something I'd never seen happen before. 'Good,' she said. 'See that you do.' To me, loud enough for Mac to hear, she said, 'I like this one, Ally.'

As heat rose to my cheeks and I became overly interested in the now pastel ocean, I heard Mac chuckle in response.

'I do too,' said Callie, earning her a frown from Matt. 'What?' she said, a picture of innocence.

Mac couldn't get the grin off his face, and Jake was laughing. 'Don't worry, mate,' he said to Mac. 'You get used to these three very quickly, and heaven forbid anyone who tries to come between any of them. Isn't that right, babe?' He pulled Tiff back into his side.

'Absolutely,' she said.

When the men went to the bar for long overdue drinks, Tiff tapped at the table to capture my attention. 'Okay, they're gone. Now, Ally, spill the details.'

'They've slept together,' said Callie, 'and Ally said it was the best ever.'

'Oh my god, you two! Seriously? Are we teenagers again?' I said, my cheeks flaming.

'And Matt – what's this whole big brother

frowning thing he has going?' asked Tiff.

Callie rolled her eyes. 'He knows what Alex's track record is as far as relationships go.'

'So?' said Tiff. 'He used to be just as bad as was I – and look at us now. Besides, Ally's not that much better when it comes to commitment.'

'Hello,' I said. 'I am still here.'

'Sorry, sweetie,' said Tiff. 'But you know what I'm talking about.'

'I do,' I said.

'I'm just glad you finally realised how you feel about him,' said Tiff. 'We've always known there was more to you two than friendship.'

'Ally said it was love at first sight for her,' Callie helpfully offered. 'I can't believe she didn't tell us.'

'How does he feel about you?' Tiff asked, suddenly serious.

'He cares about me; I know that. We're great together, but as far as a long-term relationship goes? I have no idea whether it's a friends with benefits thing with him or …' I shrugged. 'When I found out about him being Callie's boss and Alex rather than Mac, and how he's this big-shot businessman, I figured I was so far out of his league, but now that doesn't seem to matter. When we're together, he's just Mac, the same as he's always been. I can't get out of my head, though, how I'm nothing like the woman he normally goes out with.'

'Which is more of a reason you're the one he wants to be with,' said Callie, ever the romantic.

Tiff narrowed her eyes. 'Would you be happy as friends with benefits for as long as that lasts?'

After shaking my head, I pulled my hair back into a ponytail. 'I thought I could be, but – and this is going to sound bitter and twisted – but I want it all. I want what you guys have.'

'Awww, Ally.' Callie brushed at her eyes and put her arm around me.

Even Tiff looked pityingly at me and rubbed at my other arm in sympathy. 'Then tell him,' she said.

When I raised my eyebrows in memory of how she denied the feelings she had for Jake for so long, she said, 'I know. I'm the last person who should give advice like that, but when you know, you know … you know?'

'I know.' I forced a smile, so glad these women were in my life. 'I've missed us three.'

Callie rubbed at her eyes again and hugged me harder. 'Me too.'

When Tiff blinked a few times and sniffed, she said, 'Bloody hormones. I was crying at a puppy in a toilet roll commercial the other day.'

And then the three of us were laughing and crying and hugging again – which is how the men found us.

'Leave you three for five minutes and look what happens,' said Jake.

'Is everything alright?' Matt asked Callie, concern in his voice.

She nodded and left us to kiss him. 'We're just all so happy to see each other.'

I caught Mac's eyes, and he mouthed, 'All good?'

I nodded and turned away before he could see the burning tears in my eyes.

Dinner was a raucous affair. Tiff, Callie and I talked at the rate we always had done when we were together. This was, though, the first time we'd all been out with partners – not that Mac and I were partners, but … It made for a different dynamic, yet one we all seemed to enjoy. The men got on well, and the banter was lively. With Mac beside me, our legs touching under the table, I could almost believe we were there as an established couple.

Callie told Tiff all about Tommy and what he'd done, and she was outraged on my behalf. 'He's bloody lucky I wasn't around,' she said. Jake shuddered visibly at the thought.

The only low point came when Callie asked Tiff and Jake about their plans after the baby came.

'You're not going to be able to travel like you currently do,' Callie said.

'No, not in the first twelve months or so, I imagine, and even then, the way we travel will be different, so we've spoken about a few options,' Tiff said. 'We'll probably do more immersive tourism at that point – stay in a country or a region for an extended period and explore, but as for the next twelve months?' She looked across at Jake, who nodded. 'We're considering selling both our places in Melbourne and buying something more permanent in Brisbane. It'll be nice to have a home base with a yard, and Jake's going to take some time and write a book – he's already got a contract. Besides, it'll be nice to be near Dad and Mary when the baby comes. I have no idea what Mum's planning on doing, but Dad's keen to be a grandparent and Mary's so excited.'

'So you'll be up here too!' Callie clapped her hands in delight before she glanced at me. My heart skipped at the look of horror on her face when she realised what she'd said.

'Too?' I asked.

Under the table, Mac's thigh pressed into mine, the contact both a warning and a comfort.

'Yes,' she said, looking quickly at Matt, then back at me. 'We haven't had a chance to talk to you about it – it's all happened so quickly.' Her voice was high-pitched, and her giggle was nervous. 'We can't afford the family home we want in Melbourne, and our buying power is so much more in Brisbane. Plus'— she looked at Matt again— 'it's important to us to be close to both sets of grandparents when we …'—she coloured prettily— 'have our family.'

'I see.' I reached for my wine glass and took a sip to compose myself. Mac had warned me this could be the case, but Callie hadn't mentioned it to me – neither had Matt. Tiff's eyes were on me, and Mac placed a calming hand on my leg. It was enough to remind me that even though I was upset, this week was all about them, and they didn't need my permission to lead their lives just as I didn't need theirs to live mine.

I took another sip of wine, followed by a shaky breath. 'So you'll both be up here then? On the bright side, it gives me an excuse to visit more often – especially during winter. Brisbane in the summer, though? You can have that!' I forced a laugh that sounded fake even to my ears. 'Tell me about the others coming on Friday night,' I said. 'I know Andi and Todd, but who else will be there?' Callie seemed to relax at my change of subject.

'Before you do,' said Tiff, 'can I just say what a truly inspired idea it was to have a joint hens and stags party that isn't really a party? Seriously, who needs one these days? In the past, it might've been one last bash of freedom before you were confined to a life of domestic drudgery and kid wrangling.' Cal and I raised our eyebrows at each other; Tiff was on one of her rants. 'But I'd like to think none of us are fool enough to marry someone who will never let you see your friends again, so why not just have dinner and drinks with your friends?'

'Thanks for your approval, Tiff,' said Matt with a laugh.

'You're welcome. Right, now that's out of the way, tell us who's coming,' Tiff said, sitting back in her chair, her hand resting on the gentle curve of her tummy.

'Well,' started Cal, 'there's Todd and Andi, of course, and Brad and Abby – who you also know.' To me, she said, 'Brad was at uni with Matt and Todd – he's a landscape gardener but does mostly corporate and commercial work for rooftops bars, and the like. Abby used to be an accountant, but now she's in the business with Brad. Then there's Emily from work.' When Mac looked quizzically at her, she added, 'Emily Porter – she started with DotPoint in February.'

'Yes, I know her,' said Mac. 'Web development and social media.'

'Emily Porter? I said, 'I think I've met her too – well, I met an Emily Porter in Ubud at the astrology conference I was at last year. I caught up with her the following week in Legian, but she was with her boyfriend then. What was his name?'

'Josh,' said Callie.

'Yes, but she called him something different …'

'Booth?' suggested Cal.

'Yes, that's it. We exchanged details but never got around to catching up once we were both back in Melbourne. I wonder if she remembers me?'

'It's a small world,' said Cal, 'but Andi also knows her – from way back … it might even be from school. Anyway, other than that, both sets of parents, Laura and Mick, Clio and Owen, and Angus. It won't be a massive night, but it should be fun.'

'It sounds it,' said Tiff. 'But I'm exhausted even thinking about it and we have a full day of wedding things tomorrow. Honestly, I've never felt as tired as I did during the first twelve weeks and even now, I'm flat out staying awake past nine.'

The rest of us laughed as we knew we should and walked out with Tiff and Jake, who were staying in one of the holiday units on the Esplanade.

'You two go ahead,' I said to Matt and Callie. 'I thought I might show Mac the beach at night.' The truth was, not only did I want to be alone with Mac, I didn't trust myself not to say anything to Callie and Matt about their impending move.

'I'd like that,' Mac said, somehow keeping a straight face.

'We might come with you,' said Matt.

'Oh darling, can we not?' said Callie. 'It's been a big week, and I'm tired. Besides,' she said, a suggestive lilt to her voice, 'I feel like I've been sharing you with everyone all day.' As she said it, she reached up and cupped his cheek.

'But—' began Matt.

Callie kissed his lips.

'You two have fun,' she said while Matt tried to work out what had happened.

As they walked away, I heard him say to Callie, 'You know what we did on that beach.'

'I certainly do,' she replied.

'What if they do the same?'

'Then I hope they enjoy it as much as we did,' she said, their voices trailing off in the distance.

'So Callie obviously knows,' Mac drawled. 'And Tiff?'

I nodded. 'Does that matter?'

'Not at all. You were the one who wanted to keep things quiet until after the wedding, that's all.'

In the dark, I couldn't see his expression, which meant he couldn't see mine. I reached for his hand and led him across the road and up to where the waves splashed against the rocks.

'Ally,' he said. 'Are you alright?'

'Of course I am,' I said breezily. 'Why wouldn't I be?'

'Because Callie and Tiff are both moving up here and leaving you behind,' he said bluntly.

I nearly replied that they were leaving me behind in more ways than one, but that would've given too much away, so instead, I kissed him.

At first, he kissed me back with as much enthusiasm as I'd had but then pulled away. As I would have turned away so he couldn't see the tears that had spilled over, he reached for my hands and pulled me towards him. 'Oh Ally,' he murmured into my hair, allowing me to sob against his chest for the second time today. 'I know it hurts.'

'I'm happy for them, I am,' I spluttered.

'I know you are, but that doesn't mean it has to hurt any less,' he soothed.

'It's easy for you to say,' I said. 'They're not your friends, and you'll probably be up here as well before too long.'

He said nothing to that but stroked my hair, letting me cry, calming me ever so gently.

'Why am I always the last one?' I said, sniffing. 'I was the one left in Sydney after they both moved to Melbourne, and now that I'm in Melbourne, they won't be, and I'll be alone again – and that's when the trouble starts with me. I begin listening to Temptation and make stupid mistakes like I did with Hayden and Luke, and … are you laughing at me?' I lifted my head and pushed against his chest. 'You are! You're laughing at me.'

'Oh Ally,' he said. 'I'm sorry, but that last little outburst made no sense at all.'

I pushed again ineffectually at his chest. He caught my hand and held it. 'What you did tonight took real love for both of them,' he said. 'I knew you were hurting and so did they, and you could've made it about yourself – no one would've blamed you, especially not after the day you'd had – but you didn't.

So next time you're beating yourself up about what a dreadful track record you have with relationships, remember that.'

I nearly told him then. I nearly said, 'I love you', but it didn't seem to be the right time. What if he'd taken it as a way of me holding on to him because everyone else was leaving? What if he ducked his head and didn't meet my eyes and, instead of saying 'I love you' back, said something like, 'Oh Ally, you know I love you as a friend and we've had a lot of fun, but I thought you knew that was all it could ever be?' So I didn't say it. I just said, 'Let's go home, Mac.'

There was a split second when I thought he might've said something else, but the second passed, and he nodded and held my hand as we started walking.

CHAPTER TWENTY-FOUR

The following day, Callie and Tiff and I did wedding things: writing place cards, finalising seating charts and putting together the wedding favours – little jars of local honey, which we had to wrap in a hessian ribbon and attach the labels with string before tucking in a spray of seaside greenery.

The men were off doing last-minute men's things – I didn't ask.

Callie had apologised first thing in the morning for not telling me about their move and again when Tiff arrived.

'I'm so sorry, Ally, it happened quickly. I mean, this whole thing has happened quickly, and I didn't know how to tell you.'

I hugged her and told her it was okay, but she knew it wasn't. Intent on making amends, she continued before I stopped her.

'No, sweetie, no more apologies, but you can talk to me about it. In fact'—I gripped her hands— 'I insist you tell me all about it.'

Her smile was tremulous but grateful. 'Oh Ally, I wish you could be as happy as I am.'

I hugged her. 'I will be,' I said firmly, almost convincing myself.

Tiff flashed me a smile that said she understood but knew I was holding on to my emotions by a thread and would therefore say nothing that could snap that it. I placed my hand on my chest to thank her.

'How many of these do we need to do?' complained Tiff after we'd been going for a couple of hours. 'And what's with this label? *Meant to bee?* Honey and bee? It's so you Callie.'

'I have no idea how many there are,' said Callie. 'I'm not putting them on the tables, though; we'll pop them into baskets and leave them for people to collect – or not – on their way out. Anyway, we'd do the same for you, wouldn't we, Ally?'

'We certainly would,' I said. 'Speaking of which, what's happening in that regard?'

Tiff sighed theatrically. 'So I'm knocked up, and now you think I need to get married to make it all official?'

'No,' said Callie patiently, fully aware Tiff was winding her up. 'I just thought you might do it because you love Jake.'

'Or it's easier to get visas that way,' I quipped.

Tiff grinned and made a ticking motion in the air with her finger. 'He's asked me to marry him, and I said I would, but not yet. And,' she added as Callie was about to spring up to congratulate her, 'that doesn't mean we're engaged; it means that one day when we get around to it and we both feel like it, we might turn up at the registry office at the same time and say yes.'

'But you'd invite us, wouldn't you?'

'As if I could get away without having you two there, Cal. I might even invite Matt and'—she shot me a cheeky look— 'Mac. Speaking of which, what do you want when you do the deed, Al?'

I sighed and laid down the string I'd been trying to wrangle into a neat bow. 'Everything,' I said. 'I want the whole meringue – with you two in matching ruffle dresses and your children as flower girls and page boys tossing petals as I walk up the aisle on Dad's arm.' And Mac waiting for me at the end – although I didn't tell them that part, I thought they already knew.

'Well,' said Tiff with a knowing smile, 'you could be in for a bit of a wait if you're waiting for our kids to walk. And I hate to tell you, but Callie has set the bar pretty high as far as bridesmaids' dresses go.'

'But I allowed you to choose your own,' she said with a confused pout.

'Exactly – and we're both very grateful to you for that, aren't we, Al?'

'We are indeed.'

•

I dressed with extra care the following night for what we'd taken to calling the pre-wedding party by choosing a wide-legged Palazzo-style jumpsuit. The fabric – mostly green but filled with massive pink and white peonies – brought out the colour in my eyes, the tie-style belt emphasised my waist, and the chiffon butterfly sleeves made it look special and dressy. My hair was loose and curly, and I added some large glitzy earrings and gold heels and swished out to the kitchen – only to find Matt. My shoulders slumped with disappointment that I'd wasted my grand entrance on my brother, but an entrance was an entrance.

'Wowsers Alley-cat, who are you trying to impress?' As if he didn't know.

I shrugged in a whatever motion. 'Where are the others?'

'Callie's still getting ready; Dad's gone to get petrol in the car. Apparently, he's heard the price will be going up ten cents a litre over the weekend, so he wants to fill up.' We shared a smile – Dad was constantly on the lookout for the best petrol prices. 'Mum's having a shower. They'll take Callie and me, and you guys are going with Laura and Mick – which is fortunate as I don't think you'll be walking too far in those shoes.'

'They're not meant for walking, big brother; they're meant for impressing.'

'Ally—' he began.

'Please don't, Matt. Not tonight. Let me have one

night without you looking all disapproving and big brother-ish.'

'But—'

'I know – you've already said it.'

'I just don't want you to get hurt,' he said.

'And I love you for that, but I'm a big girl.' I smiled to take any sting out of my voice. 'Answer me this: how would you have felt if someone tried to talk you out of Callie once you knew you were in love with her? Or worse, warned her about what you were like – or, rather, used to be like. You know I could've done that. She's my friend, and I should've done that, but I knew how she'd felt about you all those years ago, and I saw you fall in love with her the minute you saw her again. As much as I knew what you used to be like, I also knew that you'd do nothing to hurt her. Besides, you're a Delaney – I couldn't have talked you out of loving her.' I hesitated and added softly, 'And you can't talk me out of loving Mac. He's the one, Matt. I knew it the minute I met him.' I patted his cheek lightly. 'I just have to hope you haven't turned him off me!'

'If I have, he doesn't deserve you,' he growled.

'You changed when you met Cal; maybe he can too?'

'Aaah Ally, always the bright-sider. Are you going to tell him how you feel?'

'Yes, and I hope our friendship still means something if he reacts badly. I don't think Cal would take too kindly to her bridesmaid and your best man shooting daggers at each other tomorrow.'

'I'm sure it won't come to that,' he grinned.

'Am I interrupting something?' Mac stepped into the kitchen looking freshly showered and, in a navy long-sleeved shirt and black jeans, completely shaggable. 'Oh Ally,' he said, looking me up and down, my skin burning where his gaze lingered.

Matt shook his head. 'I give up! I'm off to chase up my delectable fiancé.'

The minute he was gone, Mac pulled me into his arms. 'You look good enough to eat,' he said against my ear.

'Is that a promise?' I teased.

He groaned as his lips claimed mine in a kiss that could've gotten quickly out of hand if Laura and Mick hadn't chosen that moment to come into the kitchen. 'Don't mind us,' Laura said. 'You must be Mac.' As we separated, she caught sight of me. 'Jesus Ally, that outfit should come with a warning!'

'You're telling me,' muttered Mac. 'And you must be Laura.'

As Mick hovered in the doorway, Laura said to him, 'Pay no attention to what Alice is wearing.'

'Right you are,' he said with a grin, stepping forward to kiss my cheek. 'Looking good, Ally, and is this the bloke Laura told me you're stuck on?' He held out his hand for Mac to shake it.

'Oh my god, Mick!' Laura scolded. 'I told you not to say that! Sorry Mac, he didn't mean to say that.' She scowled at her husband, who shrugged nonchalantly.

'No problem,' said Mac tightly. In my embarrassment I didn't dare look at him, but the mood in the room felt as though it had dropped and I had no idea why.

'Okay,' said Laura, her eyes darting between Mac and me, 'have you got your bag? Mum said you're staying in Mooloolaba tonight with Callie and your other friend.'

'Yes, we are, but we checked in earlier and dropped our bags when we were there getting our nails done.' I waggled my freshly manicured fingers at her. 'So, we're right to go whenever you are.'

Despite the heat of the kiss we'd shared earlier, something was wrong with Mac. Where he'd been by my side on the other occasions we'd been out with a group, tonight he was absent. He did, however, seem to be having a good time. Whenever I caught sight of him, he'd be chatting to Matt, Todd, Brad or one of the other men. He even engaged in an animated discussion about something with my father. He just wasn't with me. I didn't think I'd done anything wrong unless … Had he heard my conversation with Matt? He'd joined us soon afterwards, so maybe he had – and this was his way of ensuring I didn't tell him how I felt about him.

I inwardly shook myself and concentrated on what Emily was saying. 'I'm so sorry I didn't look you up when we returned to Melbourne,' she said. 'My only excuse is that I went travelling for another couple of months, and when I got back, well, it all seemed too late.'

'Don't worry about it,' I said. 'I could easily have called you too.'

Someone walking by jolted me, and I stepped backwards, catching my heel in the hem of a coat hanging over the back of a chair. As I was rehanging it, Emily said, 'I probably shouldn't have left it there, but I have such a dreadful habit of forgetting things, and I thought it would be cooler in here than it is.'

There was something about it – blue suede button through – I'd seen it before, I was sure of it. 'It's a great coat,' I said. 'Vintage?'

'Yes. I bought it from a vintage store in Fitzroy last year and virtually lived in it. A funny story, but it had a—'

'Bucket list in the side pocket,' finished Cal, who'd joined us.

As she said it, the pieces dropped into place.

'How did you know?' asked Emily, surprise in her voice.

'It used to be mine,' Cal said. 'I wondered what had happened to that bucket list. I can't even remember what was on it. Don't tell me because I'll probably be embarrassed.' Callie's giggle was high-pitched.

'This is so weird,' said Emily. 'If it wasn't for that bucket list, I don't think Booth and I would be together today.' A broad smile ran across her face. 'Another reason I should be thanking you.'

'Another one?' asked Tiff, who'd come in halfway through the discussion. 'This coat was part of the great purge when Callie split from her ex-boyfriend, Jamie Aldridge, a total dick.' She examined Emily through narrowed eyes. 'I've just realised where I've seen you before.' And then, unusual for Tiff, she clamped her hand over her mouth and said no more.

'It's okay, Tiff,' said Emily. 'Callie and I have already been through it. She recognised me when I first started at DotPoint.'

'It was such an awkward conversation too,' said Callie, rolling her eyes.

'I'll say,' Emily said with a chuckle.

'Does someone want to fill me in?' Tiff asked.

'Okay,' said Callie. 'Remember I told you about the night Jamie manipulated me into going on holiday with him—'

'Even though you already knew you were in love with Matt,' I finished.

'Yes, even though I knew I didn't love Jamie anymore. Anyway, a woman approached him that night, and I got the impression they were involved.'

'I remember you telling us that. Then you and Tiff

saw the same woman in a coffee shop in Abbotsford with someone you thought might also have been involved with him. It's the reason you didn't get on that plane,' I said.

'I remember that night in Bourke Street,' Emily said quietly. 'It was the night Booth and I got together for the first time. I remember the coffee shop too. I was with Suse – the three of us, Booth, Suse and me used to be like you three, but Suse cheated on her husband with Jamie, and I haven't seen her since that day.'

Her expression was pensive, then she blinked and forced a smile. 'I still miss her,' she said. 'Both of us do.'

Tiff, Callie and I looked between each other, all of us, I was sure, thinking the same thing – how lost we'd be without each other.

'So the way we figure it,' said Cal, putting her arm through Emily's, 'we're even.'

Tiff raised her eyebrows. 'How so?'

'I credit Cal's bucket list and seeing her with Jamie for pushing me towards Booth, and she credits me with changing her mind about getting on a plane with Jamie.'

Tiff thought for a minute, her brow furrowed. 'You're right. If I weren't pregnant, I'd drink to that.'

Across the room, Booth was talking with Mac and beckoned Emily. 'I'd best see what my boyfriend and my boss are after,' she said, rolling her eyes.

'Talk about coincidence,' Tiff said when she was

gone.

'I'll say,' I said. 'What was on that bucket list?'

Callie plastered on a look of pure innocence and said, 'You know, I can't remember.'

Once we'd finished laughing, she said to me, 'Ally, even when we move, you know we'll always be there for you.'

'I know,' I said. 'Mac's also thinking of relocating.'

'Oh Ally.' Callie put her arm around me from one side and Tiff from the other.

'Was that before or after you hooked up?' asked Tiff.

'Before, but—'

Tiff squeezed my hand. 'All I'm saying is things might have changed since then.'

I swallowed hard and bit the inside of my mouth. 'Maybe. I'm just going to'—I pointed vaguely in the direction of the river— 'get some air.'

'Do you want us to come?' asked Callie.

I patted her cheek. 'No, sweetie. You stay here and be the bride-to-be. I'm just having a moment, and then I'll be fine.'

Their eyes followed me as I weaved through the guests, out the doors and onto the deck. Turning left, I walked along the wharf until I got to the river's edge and stumbled onto the grass, my heels sinking into the soft earth. Leaning back against the outside of the pub, I concentrated on my breathing. This was Callie's night – Callie's and Matt's. Whatever was going on – or wasn't going on – with Mac and me didn't matter. We could resolve that after the wedding. My priority was making sure that tomorrow she had the day she'd dreamt of since she was a little girl.

'Hey,' Mac said softly, sneaking around the edge of the building to where I stood. Standing beside me he leant in to bump my shoulder lightly. 'You okay?'

I nodded mutely and snuck a sideways glance at him. Mac's eyes were on the river rather than me. I took another steadying breath. 'Yeah, fine. There was just this weird coincidence … anyway, it's a long story, and I'll tell you later.'

'Ally,' he started.

'Yes …' I turned to look at him but his attention was still on the river, the lights from the mansions across from where we stood reflecting across the water.

'I overheard you and Matt before.' His tone was flat, his jaw tense.

'Oh.' My tummy flipped, then flopped, leaving an empty pit where it used to be. 'Is that why you've avoided me tonight?' I asked, squeezing the words past my heart, which was now in my throat.

He barely nodded. 'I didn't want to hear it. I'd allowed myself to think …' He shook his head slightly, then said again, 'I didn't want to hear what you were going to tell me.'

'I see,' I said bleakly. The urge to walk away and return to the hotel was strong. 'Well, that's it then, I suppose.' My breath came out in a quiet shudder. 'The thing is, Mac, I can't do the friends with benefits thing—'

'Ally …' He finally faced me, his hand reaching out to tuck a strand of hair away, his touch so gentle it was almost unbearable.

'Please, Mac, you mightn't want to hear it, but I need to say it. Our friendship has been too important for me not to.'

'I know it has been, and that's why—'

'I understand that it's not what you want to hear, and I thought I'd be happy with any little part of you I could get, but I'm not. I want it all, Mac. The whole happily ever after – and I want it with you. I probably shouldn't have told you until after the wedding, but I hope we can still be friends tomorrow and this won't be too awkward …'

'Sorry? What did you say?' He peered at me through the darkness, and I wished I could see the expression in his eyes.

'It should be raining for a scene like this, shouldn't it?' I forced a smile. 'Us in the dark in the rain in the middle of the road, me telling you how much I love you and how I've loved you since the minute I first met you, and you holding me and saying you love me too, but not like that and how you wished you could.'

Tears came to my eyes then, and I couldn't seem to stop them from overflowing. 'It should be raining, and I should walk off into the rain, alone.'

'Oh Ally.' He reached for my hands. 'I asked you to repeat yourself because I thought you were going to tell me you weren't interested in a relationship, and I didn't want to hear that.'

'But you said you'd overheard Matt and me.' A little kernel of hope, the tiniest chink of it began to glimmer.

'I did. You said that you hoped I wouldn't react too badly to what you had to say and that you hoped our friendship would mean we could hold it together for tomorrow.'

'So … you missed the part where I told Matt that you were the one and I was going to pull my big girl's undies on tonight and tell you.'

'Yes,' he said sheepishly, 'I missed that part. You see, I'd decided that tonight would be the night I would tell you I loved you and wanted everything with you. You're my one, Ally. The one I've been waiting for and every other cliched and corny line you can come up with. Then I heard what I heard and thought that you were going to tell me, well … I thought you were going to tell me the opposite and I didn't want to hear it.'

'Oh,' I breathed.

'Oh,' he replied, a smile curling at the end of his

lips. 'Had you practiced what you were going to say to me?'

I nodded. 'I had it all worked out.'

He brought one of my hands to his lips, kissing my knuckles. 'Set the scene for me.'

I grinned back at him. 'Well, we've come outside to look at the moon …'

'There isn't a moon, though,' he interrupted.

'Maybe not, but in my fantasy, there is – a lovely big silvery full moon. And we're looking at it, together, of course, and you put your arms around me from behind …'

He pulled me away from the wall and turned me so he could put his arms around my waist. 'And what happens then?'

'You're kissing me – down my neck, the way I like …'

He dropped kisses down my neck and back up again, gently pushing aside my hair so he could nuzzle in behind my ear. 'Like this?'

I moaned and nodded; at the same time, a buzz filled my core. 'Exactly like that. And then I say, "Mac, this is no good. I love you, I've always loved you, and you're my person."'

'And what do I do?' I didn't need to see his face to hear the smile in his voice.

'Then you turn me in your arms and say, "I've been waiting for you to say it, Ally, because I love you too."'

He turned me in his arms and said, 'I've been waiting for you to say that, Ally, because I love you too – and have done almost since the start. Now what happens?'

'Now you kiss me.'

So he did.

CHAPTER TWENTY-FIVE

'You look beautiful, Cal,' I said, my eyes welling at the sight of my best friend ready to get married.

I suppressed a smile as Tiff dabbed at the corner of her eye with her pinky finger so as not to damage her make-up. Loving Jake had mellowed her and allowed her to be loved, but pregnancy had softened her further. I couldn't wait to see how she adapted to motherhood, although knowing Tiff, it would be with the same mix of practicality and deep love – with a smidgeon of 'it's for your own good' firmness – she'd always shown us.

As the three of us gazed at our reflections in the mirror, it hit me again that while we all looked the same on the outside – except for Tiff, of course – the three of us had changed so much. Our circumstances had changed.

Last night when we staggered home after the party – not too late or too drunk, we did, after all, have a wedding today – we'd sat up and talked in the way we used to talk. Cal sprawled on the lounge, Tiff upright in a soft chair, me cross-legged on the floor. The main subject had been Mac and me.

When we'd finally come back into the bar, we'd been holding hands, and he scarcely left my side for the rest of the evening. Cal beamed. Tiff professed to have known it from the second she saw us together, and Matt frowned some more when he thought I wasn't looking. Mac finally took him aside and assured him he wouldn't hurt me and that this was the real thing for him.

'I love her, man,' he said simply.

Matt had nodded once and slapped him on the back before giving Mac a one-armed man hug.

'You're a better man than I am to think about taking on Ally – although you've had plenty of time to be warned, I suppose.' To me, Matt said, 'Take care of him, Ally; I don't want to lose a good mate.' His subsequent grin didn't stop me from punching his arm. And the fact that it was a light punch didn't stop him from rubbing his arm dramatically. After that discussion, however, there were no more frowns.

When we parted, Mac kissed me thoroughly, and we both said how much we wished we weren't going to be apart that evening.

'I've booked a room for tomorrow night, Ally,' he said. 'And we'll finally get the night we deserve – no dodgy motel, no wet dogs, just us. Then we'll head into the hinterland for a couple of days.'

I couldn't wait.

Now, though, it was time to get Callie married.

'Well, girls,' said Tiff. 'This is it. Any last-minute change of heart?' she asked Cal. 'It's not too late, you know.'

'None at all,' she said, her eyes gleaming. 'I've never been surer of anything in my life.' She linked arms with us. 'And I couldn't imagine doing it without you two.'

'We wouldn't let you,' I said, leaning in to kiss her lightly on the cheek.

'Hey,' said Tiff, a catch in her voice, 'don't mess with the make-up.'

The three of us picked up our bouquets of wildflowers and walked out of the hotel, Tiff and I in our floaty floral knee-length dresses, Cal in her vintage wedding dress, through the crowds of people gathered in the cafés on the Esplanade, and across the road to the beach where Cal's father was waiting for her.

Tiff and I kissed her cheek. 'Good luck, sweetie,' I whispered.

'Go get hitched,' said Tiff.

Then Tiff and I paused at the start of the sand. Down on the beach, a whitewashed timber frame had been erected and festooned with flowers and greenery. From the centre of the frame hung, incongruously, a disco ball. I laughed aloud at the sight of it.

Two pelicans flew across, inches above the water, their wings spread wide. As they reached the level where the wedding was taking place, they rose high into the air, heading over the surf club for the river.

The guests had gathered, but I only had eyes for my man waiting at the end. As Tiff began walking, Jake's gaze never left her. Even from here, I could see the way he felt about her. Then it was my turn.

As I drew closer, Mac mouthed, 'You look beautiful.' Then, 'I love you.'

'I love you too,' I mouthed back.

Almost exactly as I'd imagined it – but better.

BEFORE YOU GO

If you enjoyed *It's In The Stars* I'd love it if you left a review in the usual places. If you'd like to stay up to date with my next happy ending, you can sign up for my newsletter at my website: https://joannetracey.com

You can also drop by and see me – virtually speaking, of course – at any of these places:

My blog; https://andanyways.com
Facebook: https://facebook.com/joannetraceywriter
Instagram: https://instagram.com/jotracey

ACKNOWLEDGEMENTS

Way back in 2010 I wrote 50,000 words of a novel I'd titled Brand New Without Tags. It was about Alice Delaney, an astrologer living in Prahran, Melbourne and it was absolute rubbish. So bad that after I lost a fat bet with my friends Shelley and Daniel and had to show them the novel when I didn't lose the weight I'd wagered, I trashed it so no other person would see it.

Alice, however, stayed with me.

She made a brief appearance in *Baby, It's You*, was back in a co-starring capacity in *I Want You Back* and *Careful What You Wish For*, and now has her own story. It seems fitting that the character who began it all is also the one to tie this series together.

Thank you as always to my editors, Nicola O'Shea and Joanne Speirs for wrangling my words into shape; to Keith Stevenson for turning those words into a physical (or digital) book; and to Louisa West for another fabulous cover.

As always my love and gratitude to Grant and Sarah whose support allows me to juggle writing alongside a day job and tolerate the soundtracks of each novel and the procrastibaking as I approach deadline.

Mostly though, thanks to Melbourne and Mooloolaba for the inspiration.

ABOUT THE AUTHOR

Joanne Tracey lives on the Sunshine Coast in Queensland Australia with her husband and a cocker spaniel who takes her role as resident flop-dog and guardian of Jo's office very seriously. An unapologetic daydreamer, eternal optimist, and confirmed morning person, Jo writes contemporary romance, romantic comedy, women's fiction and cosy crime. When she isn't writing or day jobbing, Jo loves baking, reading, long walks along the beach, posting way too many photos of sunrises on Instagram and dreaming of the next destination and the next story.

Jo's life goals (apart from being a world-famous author) are to be an extra on *Midsomer Murders* and to cook her way through Nigella's books.

ALSO BY JOANNE TRACEY

The Philly Barker series (cosy crime)

Philly Barker Investigates

Philly Barker Is On The Case

The Melbourne series (contemporary romance)

Baby, It's You

Big Girls Don't Cry

I Want You Back

Careful What You Wish For

It's In The Stars

Christmas At Mannus Ridge *(coming soon)*

Escape To The Country series

Wish You Were Here

Happy Ever After

The Little Café By The Lake

Escape To Curlew Cottage